Frozen Footprints

Therese Heckenkamp

Ivory Tower Press

www.ivorytowerpress.com

Fleuron by Foglihten DecoH02

Cover design by Robin Ludwig Design Inc.
www.gobookcoverdesign.com
Cover photos: 9751858 © Peter Zelei, iStock.com;
41494481 © Happymelvin, Dreamstime.com

Published by
Ivory Tower Press
www.ivorytowerpress.com

Printed in the United States of America

Also by Therese Heckenkamp:

After the Thaw (Coming early 2016)

Past Suspicion

To my brother Jerome
and to my father,
for all the memories we've shared,
particularly our northern adventures
and snowboarding trips.

"His truth shall compass thee with a shield:
thou shalt not be afraid of the terror of the night."

— Psalms 90:5

Prologue

*H*is prayers, as he dug hungrily into the black earth, were not heavenly. They reeked, as he did, of all that was foul and rotten. The Bible lay open in the dirt beside him as he labored by candlelight. Stones and earth flecked the pages. The book appeared discarded, forgotten. But it wasn't forgotten. He never forgot anything.

Memories haunted him.

Memories of his wife, and how she had been stolen from him.

Stabbing at the earth with his rusty shovel, he worked fiercely while Bible verses churned through his mind.

"Revenge is mine, and I will repay them in due time, that their foot may slide. The day of destruction is at hand, and the time makes haste to come."

A raspy cackle broke through his dry lips. It amused him to use his Bible knowledge this way. All those years of study had paid off after all.

"Revenge . . ." The word seeped from the man's mouth like poisonous vapor, slow and deadly. He savored the savage sound, the raw roughness of the "R," the sharpness of the "V," the brief sting of pain as his teeth cut into his bottom lip, the way the word heated his throat and burned deep in his belly. Burned like the fire in his gut when he thought of his wife.

His blood sizzled with each vicious thrust of the shovel into the dirt. He grunted with exertion, but he was pleased, very pleased. His plan was perfect.

This is for you, my love.

The pit was growing daily. Not much longer now.

Soon, my love, soon.

He paused to survey his work, swiping a grubby arm across his face, leaving a streak of soil. He breathed in deeply, letting the dirty air fill his lungs while his mind moved to Proverbs.

"Let us swallow him up alive like hell, and whole as one that goeth down into the pit."

His big hairy arm reached down, gorilla-like, and he snagged a beer can. The last one. He'd have to go up for more soon. Lifting the can, the flimsy plastic packaging still encircling the rim, he took a long, sloppy, satisfying chug.

Finished, he tossed the can against a shadowed dirt wall. The shadows shifted and twisted with possibilities. A toothy grin spread wide across his face, and he reached to his side for the snake-handled knife.

As he pierced the dirt wall with the blade, he thought of *Them.*

He spat.

Them, with their wealth and power and pride.

The simple carving didn't take long. He wiped the knife-blade clean on his finger, purposely leaving a thin slice in his flesh. He watched as the blood came: at first a thin red hair, then an oozing scarlet worm that began to *drip, drip, drip.*

"And man shall be brought down, and man shall be humbled, and the eyes of the lofty shall be brought low."

A good verse. A very good verse.

I'll start with the boy.

Chapter One

Three months later . . .

*M*ax went missing on a Friday, the day after Christmas. I should have been with him, but instead I was at the mall, shopping for bargains I didn't need, with only my twin intuition to tell me something was wrong.

I had just handed my credit card to the sales lady and was surveying the department store's glaring lack of Christmas decorations, when an arctic chill swept my body—a chill that came not from outside, but from inside. It started in my heart, a frigid shock, and rushed outward through my limbs and up my neck. I half expected my curly mop of brown hair to spring up electrocution-style.

Instead, my scalp prickled and goosebumps popped out on my arms. Dread filled my stomach like a brick of stale fruitcake. I felt my face pale.

"You all right, Charlene?"

I blinked, momentarily distracted. *How does she know my name?*

Click, click, click.

Following the sound, I saw her shiny red nails tapping against plastic—my credit card. *She read my name,* I realized. Or maybe she just recognized my Perigard face. After all, the magazines and tabloids constantly featured my billionaire grandfather, so Max and I couldn't help but receive some residual recognition.

"Wise and distinguished," my grandfather termed his own Perigard profile. "Proud and pompous," many others called it. For my part, I saw no resemblance in myself, physical or otherwise, to my grandfather. Honestly, what eighteen-year-old girl would?

"You need to sit down or something? You don't look good." The cashier's penciled eyebrows pinched together with concern, and she glanced over her shoulder, probably searching for help.

Unable to find my voice, I shook my head, but my foreboding grew stronger. I had felt this before, the night Max was arrested. The party, the booze, the drugs, the fighting . . . I hadn't been there, but I had sensed something was not right in his world and, therefore, it had not been right in mine, either.

Just like now.

I grabbed the credit card and turned to go.

"Wait! Don't you want your things?" shrilled the cashier.

I didn't pause to reply. Urgency tugged me out of the store and across the dim parking lot to my silver Lexus. I struggled to brush snow off the windshield while more of the falling white stuff bombarded me. Then I, who never speeds, raced onto the slick streets, heart hammering.

This is ridiculous. Illogical. I tried to reassure myself, one thought tumbling after another like the frantic snowflakes. *It'll all be fine. I'll find Max at home, reading comics or practicing magic tricks.*

Then why this horrible fear?

Because twin intuition doesn't lie.

If only I could talk to Max . . . I let out a short laugh, then reached across the seat and dug my hand deep into my Prada bag. My fingers skimmed over wallet, keys, and compact, searching blindly for my metallic green phone. At last I plucked it out and discovered eight missed calls. Eight! Two from Grandfather and six from Max. My stomach plummeted.

Why, oh why, had I left my phone on vibrate the entire day? I hadn't stopped to think it odd that I hadn't received any calls, because I very rarely did. Unless Grandfather was checking up on me (and I was always happy to miss those calls), my phone stayed conspicuously silent for a teenager. I didn't have a gaggle of girlfriends to chat with. Mostly, my

4

phone was for emergencies.

Glancing up at the road just in time to notice red taillights, I hit my brakes and narrowly avoided skidding into the van in front of me. Muttering under my breath, I glanced back at the phone. Eight missed calls, but no messages. Not reassuring. Max didn't usually call me—certainly not six times in a row. *Something's definitely up.*

I punched the callback button and waited without breathing. *Come on, Max, answer.*

When I heard his voicemail kick in, I hung up and tried again.

Traffic began moving, so I eased forward. A flashing kaleidoscope of emergency lights came into sight on the side of the road. Cop cars, fire truck, ambulance, and two dented cars in the ditch. As rarely as I prayed these days, an accident still always brought a prayer to my lips. Now I added another one for Max.

The falling snow thickened, visibility lessening as I left the accident behind. My eyes flew from phone to windshield, the continuous back-and-forth making me dizzy. I wasn't used to this whole using-your-cell-phone-while-driving thing.

Still no answer from Max's phone, so I tried calling home. Jennifer, our head housekeeper, answered in a very professional, yet clipped, tone. "Hello, Perigard residence."

"Hi, Jennifer. This is Charlene. Is Max there?"

"No, I don't believe so. I haven't seen him recently, and I just finished cleaning his room."

Ugh, I couldn't help thinking, *that job probably took all day.* "Okay, thanks."

I turned carefully off the highway onto a smooth, snow-powdered side road. I'd be home soon enough to search for Max myself. In the meantime, I tried his phone again.

My foot jumped on the gas pedal when I heard the phone pick up. "Max!" I cried, steadying the wheel.

No answer.

I was about to speak again, when I heard something . . . the white noise of a bad connection? No, it was the sound of

. . . breathing. Deep, heavy breathing.

"Max?"

More breathing. I pictured a fanged animal salivating.

"Answer me!" I fought the tremble in my voice as the breathing continued. Dear Lord, if Max was playing a trick on me—

The breathing paused. Then a low, raspy voice whispered slowly, precisely, "Hello, Charlene."

Quivers of horror raced up my back. "Max? Max, is that you?" I cried, stupidly, because I knew it was not him. "Who is this?"

Beep, the connection ended.

I was left holding the phone pressed painfully to my ear. My left hand clutched the steering wheel in a death-grip. I'd completely forgotten I was driving, yet somehow, here I was gliding onto my exclusive street, Perigard Place. The great black iron lampposts shone with haloed globes in the falling snow.

Shaking, I thumbed the number to call Max's phone back. Instead of ringing, this time it went immediately to voicemail. *What does that mean? Is his phone suddenly turned off? Destroyed?* I gulped down my panic. Breathed in and out. *Slow down, slow down . . .*

Grandfather's towering gray brick mansion loomed to my right. Ensnared in shadows, it seemed more like a sinister old castle than a modern architectural marvel. Across the street, our stone, glass, and cedar mansion sat modest in comparison.

Stopping at the gated base of our driveway, I touched a button on my visor and the metal gate swung wide. I redialed Max's phone as the gate clanged shut behind me, but no matter how many times I tried calling, no one picked up again. It was almost as if I'd dreamed the incident, the nightmare voice. I shivered. *Who was it? And why did he have Max's phone?*

At last I parked my Lexus beside my stepsister's cherry-red Ferrari in our spacious four-car garage, a garage made even more spacious by the fact that both Max's black Maserati and my stepmother's navy Porsche were absent. Max's car had been gone for a month now, "repossessed" by Grandfather after Max's latest speeding ticket.

Stepping from my car, I felt a prickle like pine needles on my skin as I recalled the scene, right here in the garage: Grandfather brandishing his fist at Max, his imperial voice echoing off the cold concrete walls as he shouted.

"Three tickets in one month! You think just because I have money, I want to throw it away to save your sorry hide? Think again. I'll see to it that you don't drive again till you're forty!"

"Like you've never gotten a ticket in your life," Max shot back. "And I'm telling you, those last two times, I wasn't going more than five over—no faster than anyone else, I swear. The cops just have it in for me."

"Excuses, always excuses!" Grandfather snarled. "The fact is, you've proven yourself a troublemaker over and over again. No cop in this town is going to give you a break."

"I'm not asking for a break." Max's hands turned to fists. "Just a fair shake. Not one set of rules for everyone else, and a different set for me. Just because I'm a stinking Perigard, I'm held to such dang high standards—"

"You bet you're held to high standards—the highest there are. And yet you insist on dragging my good name through the mud every chance you get. No more!" Grandfather turned to his waiting mechanic and bellowed, "Take it away!" while swinging his arm at the Maserati.

"Take it then," Max said, jaw clenching. "But don't say it was a gift, you hypocrite."

I stood in Max's shadow, hating the scene but unable to tear myself away. He needed my support. I glanced at my prized Lexus, a gift, as Max's car had been, from Grandfather on our eighteenth birthday.

"Real gifts don't come with strings attached," Max continued. "I don't need your charity, anyway. You and your tactics. You thought if you gave me the car, I'd hang around, keep playing your games. I'm not. I'm through with you and through with this place, this prison. I'm out of here."

"We've all heard that before," Grandfather said mockingly.

7

"Don't kid yourself. We all know you couldn't make it on your own. Who'd pay your bills?" His chuckle bounced behind him as he left the garage to purr home in his Jaguar.

"That's it." Fuming, Max threw a punch at the wall. "I'm outta here for real this time, and I'm not ever coming back."

I grabbed his arm and pleaded with him to stay. "Please, Max. You can use my car."

"Char," he said, exasperated, "it's not about the car. It's about how he rules our lives and treats us like dirt."

"Things will get better, you'll see." As much as I disliked Grandfather's attitude, at least we were well provided for. Very well provided for. And this life was all I knew. "I couldn't stand it here without you, Max. Please. You're my only real friend. Please stay."

And he had.

But now . . . standing alone in the cold concrete garage, the memory churned my stomach, and I felt sick. It was no secret to me, or anyone in the family, that Max constantly threatened to leave. What if he'd finally made good on the threat?

No. He wouldn't do that to me.

Would he?

Chapter Two

I burst into the house, plunking down my purse and kicking my wet boots off on the stone tiles as my mind fished for explanations, snagging on the most comforting: Maybe Max was still here at home, having a huge laugh at my expense. Yes. He was a guy, after all, and no matter how much he loved me, freaking me out was always high on his list of amusements.

Like the time he told me he'd stumbled across some human bones in a drainage ditch by the highway, bones so old that they probably belonged to some long-ago unsolved murder. I didn't believe him until he took me to see them and I laid eyes on the brittle yellow, porous pieces. My swirling emotions got the best of me, and it wasn't until I started dialing the police that Max started cracking up—and I realized the pieces were really just old animal bones.

"Max? Max?" I now called as I raced up the curving stairs, my hand sliding over the polished mahogany banister, the scent of lemon-cleaner fresh in the air. Rounding a curve, I almost bumped into Jennifer, who was hurrying down with a white plastic sack in hand.

"Pardon me, Miss Charlene." She gave a prim nod as she maneuvered past in her stiff black and white uniform, the mandatory black silk bow perched incongruously in her short gray hair. A moment later, Mitsy darted past me, a silver blur on silent cat-paws.

"Max?" I pushed open his bedroom door, ignoring the metal stop sign nailed to the front. (I'd avoided asking him how he got it, because I was sure I'd rather not know.) The cleanness of the room amazed me. Jennifer had done a thorough job of eliminating all the food fragments, wrappers, dishes, and other assorted clutter. Magazines and comics were shelved perfectly. There wasn't a wrinkle on the smoothly made bed, and clothes hung orderly in the closet. The adjoining bathroom was scrubbed shiny and smelled of bleach.

I darted in and out of the many remaining rooms, sweating in my blue coat as I searched for Max, first upstairs, and then down. At last I found my stepsister Gwen in the great room, a room lined with tall windows swathed with swooping arcs of burgundy silk. She lay sprawled across the leather sofa with a box of chocolates perched atop her fingertips. Her face had a zoned-out look as she watched a talk show on the giant flat screen. Flames blazed in the oversized stone fireplace. A colossal pine tree towered in the corner, decorated so professionally with sheer ribbons and strands of pearls that it looked more like a model evergreen out of a glossy magazine advertisement than a family Christmas tree.

I hurried across the ebony floor and skidded to a stop at the Persian rug. "Have you seen Max?"

"Nope," Gwen said without taking her eyes off the screen. "He's not here. He ran away."

A sound like waves crashed in my ears. "How do you know? Did he—"

"Your grandfather called," she continued with a dramatic toss of her wavy blond hair. "Apparently, they had a huge argument this morning, and Max ended up swiping one of his cars. The Jaguar." She licked chocolate from her polished fingertips. "One of the staff saw him take off with it, thought your grandfather had given Max permission. Why anyone would think that, I have no idea. Must've been one of the new guys, because if he knew anything at all about your grandfather—"

"Gwen," I picked up the remote and zapped away the television chatter, "Max didn't run away."

"Think what you want." Her voice was almost sing-song. "But you know he's done it before, and—"

"Oh come on, that barely counts. He just camped out in

the woods one night." That had been two years ago, right after our father died tragically and Grandfather had been laying down a ton of new laws. And Max had told me his plan ahead of time, so I knew not to worry. "He didn't run away." My voice lowered, taking on the tone of a death sentence. "It's something worse. Much worse."

"Oh man, what a Ms. Gloom and Doom! Don't tell me it's that 'twin intuition' thing again."

Fine, I won't. Instead, I told her how I had tried calling Max and a strange creepy voice had answered.

Gwen blinked. "A creepy voice? So? It was probably just Max being lame."

I shook my head. "It wasn't. I know his voice."

"Fine," Gwen said in a tone that told me she wasn't convinced. "What did the creepy voice say?"

" 'Hello, Charlene.' "

Gwen's mouth gaped. "That's it? Sheesh, I thought you were going to say it was a death threat."

"It was the *way* he said it."

"Come on, Charlene. Max is just messing with you. Again. Man, you are the most gullible person I know. Remember that time when you walked into a door and smashed your nose, and—"

"Yeah, yeah," I mumbled. I didn't need her to repeat the embarrassing details which I recalled quite clearly, how Max had easily convinced me that I'd permanently damaged my nose.

"Don't worry," he'd assured me, "it's not crooked enough for anyone but me to really notice. Well, me . . . and maybe a few other guys."

For the next couple days, I'd wasted hours examining my nose with mirrors from every possible angle, before I finally realized he'd duped me again.

But that had been relatively harmless fun. This . . . this was cruel. I leaned over both Gwen and the sofa to peek through the bamboo blinds. Snow flew and howled like a million wild banshees. I let the slats fall shut, then finally shed my coat

11

reluctantly. I wouldn't be going back out tonight, not in that weather.

Gwen stretched and yawned. "So you really don't know where he is? Max never tells me anything—thank goodness—but your grandfather was sure you'd know where he is. He gave me this message." She tipped her head back, scrunched her eyebrows together, deepened her voice, and quoted, " 'Tell Charlene to call me as soon as she returns from wasting my money. I want my car back, and I want Maxwell studying.' "

I was saved from replying, because at the other end of the house, a door burst open. "Oh my gracious word," my stepmother Joy gasped. "It's a snowstorm out there. You should see the drifts. I'm lucky I made it home at all!" A moment later she swept past us and into the dining room. "Let's eat, girls," she called. "I'm starving."

I followed Gwen into the dining room and stood beside the walnut table, already laid with fine white linens and a scarlet table runner threaded with gold. A large vase held a glittering assortment of red and green glass ornaments and scented pine-cones with spirals of silver twirling out at all angles. Joy deposited her latest Coach purse on a side table, then un-clasped her hair. It tumbled generously over her shoulders, framing her smooth face in bouncy golden tresses and making her look young enough to be Gwen's sister.

Gwen, always bubbling with gossip, announced: "Max did it. He finally ran away." As she began filling her mother in, Fiona, another maid, sailed in and out with silverware, water goblets, crusty bread and steaming soup. Joy and Gwen sat, but I remained standing.

"That boy's like his father," Joy said above the Frank Sinatra dinner music crooning from a hidden ceiling speaker. "You never know what he's going to do next. Although I can't even count how many times I've heard him threaten to run away." She lifted a dainty spoonful of soup and paused mid-air. "But I wish he'd try just a little harder to please his grandfather—you just never know when the old man will get angry enough to take everything away. From all of us." Joy and Gwen shuddered simultaneously. They'd had ten years of living the rich life, and now with my father gone, they likely felt their place here was precarious—at least enough so that they didn't want any waves made.

"Max talks big, but he didn't run away," I insisted. But my conviction was crumbling. I plopped into a chair. "He would have told me. And he would have taken his stuff. I checked his room, and it's all still there."

"Oh Charlene," Gwen said, rolling her eyes, "everyone knows you can buy new *stuff*."

"Not without money," I muttered. Then an important thought occurred to me. There was something, one very important, irreplaceable thing in Max's room that I hadn't checked for.

"Try not to worry, Charlene," Joy said. "I'm sure Max is fine."

I nodded as I stood up, thinking only of searching Max's room again.

"Anyway," Joy continued, "I'm sure he'll come back soon enough, like last time. Sit down, dear, and try the soup. It's divine!"

Shaking my head, I barely set foot outside the dining room when Fiona brought me the cordless home phone. "It's Mr. Perigard," she whispered, her pretty young eyes open wide and scared. She trotted away the moment I took the receiver, her black hair bow bouncing and satin ribbon tails swishing.

"Hello?"

"I knew you were home. I knew you wouldn't call."

"Uh—Grandfather!" I made my voice sound bright. "Merry Christmas!"

"Christmas is over. Wasn't one day of forced, false well-wishing enough? You know why I'm calling."

Of course I did. Grandfather never wasted time or money with chitchat. Which was a relief, I supposed, because what would we talk about? His collection of European paintings and Roman sculptures? His success as a giant oil tycoon and how his hard work had made him rich? I'd heard enough versions of that story to write twenty books. Twenty very boring books.

"Where's Maxwell?"

A burst of laughter exploded from the carefree world of the dining room. I turned my back and placed a hand over my left ear. "I don't know."

"Why not? He's your brother."

And he's your grandson! I wanted to retort. *Not that you have anything to do with him, unless he's in trouble.* But I bit my tongue. Ranting would accomplish nothing. Sometimes I thought Grandfather's ears, head, and heart were clogged with his thick, black, ugly oil.

In the superior tone he used—but unfortunately did not save—for speeches, Grandfather continued. "I want him found, and the moment he's found, I want him brought to Gardburg." Gardburg was the name of Grandfather's grand estate. To me, it sounded like the name of a prison.

"I want him found, too," I said. "You should send out a search party."

"Bah! The boy left on his own, he can come back on his own. I won't go begging for him. Serves him right if he gets stuck out there. Teach him a lesson."

My grip on the phone tightened savagely. "What lesson? How to freeze to death in one easy step?"

"Don't get smart with me, Charlene. You're not trying to cover for him, are you? If you are, I'll find out. I—" Grandfather gave a dissertation on what he would do to me, including marrying me off to a strict, old husband who'd teach me to respect my elders. Then he hung up without a goodbye, which was the only way he would end a phone call.

"What a tyrant," I muttered. "Why do I even bother trying to please him?"

"Yeah, he's a tyrant all right," Gwen agreed, "but some things are worth putting up with."

I hadn't realized she and Joy had stopped their chatter to listen to my phone conversation.

Gwen dabbed her lips with a linen napkin before continuing.

"Pacify him, or the two of you are going to blow it for all of us. Have you ever thought about what would happen to us if the old man gets rid of you two? Sheesh, sometimes you're just so selfish."

Not trusting myself to respond, I hurried back up to Max's room. I headed straight to his bed and slid my hand under the mattress. Nothing. So I awkwardly hoisted the entire queen-size mattress and did a thorough search over the box-spring. Still nothing.

The book I was searching for was a thin, ragged notebook, but very valuable to Max. He had written *Magic Secrets of a Master Magician* on the yellow cover in black marker. The notebook contained important irreplaceable notes about magic tricks. He'd begun the journal when he was eleven, and though he thought he'd kept it top-secret, I had known about it from day one.

I dropped the mattress back down, then smoothed the rumples out of the black comforter, not sure how I should feel about the missing journal. Did Max take it? If so, did that mean he really *had* left for good?

On the other hand, if he hadn't taken it, why was it missing?

I searched the rest of the room, including the bookshelf, tearing apart all the order that Jennifer had carefully accomplished.

Suddenly, an image of her hurrying down the stairs with a bag in her hand popped into my head. Maybe she had come across the journal and moved it when she was cleaning.

Fighting a headache, I ran downstairs and located her in the library, dusting books. "Jennifer, did you take anything from Max's room?"

I saw her defenses go up like armor. "I would never take anything that wasn't mine, Miss Charlene. All I took was garbage." She brushed a Giovanni table lamp viciously with the feather duster.

"I'm sorry, I know you would never take anything you weren't supposed to. But this thing—it's an old notebook—

15

you might have thought it was garbage, or maybe you moved it somewhere?"

Jennifer's stone expression didn't waver as she shook her head.

I shifted my weight. "What was in the bag you were carrying down the stairs earlier?"

Her black eyebrows arched. "Kitty litter, Miss Charlene. Would you like me to show you?"

I gave a small laugh. "No. Thanks. That's all." I turned and left.

Retrieving my cell phone from my purse, I tried Max again and got nothing but his voicemail. I ended up back in the great room and dropped onto the sofa. I stared at the dead fireplace a moment before pulling up my saved phone numbers. Then I began calling Max's friends, but no one knew where he was—or if they did, they weren't saying.

Finally, I tried Wayne. Maybe I'd left him till last because, as Max's best friend, he was most likely to know something. They were always hanging out together, practicing the latest magic tricks and planning their futures as traveling magicians. As if Grandfather would ever allow Max to devote his life to such a frivolous career. But the phone just rang and rang while my stomach knotted tighter and tighter. An answering machine beeped on, so I left a message.

"Wayne? I'm calling about Max. Have you seen him lately? Do you have any idea where he is? Let me know as soon as you can . . . Call anytime—even after midnight." I hung up wishing I hadn't added that last part. It made me sound desperate.

"Max, your little mother was calling for you," I could almost hear Wayne taunt. Max wouldn't thank me for that.

I returned to the deserted dining room, almost wishing it was still dirty so I could clean it and actually accomplish something. But of course, the maids had beat me to it. By this time, Gwen and Joy were nowhere to be seen, probably watching a movie in the downstairs theater room. So I wandered back into the great room. With no fire and so many large windows, the room was already beginning to take on a chill. Not caring, I sank down on the sofa and stared at the stiff blinds, the little slits of darkness leaking through.

Darkness.

The word echoed ominously in my mind, and I didn't know why. I shivered and shifted my gaze. Unlit, our Christmas tree stood huddled in a shadow-shrouded corner like a monster waiting to attack. I turned my eyes on the nativity set at its base, a cluster of little silhouettes, offering nothing but childish illusions of faith and hope.

I forced out a prayer anyway, but it left me feeling empty.

Lonely.

All night long I stayed on the sofa, waiting for Max. Weariness eventually dragged me into a restless sleep, despite the cold.

So cold.

I reached blindly for a blanket, but found none.

As the morning dawned gray, into my bleary brain slithered the sinister voice. *"Hello, Charlene,"* it whispered slowly, tauntingly evil.

And it was almost as if I heard the voice add: *"Go ahead, try to save your brother . . . if you dare."*

17

Chapter Three

*F*ear thrummed in my heart as I tugged on my coat and left the house. I could feel the weight of sleeplessness hollowing my eyes, eyes that smarted and watered when they met the winter air. Sunlight glared blindingly on the fresh snow, and immense mounds of white flanked the road.

I walked with quick strides, my chin tucked deep in my cashmere scarf, braced against the wind which lacerated my cheeks. No one went to see Grandfather without an appointment. Particularly his grandkids. He didn't want us getting special treatment. But he was going to see me this morning, and I didn't care if I had to break in.

I carried this strong resolve to the iron entrance gate, which stretched at least two stories high, making it almost impossible to read "Gardburg" scrawled in iron letters across the top. Two granite, sword-wielding angels flanked the entrance, staring me down with cold stone eyes, daring me to come closer. I lifted my arm and waved to get the guard's attention. He scampered out of his round station house like a rabbit from a burrow.

"Max!" he called. "It's about time! Your grandfather—"

"It's Charlene!" I yelled, too cold to feel the heat of annoyance at the common identity mistake.

The guard, a coffee cup plastered between his mittened hands, drew closer and squinted at me.

Exasperated, I pulled off my woolen hat and shook out my bountiful chestnut curls.

"By golly, you're right!" he said. "But you look just like your brother, no kidding."

Everyone told us this, and it amazed us that people expected us to take it as a compliment. As if I wanted to hear that I looked like a boy, and Max, like a girl. Anyway, we had our differences. Our hair was the obvious one; I'd purposely grown mine very long, while Max cropped his so short, you'd never know it had a tendency to curl. My eyes were brown, while Max's were green. He also stood four inches taller than my five feet four inches. But this was not the time to quibble.

"I need to see Grandfather right away. It's urgent."

"Sorry." The guard snuggled his face into the steam billowing from his cup. "I have my orders, and I'm not about to bend them—not even for you. Your grandfather's not expecting any visitors."

I clamped my gloved fingers around the iron bars and actually tried to shake the gate. "You don't understand. This is urgent. It could be a matter of life and death."

The guard looked uncomfortable. "I'm sorry, but your grandfather's rules are law. You've got to know that. The guard yesterday made that mistake—let your brother in—and look what that got him—fired. No sir, I won't make that same mistake."

My heart softened. "You're right."

He took a sip of coffee, eyes fixed doubtfully on mine over the dirty rim.

"I understand." *It must be horrible working for Grandfather.* "I don't want you to lose your job. Only . . . isn't there something you can do? Some kind of compromise? Could you call up to the house and ask for permission? I just need to talk to him. It won't take long. *Please?*"

The guard stared searchingly into his cup. Then with a flick of his wrist, he tipped it. Brown liquid splashed on the frozen concrete, sending up a hissing trail of steam. "Ridiculous," he muttered. "A girl shouldn't have to beg to visit her grandfather." He took out a key with a furry mittened hand. "Here's what I'll do," he said while unlocking the gate. "I'll get you an escort, and if your grandfather has a problem with that, so be it."

"Thank you."

In answer, he reached into the guard station and pulled out a radio and called something into it that I couldn't hear. I waited, looking up the driveway. In less than a minute, a guy wearing a yellow jacket—much too thin to block the cold—appeared and skidded to a stop at my side.

"I'm from the big house," he said with mock formality, "and I've come to escort you up the driveway, Miss Charlene." He held out an ungloved hand, too tan for the dead of winter.

I shook his hand awkwardly, saying, "I haven't seen you here before." He looked to be at least thirty-five, but he smiled like a kid. "Are you new?"

"Not that new. You must not visit much, hey?"

"Not really." I felt like he thought I was a neglectful granddaughter, but surely he knew what my grandfather was like.

As we walked, the guy's black hair bounced against his forehead, which was smooth and also quite tan. "Whoa—" he reached out to steady me—"be careful of ice patches. You can't see them on this concrete, but they're everywhere."

"Thanks for the warning." I slowed my brusque steps.

"My name's Robert, by the way. Call me Rob. Can I call you Char?"

"Please . . . I'd rather you didn't." I tried to make my reply kind, but I didn't want to explain that, to me, Char sounded like something old and gray, like a pile of ashes in a dead fireplace. I didn't let anyone call me by that name, not even Max, though that never stopped him.

My ears focused on the sound of our feet crunching through snow and ice. I noticed Rob wore tennis shoes. "Aren't your feet cold?"

He laughed. "Hideous shoes, hey? My wife hates them. She keeps trying to throw them out, and I keep rescuing them. I've never owned a more comfortable pair."

I'm surprised Grandfather allows them to touch his floors.

We climbed a flight of concrete steps to reach the mansion's entrance, huge double oak doors set with hexagon glass. "Not even a wreath," I said.

"Yeah, he's a scrooge all right. No offense," Rob added as he began searching his pockets. "But it's nice you came to visit him today."

"Yeah, 'nice'. . ." *If only.* It was difficult for me to focus on small talk with my mind so consumed by my purpose. *Max, hang on. Help is coming.*

It seemed to take Rob forever to unlock the door. "How was your Christmas, by the way?" he asked as he led me inside.

"Nice," I repeated lamely. We lingered in the entrance hall, which was like a grand museum. Pillars of marble supported the domed ceiling, its crowning glory a chandelier dripping with diamonds.

A crackling noise suddenly preceded Grandfather's commanding voice, and I realized it was coming from a radio that Rob wore.

"Rob, I need you to go pick up donuts, coffee, and Advil. Pronto."

"Got it," he replied.

"Interesting breakfast," I commented.

"Breakfast?" Rob looked amused. "Nah, this is his before-before-lunch snack. He's already had a couple of breakfasts. Do you mind if I take off? Your grandfather hates waiting. He's in his train room. Know where that is? Okay, I'll leave you then. Nice meeting you."

"You too." The marble floor was slick, so I walked carefully. I followed the sound of a lively fountain, and upon finding it, gave a warped grin. Not a single wishing penny lay at the bottom.

Continuing on my way, I observed how the walls were bare of family photographs. Framed pictures of oil rigs took their place. Behind me, I heard an increasingly loud clicking sound, then felt the heat of a panting dog at my hand. I absently patted two Rottweilers, "Grim" and "Reaper," only to be snapped and growled at. "All bark and no bite," I said, and they retreated.

21

Now here was something impressive: A bronze arm and hand reaching with talon-like fingers for a dollar bill—the first Grandfather had ever earned. Sickly dramatic. "Reach for your goals" read the base of the statue. As a child, the display had freaked me out. I feared the hand springing to life. It still disturbed me, and I gave it a wide berth.

After some wandering—because I'd been to Gardburg far too few times to know my way around, though I hadn't wanted to tell Rob that—a tooting train whistle led me to the room. It had once been my ambition to draw a map of the estate, but I'd never become sufficiently familiar with the layout.

The room smelled of smoke and sparking metal. I shouted to make myself heard above the clickety-clack, chugging, and hooting of multiple miniature trains as they wove around model trees, hills, buildings, over bridges, and through tunnels—all meticulously built to scale. Though I knew model trains were Grandfather's hobby—or better yet, obsession—it still amazed me to see a whole room—larger than some houses—devoted to this stuff.

Grandfather's gray head popped up from behind a snow-capped mountain. "Who let you in here?"

"Rob," I said, purposely not mentioning the guard.

"Ah, Rob. I like him. He's got character."

A train whizzed by me, shrieking like a bird in pain. I reached out and flicked off the nearest switch. The engine came to a labored halt. "I didn't come here to watch your trains." Remembering what I did come for, I suddenly wished there was a chair in the room so I could sit. Wall to wall stretched a maze of landscape and tracks that made me feel like a clumsy, towering giant, afraid to take one step for fear I'd crush something.

"Well, I should think not. You've come to tell me that you've found Maxwell and he is returning my Jaguar and will be over shortly to apologize and beg my forgiveness." Grandfather's tone challenged me to deny it.

"Not quite," I said dryly. I glanced at his thick hair, skipped over his intense eyes, and spoke to his mustache, which I suspected he wore to help shield his pug nose. Instead, the mustache accentuated his nose by sprouting, weed-like, from his nostrils. "I came to tell you that we have to start an investigation. Right now. Call the police, get a search party going. How can you just stand there, not worried? Max would never disappear without telling me. Something's very wrong. We need to find him before—" I couldn't bring myself to finish the sentence, so I just shuddered.

"Get ahold of yourself, girl. I know exactly what's going on, as well as what I'm going to do about it."

"You do?" I crossed the room to his side. "Have you heard from Max? Has he contacted you—"

"As a matter of fact, he has." Grandfather held out a piece of paper, and I grabbed it.

My stomach dropped as I read the small typed note:

Maxwell Goodwyne Perigard I:

I want two million in unmarked bills. Put them in a backpack and lock it in locker #38 in the Whitecap Mountain Ski Resort lodge. Tie a string on the locker key and lower it through the floor drain in the farthest stall in the ladies' room. Tie the end of the string around the drain's metal grate. Don't involve the police, or you'll never see Maxwell III again.

I closed my eyes against the glaring note, but the words burned in my mind.

Max. Kidnapped.

Maybe this was what I'd feared all along. After all these years of being warned by Grandfather, his prophecy had finally come true.

"You're Perigards. People hear that name and think money," he'd say. "You're solid gold bars walking around. Never forget that. Don't talk to strangers and never get yourselves into isolated situations. If you get kidnapped it will

23

be your own fault, so don't expect me to bail you out."

As a little kid, the warning had terrified me; but as I grew, it became obnoxious. Still, whether conscious of it or not, the warning had seeped into me, become a part of me, and I lived with it from morning to night. It was something I accepted, along with the cold shoulder from kids who assumed I was a snob simply because my family was wealthy.

But Max—I groaned—Max had never been careful. Yes, at least he had friends, but look what it had gotten him: Kidnapped.

"Don't stand there gaping like an idiot." Grandfather snatched the note back from me. "This is a hoax. Your brother's playing games. He thinks he's found an easy way to make money—by extorting it from me."

I opened my mouth, but the words took time coming. "You're saying—that *Max* sent this?"

"Precisely." He snapped the paper in the air. "This is obviously the work of an amateur."

"Why would you think that?" All Grandfather's warnings about not helping—I'd thought that was to scare us. Not in a million years would I have thought he could be so callous as to carry out his threat. If he wanted to gloat over the note, with maybe a superior "I warned you," fine. But now I expected him to spring into action, to do *something* to help. He was the only one who could.

I shook my head. "Max would never do this. Not to me and not even to you. There *is* a kidnapper. I heard him." Quickly, I explained how the strange voice had answered Max's phone. "That's proof!"

"No, that's Maxwell. Do you know what his parting words to me were yesterday? 'I'm through with you, old man. You ain't ever gonna see me again!' Now *that's* what I call proof. He told me he was leaving, and he did." Grandfather leveled his eyes at me. "Now Max is out in the real world and he's realized he needs money if he's going to last more than a day. Well, he's not swindling it from me."

Frustration overwhelmed me. "How can you be so cold-

24

hearted you—you—scrooge!" I spun my gaze wildly about the room. "Look what you pour your money into—useless toys—" My eyes jumped back to his, accusingly. "And you've had this note how long without telling me?"

"It only came this morning, but I knew you'd be along soon enough to pester me."

"You call concern for my brother *pestering?*" Suddenly, I felt the urge to pull out my hair. "Don't you have a speck of a heart? Or are you trying to prove what everyone says about you is true—that you're a cruel, insensitive, greedy monster!" I couldn't believe these words were flying from my mouth. I'd never flared up at Grandfather before. Max had always been the one to do that, but he wasn't here to do it—might never be again if I couldn't convince Grandfather that this situation was real.

Grandfather flipped a switch and the train resumed chugging merrily around the track, shrieking and doing its best to drown out my words.

But I wasn't finished. My brother's life was on the line, at the mercy of our merciless grandfather. He held the money and, therefore, the power.

For a second I was even angry at Max as I remembered the story of "The Little Boy Who Cried Wolf" that our mom used to read to us back in those happy, simple days before the sickness took her. Similar to the bluffing boy, Max had threatened to leave way too many times, and now when it mattered, Grandfather would not believe the truth.

"Look." I pointed at the ransom note, but it was useless. Grandfather was back to watching his trains. "It says, 'Maxwell III.' Max would never call himself that. He hates it. He goes by Max—you know that!"

"I know that he's merely trying to make it appear as genuine as possible. He is a Perigard; he's not stupid. But neither am I, and I'm a lot smarter than him. I didn't get where I am today by letting people take advantage of me. I recognize a scam when I see one. Do you know how many letters I get every day from people claiming to be long-lost relatives? Or at death's door, and all they need is so many thousand dollars for a life-saving operation? Then there are the unimaginative ones who flat out beg for money, groveling at my feet. They're all trying to take advantage of me because I'm a billionaire and they think I owe them a piece of my fortune. If I gave in to those people, do you know where we'd be living? Out on the streets, that's where."

"But we're not talking about some beggar, we're talking about your grandson."

"Precisely. The note came from Maxwell."

"How was it delivered?"

"By mail."

"Was there a postmark on the envelope?"

"Yes, mailed yesterday, here in town. Rather convenient, eh?"

"Yes, for the *kidnapper*." I clenched my teeth. "So you're going to do nothing?"

"Patience, Charlene. This is a waiting game. Let me tell you a little story. When I was young, my friends and I used to see how long we could stand on the train tracks. The whistle would screech. We'd look the train in its gigantic eye. But always, eventually, we had to jump."

I almost said, "I wish you hadn't."

"I always wanted a toy train," he continued. "I'd look longingly in store windows at Christmas time. All I ever found under the tree were necessities. Socks, boots, a coat if I was lucky. Extras, I learned, we must earn ourselves."

He eyed me intently. "What kind of grandchildren am I raising? How do I know you're not in on this? Two million split between you would make a nice beginner's fortune."

"You're impossible. How can you even think such a thing?" I swallowed rapidly, forcing down the horrible words that would only worsen my chances of helping Max. "What will it take to convince you?"

"Proof this isn't a hoax."

"Proof? What kind of proof? A dead body?" I nearly choked on my words.

"Have you forgotten Maxwell took my Jaguar? Of course you have. People who let their emotions get the better of them cannot think rationally." He spoke slowly, as if to an ignorant child. "One who is kidnapped does not drive away to captivity, let alone in a Jaguar. Also consider the fact that this is winter break—a convenient time to stage a disappearance. Right now, Maxwell is surely sitting back, relaxing and waiting for his unearned money to roll in. I'm not going to let that happen."

"You don't know the circumstances of the kidnapping. For all we know, the car could be stolen too, or abandoned somewhere. We should look for it. What's the license plate?"

"JAGRRR," Grandfather said with an obvious note of pride.

It wasn't hard to commit to memory. "And this being winter break doesn't mean—"

"Charlene, you are getting tiresome. Do I need to call Rob to have you removed?"

"Rob isn't even here, remember?" I retorted. "You sent him out on some stupid errand."

In my anger, I looked around for something to smash. But there were too many options—mountains, buildings, bridges—that I couldn't decide. And from the weird way Grandfather's mind worked, smashing something would likely give him satisfaction. Justification for throwing me out.

"I do have other servants who could remove you," he challenged.

"Remove" me. As if I'm a stain on the carpet.

Scrounging together what remained of my dignity, I said, "That won't be necessary. I'm leaving now. If you're not going to take this seriously, then I'm going to the police." I flicked my scarf over my shoulder like it was mink. Somehow, I managed to close both the train room door and the front door without slamming them.

Outside, the winter wind blasted away the remnants of my anger, leaving behind weakness and fear. I hurried out of the mansion's shadow into the emptiness that lay beneath the hollow sky. Underfoot, snow crystals glittered like precious gems.

Hardly knowing what I was doing, I swung my arm to the ground and, catching a fistful of snow, packed it into a ball. Turning, I hurled the snowball at the door. *Bang!* Snow rained onto the welcome-mat-free porch.

I stalked down the driveway, heedless of the ice patches. How could Grandfather turn me away like this? Even if the ransom note didn't convince him, you'd think the tiniest sliver of doubt would make him do something, at least investigate. It was true what his enemies said about him—he was an insensitive, greedy monster.

What's two million to him, anyway? I kicked a crusty black chunk of snow off the sidewalk. *Pocket change. He probably spends more than that on his trains.*

As for his insinuation that I could be in on such a scheme—me!, the one who never ran a yellow light—you'd think I'd have earned a little credibility for always being the calm, cool, responsible one.

I'll show him, I thought as I crossed the street. *I don't need him. The police will know what to do.*

Chapter Four

My mind still reeled from the confrontation with Grandfather as I jammed the key into my car's ignition. I could not fathom how his mind worked. I'd always thought his heart was cold and shriveled, but no. He simply didn't have one.

I barreled toward the gate and opened it just in time. My body shifted and strained against the seatbelt as I rounded turns, screeched to stops, accelerated, and sped. What a way to drive to the police station, but my adrenalin-pumping body left me no choice.

"Don't involve the police, or you'll never see Maxwell III again." The words from the ransom note pulsed ominously in my head as I entered the green-roofed police station. *This is the right thing to do,* I assured myself. *Doing nothing at all would be worse.*

"I need to talk to a detective right away. It's an emergency," I demanded at the front desk. "It's about my brother. He's been kidnapped—"

"Charlene Perigard?" a heavy voice overpowered my own.

I turned to see a large-chinned, middle-aged man in a gray suit. "We've been expecting you. Step into this room, please, and we'll discuss your concern."

"Expecting me?" I narrowed my eyes as I entered the small, paper-cluttered office. Filing cabinets lined the rear of the room. My eyes fell on a phone. "He called you, didn't he? My grandfather. 'Pay no attention to Charlene. She doesn't know what she's talking about. She's just overreacting, emotional—'"

"No need to get defensive, Ms. Perigard." The man gestured to a gray swivel-chair before settling into a cushier one behind a large computer desk.

I sat, trying to pull myself together. This was not going well so far; I couldn't let my agitation ruin my chances of being taken seriously. That's what Grandfather wanted. I took a deep breath, but the big-chinned man spoke first.

"The name's Detective Donnelly." He shook my hand and gave me his card. "And yes, your grandfather called. Now I'd like you to go ahead and tell me your story. I'll just be taking some notes as you talk, so don't mind my typing."

"Okay. Thanks." I focused on the deep wrinkles on Donnelly's forehead as I began relating the details of the last twenty-four hours, including Max's disappearance, my missed calls, the strange voice, the ransom note, and Grandfather's lack of concern. Every now and then Donnelly interrupted to ask a question. The tapping of his keyboard was constant.

Finally, I finished with, "That ransom note is real, and Max is really kidnapped, no matter what my grandfather claims. So we have to do something." The weight of the horrible situation lightened a little now that I'd shared it with someone capable.

His eyes met mine over the top of his computer screen. "You did the right thing in coming here, Ms. Perigard, and we appreciate it. Rest assured that we'll handle the matter from here."

How easy it would have been to stand up and leave, comforted with the thought that Max's welfare was now high priority, but I didn't budge. There was something vague and evasive in Donnelly's words that worried me. My grip tightened on the plastic armrests as I leaned forward. "So what's your plan? Are you going to start looking for Max right away?"

He crossed his arms and gave me an assessing look. "You're an intelligent young woman, Ms. Perigard, so I'm going to give this to you straight. We'll do all we can, but this case isn't top priority."

The full weight of fear slammed back down on my shoulders. "You can't mean that. Max's life is in danger. Surely that makes it top priority."

Donnelly rolled a pen between his thick fingers. "I'm sorry, but I'm more inclined to believe your grandfather's version. I think Max is having a little fun and hoping to make some fast money. After all, he doesn't exactly have a good track record." Donnelly picked up a paper from his desk and scanned it. "Drugs, underage drinking, trespassing, vandalism—"

"Other teens do that kind of stuff, too. I'm not saying it's right, only don't abandon him because of some past mistakes. He went through a troubled time. Our father died suddenly, tragically." I fought the tremble in my throat.

Donnelly set the paper back down. His thick gray eyebrows drew together, and I wondered if his brain, too, was thick. Thick and impenetrable.

He cleared his throat. "I'm sure it was a troubled time for both of you, and I'm sorry, but that's not an excuse to go out and create trouble. You didn't. Others don't. Heck, we've all got personal problems of one kind or another, but that's no free ticket to break the law."

"Getting kidnapped isn't breaking the law," I retorted. "And I know Max better than anyone. He would never fake this." My mind searched frantically for more ammunition. "Don't you have to look for him if he's reported missing? He's practically still a kid."

"Practically doesn't cut it. Fact is, he's not a minor. He's eighteen."

"Just barely!" I sensed I was about to be dismissed, so I tried another tactic. "What about the strange voice that answered his phone? Can't you trace the call, or at least Max's cell phone?"

Donnelly looked thoughtful. "I'll see what I can do, but there are certain procedures to follow. And are you one-hundred percent sure the voice wasn't Max's?"

31

"Yes."

"You said it was a low muffled whisper?"

"Yes," I admitted grudgingly. "But I *know* it wasn't Max."

"Hmm." Donnelly leaned back, his chair grunting. "I'll look into all this and get back to you." His phone rang and he reached for it, saying, "If I were you, I'd go home and relax. Before you know it, Max will probably turn up on his own."

" 'Probably?' You think I can relax with the assurance of probably? Unbelievable. You're just like my grandfather. You say it nicer, but the end result is the same: You don't care!" I stood suddenly, and my chair went rolling back, hitting the wall. "Well, I do care, and if I have to, I'm going to find Max myself. Thanks for nothing!"

I half expected to be tackled, cuffed, and taken into custody for getting angry—or whatever they officially called it—at a police officer, but Donnelly let me run out of the station like a maniac, and I pictured him calling Grandfather and reporting my visit verbatim. After all, he'd typed a transcript of everything I'd said. *Grandfather's probably paying him off,* I fumed in my car.

Confronting Grandfather and Donnelly had taken a lot more out of me than I cared to admit. The knowledge that I was now utterly on my own was an iceberg on my shoulders. I was used to responsibility, but this was too much. But I wasn't ready to go home and wait, as Donnelly advised.

So what next?

I pulled out my silent phone and frowned at it. No missed calls, but surely Wayne had gotten my message by now. I started dialing, then hung up. It was too easy to ignore a call.

Twisting the steering wheel, I turned my car and headed back through town. Before too long, Grandfather's sprawling estate forced its way into my line of vision. Without even trying, I saw the spire of his private chapel pointing skyward, a testament to his self-righteousness. I had been inside the chapel many times. I liked Father Selton, an old priest who was very traditional without being severe. I may even have attended more often if I weren't so turned off by Grandfather's false pious attitude, and knowing he'd be watching me from his specially reserved "Perigard pew." I could tell he thought that having his own chapel made him holy, as if God measured holiness by how many bills a person dropped in the collection basket.

I kept driving.

Several minutes later, I wedged my car between two snow banks on the side of the road and turned off the engine. Across the street, the gaping garage of Wayne's blue ranch house contained two cars, making it obvious that at least someone was home.

Snow from last night's storm covered the driveway in a thick, deep and unblemished layer. As I plodded through, I saw Wayne emerge from the garage toting a snow shovel. When he caught sight of me, he hesitated. But he continued in my direction, even though he appeared to be scowling, or maybe he was just squinting in the bright light.

"Hey, what's up?" he asked as we met in the middle of the driveway.

"Did you get my call?"

"Your call?" He cocked his blond head, and his earring caught the sunlight and glinted silver. "What call?"

"I left a message last night."

"Sorry. I don't check the machine." He planted the shovel in the snow and supported his lanky body with the handle. "My sisters think they own it, so I leave it to them. That all you wanted?"

I shook my head. "The message I left, it was about Max. I'm worried about him. He—" I swallowed the quiver in my voice.

A hint of something discomforting flashed across Wayne's face, followed by a shadow. Was it concern? Wariness? Or annoyance?

"Max never came home last night," I continued. "Do you have any idea where he is?"

Wayne's gaze flickered away from me.

"Did you see him yesterday?" I prodded.

He shrugged. "I saw him around. He's not here now, if that's what you're after."

"Wayne!"

I looked up to see his mom poking her head out the front door. "Hurry up and get started on that driveway! We have to leave in— Oh, hi Charlene!" With a quick wave, she disappeared back inside.

Wayne glowered and began attacking the snow. I cringed at the ferocious grinding noise as the metal shovel scraped the driveway. The blade swooped a little too close to my feet, and I stepped back.

"Wayne?" I attempted. "About Max . . ."

He chucked a load of snow onto the already large piles lining the driveway. "Look, Charlene, it's no big deal. Why can't you ever just butt out? Give Max some space. You don't have to be looking out for him all the time." In a low mutter, he added, "Man, I'm glad my sisters aren't like you, always on my case."

An acidic response rose in my throat, but I swallowed hard.

"Just let it be." Tossing more snow, he grunted. "A night away from home isn't the end of the world. Max is fine. I'm sure he'll call you one of these days."

"One of these days may be too late. You don't realize how serious this is." It was on the tip of my tongue to tell him about the ransom note, but that would mean trusting him with Max's life. I couldn't do that. Not yet, anyway. So I settled for a passionate "Max is *missing!*"

"Maybe he *wants* to be missing! Ever think of that?" Wayne turned his head and spat. "Just leave it alone."

"I can't," I insisted, almost tearful.

He shifted his weight. "Look, I've gotta get this job finished and get packing. My whole family's leaving on vacation tonight."

I stared at him. He was Max's best friend. Why was he not worried? As he faced me, his stance was defiant; but he was finally not moving, not pitching snow, and I noticed something. My eyes narrowed as I peered closer at the large white tag hanging from his winter coat. A ski lift tag. And it had yesterday's date stamped on it, along with the words "Whitecap Mountain."

Realization zapped me. I met his eyes as my pulse quickened. "You went snowboarding with Max yesterday, didn't you? At Whitecap Mountain?"

His mouth opened slightly. After a pause, he admitted, "Yeah, so? We went snowboarding. What of it?"

Snowboarding.

The back of my throat constricted. Max was always hounding me to go snowboarding with him, but I always refused. I was too scared. So this time, he didn't even bother asking me. *I could have been with you. I should have been.* And somehow, I was convinced that if I had been, he wouldn't have been kidnapped. Guilt welled up inside me.

"You okay?"

Wayne looked at me with concern, and with monumental effort, I peeled my tongue from the roof of my mouth. I had to keep asking questions. "Did you drive to the hill together?"

"No." He picked up a load of snow and pitched it. "We took separate cars and met there."

"Did anything unusual happen at the hill? Did you meet other people, or did you snowboard with each other the whole time?"

"Mostly with each other, but we split up a few times. I had to go inside to warm up." He planted the shovel back in the snow. "We did join a few girls, but they left early, and we didn't talk to much of anyone after that. The janitor was a real jerk, though," he added. "I tried to tell him the garbage in the cafeteria was totally reeking the place out, and he gave me this glare that would burn a hole in a snake."

"Thanks for the mental picture." Strangely cooperative as Wayne was suddenly being, I couldn't shake the feeling that he was holding out on me, trying to sidetrack me, or both. "Anyone else?"

He wrinkled his brow. "The usual people at the ticket

window, rentals, and cafeteria."

"Did you leave the hill at the same time?"

"Just about. Around four or five. When I left, Max was about to leave, too. As soon as he returned the board he'd rented."

"Did he say if he was going straight home or not?"

Wayne seemed to debate his answer. "Maybe. I'm not sure." He picked up his shovel. "Look, I've told you what I know, and I've gotta finish this driveway."

"But have you told me *everything* you know?"

He clamped his mouth shut and resumed shoveling. I had to move to avoid the blizzard he was creating.

I was walking away when I heard him call out, "It'll all be okay, Charlene. Don't worry so much."

But I have to worry. I'm the only one who is. Fear rippled through me, followed by a wave of panic. Suddenly I thought, *And if I was kidnapped, who would care? Grandfather? No way. Gwen and Joy?* They'd miss me, I supposed, but they wouldn't be devastated. Max was the only one who would really care.

I had to find him.

In my car, as I turned the key and the engine growled, I knew exactly where to go next. As I drove, I pulled out the card from Detective Donnelly and dialed his number. He picked up on the second ring. "Detective Donnelly."

"Hi. This is Charlene Perigard." I had no doubt he remembered me. "I thought you should know that Max was last seen at Whitecap Mountain Ski Resort. He went snowboarding there yesterday with a friend."

"Yeah?" His voice reflected mild interest. "Who was the friend?"

"Wayne Shwartz. You need to question him, and soon because he's leaving on vacation this evening. He knows more than he's telling; I'm sure of it. I just left his house and I'm heading to the ski hill now. Just thought you should know."

"All right, thanks for the info. Have fun at the hill."

"Have fun? I'm not going there to have fun. I'm going to

look for—" I heard a click followed by dead silence, and I knew he'd hung up. I slammed my phone onto the seat.

The lengthy drive helped cool my anger, however, and I knew I'd continue to update Donnelly, even if he didn't appreciate it. I would do it for Max. At some point, I'd convince the detective to take this case seriously.

When I reached Whitecap Mountain, I crawled along in search of a parking space, feeling like a rejected puzzle piece that would not fit no matter where it tried. I pressed the brake more often than the accelerator as daydreaming couples, preoccupied parents, and careless kids crisscrossed my path.

I'll have every vehicle in this lot memorized by the time I find a spot. Toyotas, Chevies, Fords, and suddenly, a Jaguar, so snow-covered, it must have been parked overnight.

I slammed the brake. I studied the car closer, but the license plate, hidden by an accumulation of snow, was unreadable.

Honk!

My gaze jumped to my rearview mirror. A black car rode my bumper. Meanwhile, an Accord backed out several spaces ahead of me. I zipped into the relinquished parking spot and flew out the door.

As soon as I brushed the snow off the Jaguar's license plate, my hunch was confirmed. JAGRRR. This was indeed the car that Max had swiped from Grandfather.

Chapter Five

*O*f course, I didn't expect to find Max inside the car—long as it had been out in the freezing cold, I *hoped* he wasn't inside—but still, this was a great lead. I tugged at the door, but it wouldn't budge. Thinking it must be locked, I almost gave up, when it flew open and threw me backwards against a neighboring van.

Poking my dizzy head into the car's interior, I saw pristine gray dash, seats, and floor, almost making me doubt Max had ever been in here. But I knew how scrupulously clean Grandfather kept his cars—he employed a car detailer for just that purpose—so I guessed it would take even Max more than one brief trip to mess it up.

A numb-fingered search through the glove box and under the seats revealed nothing of help or interest. I stepped out and closed the door, ready to call Donnelly, when my eagerness collapsed into dread. I pivoted to face the Jaguar, as if it really were the terrible cat it was named after. I hadn't checked the trunk. I swallowed. *The perfect place to hide a body.*

I would not allow myself to think of my brother lying dead in there. Unfortunately, this very resolution created the image of a frozen corpse. The sleek silver Jaguar was a hearse. The trunk, a coffin. And I had to open it.

I leaned into the car and pulled the lever to pop the trunk. Then I trudged to the rear of the car, set my jaw, and began to lift the trunk. Would Max's mischievous green eyes be open in a dead stare? His lips, blue? Long lashes glazed with ice? Or would he be covered by a bag or blanket?

A shiny black garbage bag lay inside, but it was scrunched into a careless ball. I touched it, tentatively. To my relief, it was empty, though I didn't know what it was I'd dreaded finding. Relishing the bareness of the charcoal colored trunk, I slid my hand over and then beneath the fabric lining. All was as it should be.

I returned my attention to my phone. Time to call Donnelly. I punched in his number and barely waited for him to complete his greeting.

"I found Max's car here, in the Whitecap Mountain parking lot."

"The car he stole? Your grandfather will be glad to hear that."

"Yes, a car is so much more priceless than a grandson," I couldn't help saying.

"Look, Ms. Perigard. A police investigation is a serious thing, and I don't appreciate your attitude."

"Police investigation! Is that what you call it? So far, I'm the only one doing the investigating. And excuse me, but I thought this information was important." *Stop it, Charlene, I ordered myself. You'll never get anywhere like this.* "I'm sorry." I took a deep breath of frigid air. "But don't you think it's important?" I asked in a softer tone.

"Yes, it is. I'll be sending someone there to check it out when we get a chance. In the meantime, cool off. Go skiing. Maybe you'll see your brother on the hill and you'll realize this was all just a teenage prank."

I hung up.

Donnelly would take his time sending someone, I was sure, and I wasn't going to wait around to meet the person. My gaze traveled over the blinding slopes dotted with people gliding rapidly downhill. How I wished Max was among them, but I knew better. A false sense of assurance was the easy, lazy way out, and neither Grandfather nor Donnelly could convince me that Max was okay. Donnelly might see the deserted Jaguar as a good sign, but I saw it as the opposite. Yes, the Jaguar was a pricey car, but why would the kidnapper take it at the risk of being caught? He wanted Max. With the ransom money, he could then buy any luxury car he wanted, and more.

I looked over my shoulder. People mingled in the lot, but no one looked at me. Could a kidnapper somehow have forced Max into another vehicle with no one realizing or caring? I pivoted on the heel of my boot, taking in the expanse of snowy pine hills as far as I could see.

The kidnapper could have driven Max away to anywhere, but Whitecap Mountain was as close to him as I could get right now. I recalled the specifics of the ransom note, demanding the money be dropped off in locker number thirty-eight at this ski hill. The kidnapper had been here, so there was a chance he was still here. If not, he would be back. I strode toward the ski lodge.

The building was decorated with large plastic snowflakes that would light up festively for night skiing. No doubt the kidnapper had chosen this place wisely. With all the people wandering around in ski masks and goggles, it was the perfect setting for a crime.

I entered what appeared to be a large, wet-carpeted basement containing blue benches, on which people sat to tug on ski pants and boots. I inspected locker number thirty-eight, but the black number on a locked gray metal door told me nothing.

I passed a fireplace around which people clustered with Styrofoam cups of hot cocoa or coffee, and ended up in a noisy cafeteria. My assorted thoughts resembled the jumble of skiers and snowboarders I saw on the hill through the large rear window. One out-of-control guy just missed crashing into a tree. He was passed by an expert little girl snowboarder. An elderly lady snowplowed her way down cautiously, followed by a guy wearing what looked like a severely stretched elf hat.

Someone's watching me. Sensing it acutely, I turned slowly and caught the eye of a bubblegum-smacking blond girl working the cafeteria register. She smiled at me with familiarity, almost as if she recognized me. Intending to question her, I stepped in line. My hungry stomach was happy with the decision. Unfortunately, by the time I reached the counter, the girl was no longer behind it. She'd been replaced by a large-boned woman brandishing a sloppy macaroni spoon.

I ate a burger while standing up, preferring this to squeezing into a table with strangers. Suddenly, I felt very much like I was in school. I never fit into the cafeteria crowd there, either. Scanning the faces, I tried to pick out someone, anyone, who looked like a kidnapper, but I knew it was hopeless. Everyone sat in clusters, as if they knew each other.

Finished with my meager meal, I entered the restroom, holding my breath as long as I could. It was typically smelly and repulsive, and I couldn't get out fast enough. I didn't even brush my teeth.

My sour breath matched my sour outlook. Answers were here, somewhere, but I didn't know what questions to ask, or who to ask. It was as I studied the line of people for the rental counter that Wayne's words replayed in my mind. *"When I left, Max was about to leave, too. As soon as he returned the board he'd rented."*

So I strode up to the rental counter line and fought the urge to cut to the front.

By the time it was my turn, I'd had plenty of time to plan my words. "Hi, I have a question," I said perkily to the hefty girl wearing a lime-green, tasseled ski hat. "I'm hoping you can help me because this is very important." Behind her, I glimpsed the bubblegum-chomping blond who'd caught my eye in the cafeteria. I sensed she was eavesdropping.

I lowered my voice. "My brother came snowboarding here yesterday and he rented a board. Do you have any way of knowing if he returned it?"

"Why do you want to know? Ya think he stole it?"

"No." I couldn't help noticing a faint mustache-like shadow on the girl's upper lip. "I—do you remember seeing him? He looks like me."

"Yesterday? I wasn't even working rentals. And ya think I remember every person who comes by here? I see hundreds of new faces a day." She crossed her arms. "Look, you're holding up the line," she said in a megaphone voice, so that

41

the whole line heard and began to grumble behind me. "I can tell ya this: No boards were reported stolen—"

"Then do you at least know who was working rentals yesterday? Please, it's very important. I need to know if anyone saw my brother, and how late he—"

"I'm not here to answer those kind of questions." She narrowed her eyes. "You're acting like you think you're a detective, but I don't see any badge. If you're not here to rent a board, step aside."

I touched my tongue to the bottom of my front teeth and pressed hard. "Thank you," I enunciated slowly, trying to remain calm, then moved away.

"Hey, over here."

I turned to see the blond gum-chewer motioning me to a corner, near a garbage can.

Irritated by my recent failure, I blurted, "Gum chewing is a disgusting habit."

She gave me a wide-eyed stare. "But I chew it to freshen my breath."

I shook my head, ashamed of myself. Since when had I become so rude? "I'm sorry. I shouldn't have said that. I didn't mean it."

"It's okay. I actually kind of agree with you. I'd prefer to just brush my teeth, but seriously . . ." She lowered her voice conspiratorially. "Have you been in these bathrooms?"

She had a point. I glanced at the overflowing garbage a few feet away and wrinkled my nose as I took a step back. "Your janitors don't do a very good job, do they?"

"It's not their fault, really. They're just short-handed this week because the day guy quit suddenly. The night guy works hard, but junk just sorta piles up during the day, you know?" She shrugged. "The cafeteria crew will get it eventually."

"Aren't you cafeteria crew?"

She smiled. "I'm all over the place. I help with anything. Anything *but* the garbage, that is. I let the guys handle that." She grimaced briefly, then smiled as she studied my face. "So you're his sister, aren't you?" She said it not as a question, but with a touch of awe. "I could tell you were Max's sister the moment I saw you."

"You know him?" *Steady,* I warned my jumping heart. I read her nametag: Cindy.

"Not really." She blushed. "I'd love to, though. He's so cute." She gave a giddy laugh, reminding me of Gwen. "He's been coming here a lot lately. I was hoping he'd be here today. I heard you at the rental counter, asking those questions, so I thought I'd help you out. I worked rentals yesterday. Max did return his board, of course. He always does. We chatted a little longer than last time, and I almost thought he was going to ask me out for New Year's." Cindy tugged at a strand of hair. "I was afraid he got the wrong impression when I told him I had plans, but I can't break tradition. My dad and I always celebrate New Year's by drinking root beer floats and watching *The Three Stooges.* But it would sound dumb if I tried to explain it."

She paused in chewing her gum to nibble her lip. "Please don't think I'm nosy, but does he have a girlfriend?" She took a deep breath, then popped a bubble.

"No."

She beamed a smile so radiant, I knew she'd willingly answer my questions. "What time did Max return his board?"

"Oh, sometime before five."

"Was he alone?"

She nodded. "But not when he got here in the morning. He was with a friend, some guy."

Right, Wayne. I filed this information away and prodded for more. "After Max returned his board, did you see where he went, or if anyone followed him?"

She shook her head. "I wish I knew." She blushed again. "I wanted to watch him, but I had to help other people." Suddenly her eyes grew round and fearful, as if the oddity of my questions finally registered. "So why do you need to know all this? Is Max lost or something?" Her voice went up a notch. "Are the police looking for him?"

"No, it's not like that." I was wary of giving too much

43

information. "But if you happen to see him anywhere, could you give me a call?"

"Of course." She whipped out a pink phone and added my name and number. "Nice meeting you, by the way. Maybe we could hang out sometime."

The statement threw me. It wasn't one I heard often. "Maybe. Thanks for your help."

"No prob. Your brother's awesome."

"I know." I also knew that, like other girls before, she was trying to reach Max through me. Only this time, I didn't mind.

"I hope you and Max come back here soon."

"I hope so, too."

"Cindy, break's over!" someone hollered.

Cindy rolled her eyes. "Duty calls," she said before disappearing.

I thrust my hands in my coat pockets and moved toward the large cafeteria window, frustrated that my investigation was giving me so little. Outside, the sky was darkening, spilling blue shadows on the glittering snow. I hated to think of another day passing with no real progress. I frowned as I watched people riding the open lifts, dangling high above the hill as they glided up out of sight. Max had sat on one of those seats only twenty-four hours ago. I pictured him in his navy blue coat, the stripe of black on the sleeves, and I saw it all so vividly.

In fact, I saw it for real. I scrambled closer to the window and almost pressed my nose to the chill glass. Yes, someone riding up the lift definitely looked like Max.

I darted outside. Knowing full well I'd never get a ride up without a ticket, I bypassed the lift. My attempt at running up the snow-packed hill was just that, an attempt. My stiff boots, the slope, and cumbersome snow forced me to trudge along the tree-line, but I still had to be alert for skiers and snowboarders sailing my way.

I watched for the blue-coated snowboarder to come cruising down the hill, but my eyes stung and watered in the cold, obscuring my vision, and the increasing shadows didn't help.

All too soon, I was panting, and my muscles burned.

By the time I reached the hilltop, all sunlight was gone. Large spotlights bleached the snow. Huffing, I leaned against a tree while a quick survey told me that there were three different routes downhill: An easy path, marked with a green square sign; an intermediate slope (which I'd just trudged up), marked with a blue circle sign; and an expert slope—meaning steep and dangerous—marked with a black diamond.

Distancing myself from the diamond slope, I took a step toward where the lift chairs swooped low to let the riders off, planning to watch for a little while in hopes of spotting the blue-coated snowboarder again. *It can't be Max. But if it is, I'll be happy I was wrong. Grandfather can tell me, "I told you so," and I won't care. As long as Max is safe.*

Through my wool hat, I heard the mechanical whirring and squeaking of the ski lift cable above. I turned my head upward just as someone yelled, "Look out!"

I dodged the first snowboarder leaving the lift, but was sideswiped by a second one and knocked to my knees. I looked up just in time to see him cruise toward the expert slope and disappear abruptly over the crest, as if it were a cliff.

I scurried out of the path of others dismounting the ski lift, and the blue-coated snowboarder I'd been watching for glided by, slowing momentarily. "You all right?"

"Yes," I answered weakly. "Thanks for asking."

He sailed off and I sighed. He was round-faced and at least thirty. Not Max.

Deciding to call it a night, I set off on the easy slope, a wide, gently winding tree-fringed path. My kind of ski slope. I expected plenty of skiers to pass me by, but none did. Glimpsing behind me, I realized I was completely alone on this oversized trail. I swallowed a cold lump in my throat and quickened my pace. Every shadow on my right and left seemed to shiver and jump. My heartbeat quickened as something occurred to me. I wouldn't recognize the kidnapper if I saw him, but he would recognize me, Max's twin, easily.

That's when I saw him. A dark, solitary figure standing in

the trees to my right, just waiting for me to reach him. I skidded to a stop, almost falling, then whirled and ran to my left, into the trees. I jumped a fallen branch and scrambled through crackling brush, emerging onto a much steeper slope. In fact, this was almost a sheer drop. The black diamond hill.

My momentum was too much, and I fell, limbs tangling and twisting. Amidst the whirling light and dark, and the ice flecks biting my cheeks, I felt a sharp pain. But I was tumbling so fast that I couldn't identify the location of the pain. I rolled like an acrobat, and I had a crazy vision of myself becoming buried in the center of a giant snowball, like in a cartoon. But it wasn't funny. I'd freeze to death. No, I'd suffocate first.

With a thud, I finally stopped rolling. I opened my eyes to a hazy purple sky, the color of a giant bruise, and groaned.

"Are you all right?" demanded a voice that was suddenly above me. I stared up into a black ski-masked face. Was it the same menacing figure that had been waiting for me in the trees?

I closed my eyes.

"Can you hear me?"

Maybe if I pretend to be dead, he'll leave me alone.

He crouched beside me and I heard static. He called for help, and I realized he was talking into a radio.

I groaned again, but not because of the pain. *I'm so stupid. He's not a kidnapper; he's ski patrol.* I took a deep breath and moved up to a sitting position. "I don't need help, really. Thanks anyway, but I can make it from here." I struggled to stand, and clenched my teeth. The pain in my ankle wasn't severe, but I'd be feeling it tonight.

"Just sit and wait for your ride," the guy said, none too kindly. "What the heck were you thinking, jumping off the edge of the slope like that?"

I felt my face flush. "I guess I got scared."

"What? Of me?" The guy stood and plucked off his mask. "That a little less scary?"

I stared mutely at the shaggy red hair, dark eyes, and broad boney nose.

"Maybe not." He shrugged, then pointed to a badge. "I'm on the ski patrol. What did you think you were doing? Being a reckless hazard, that's what. Especially to yourself. You don't even have a ticket and skis, and you probably broke your ankle."

"It's just twisted," I said, attempting once more to stand. The guy put a firm hand on my shoulder and pushed me back down. "Stay off it. The stretcher will be here any second." Sure enough, the emergency snowmobile roared up moments later with a long sled-like stretcher on the back.

As it turned out, I was right. My ankle was only twisted. "It's not too severe, but you should still try to stay off it and ice it," I was told. "Anyone you want us to call?"

"No, I'll be fine." I hobbled back to my car. As I pressed the accelerator, I was grateful that the twisted ankle wasn't my right one.

I arrived home to find Gwen and Joy gone. *It's just as well.* I didn't feel like reliving the unsuccessful and humiliating day by describing it to them.

I entered the large kitchen, shining coldly with its stainless steel appliances, and headed to the fridge to see what our cook had left for me. A covered china plate held a generous slice of roast beef, green beans smothered in hollandaise sauce, and garlic mashed potatoes drowning in mushroom gravy.

Suddenly famished, I zapped the food in the microwave, then sat on an upholstered stool at the marble counter. I swirled the seat this way and that as I ate, nervous and fidgety. The house was too large and quiet. All the help had gone home for the night, and all I heard was the relentless ticking of the grandfather clock.

Grandfather. Not who I wanted to think about right now.

My appetite gone, I limped tediously through the mansion, checking that all doors and windows were locked, all the blinds closed. Usually this ritual made me feel cozy, and with the peace of having the place to myself, I would have savored the time to curl up and work a crossword puzzle in the overstuffed chair that Gwen usually claimed.

Tonight I went through the motions but the sense of security was lacking. Tonight the crossword squares stayed blank, and I actually began nibbling my pencil. As if sensing my unsettled mood, even Mitsy the cat avoided me.

I'm not nervous, I told myself, but then the mansion began making noises that I'd never heard before, and I began wondering what I would do if the kidnapper came for me. I knew I shouldn't entertain such irrational thoughts, but darkness and solitude were skillful at canceling common sense.

As if I'd be any safer if Gwen and Joy were home, I thought, attempting to lighten my mood. *They'd probably open the door wide and invite the kidnapper in for a makeover.*

Though I knew it was childish, I pulled an iron poker from the fireplace and carried it upstairs with me. When I went to bed, I slipped it under the sheets and fell asleep hugging it, the way I used to hug my stuffed unicorn.

Maybe it was Gwen and Joy arriving home that woke me; but when I listened, all I heard was silence—a prickly silence, the kind that plays a game, seeing who will break it first.

I lay in bed, listening for something, and all the horrible kidnapping cases I'd ever heard came creeping back to me, accounts of people never being found, or worse—turning up in a sack, at the bottom of a lake, buried in a woods or in someone's backyard or basement.

Then there was the disturbing fact that most kidnapping victims were killed within the first twenty-four hours. Not a comforting statistic.

Thinking back on the day, guilt crept in. What a jerk I'd been to Cindy, and how nice and helpful she had been to me in return. But everyone else had been so uncaring. *It's a rotten world.*

I recollected how Grandfather had termed me an idiot, a pest, and tiresome; Donnelly accused me of having an attitude and being defensive; and the ski patrol worker had called me a reckless hazard.

They're all correct, I admitted, *but they forget one: Failure.*

Because I was able to snuggle into a warm, safe bed, while Max was still out there somewhere, cold and afraid, relying on me to save him.

If he was even still alive.

I buried my head in my pillow and cried.

Chapter Six

*W*hen I awoke, it was morning, and I must have been in a deep sleep because I saw the iron poker had fallen out of bed during the night and the noise hadn't disturbed me. I stepped over it and tested my ankle. Tender, but ignorable. No way was I staying off my foot today. I showered, threw on my clothes, and hurried across the street to Grandfather's.

Only when I reached the gate, did I remember today was Sunday. So I told the guard I was going to Mass, and he let me through with no hassle. A faint hymn wafted to my ears as I approached the little stone building.

I hesitated in the chapel vestibule, glancing down at my jeans and boots. True, the jeans weren't dirty, frayed, or adorned with colors or holes, and my black boots looked brand new; but this was not what Grandfather would consider proper attire for attending Mass. Even from here, I could see that the women—hired help, I assumed—were all wearing long skirts, dark coats, and veils or hats to cover their hair.

I pulled my wool cap down tight around my cold ears, thankful for it. Without it, I would have been expected to borrow a head veil out of a basket which had been provided by Grandfather for just such an emergency. I remembered how, back before he'd had this ingenious idea, I once had to wear a tissue on my head. Max had kept grabbing it and pretending to blow his nose on it. Now, respectful as I wished to be in church, I couldn't get past the thought of putting something on my head that had been worn by countless strangers.

During the sermon, the way Father Selton spoke about religion being more than an outward show, and that in order to get anything out of it you had to give, made me pray Grandfather had his hearing aid turned up full volume.

I could tell Grandfather was still angry at me, because after Mass he didn't mention my unsuitable clothing. He simply said, "*You* again," while charging past me and barreling through the church doors. "Have you come to apologize for Maxwell, who's too cowardly to come himself and ask for forgiveness?"

Ask? Yesterday it was beg. Are you softening? "He's not back. But I am, and I need you to listen." I hurried to keep up with Grandfather's stalking strides, and I wondered how he could walk that way on the icy drive without slipping. Probably because it was his ice and it wouldn't dare slip him; he'd have workers outside in seconds, blasting it away with blowtorches. It had no qualms about sabotaging me, however. My feet flew out from under me and I landed with a painful thud.

"I saw that," said Rob, who answered the door when I finally made it up to the house. Grandfather had long ago disappeared from sight. "You all right?"

"Yeah, I'm fine. Thanks." I pushed my way inside and tried not to limp. "Where's my grandfather?"

"Eating." He pointed toward the dining hall.

Eating is an understatement, I thought upon arrival. *Feasting is more like it.* Still wearing his pinstripe suit, which made him look like a gangster, I found Grandfather seated in a throne-like chair with carved armrests. Before him lay a spread of sumptuous food, including a buffet of eggs, bacon, sausages, gravy, toast, fruit, cream, syrups, waffles, pancakes, and donuts, all laid out in sparkling serving dishes on a long polished wooden table, while a chandelier dripped rainbow crystals from the ceiling.

The dogs sat one on each side of Grandfather, alert as guards, but eyeing the food greedily. "Breakfast time, Grim." Grandfather handed him morsels too grand to be called scraps. In fact, they could have fed a hungry family. "Here you go, Reaper. Only the best sausages for you," Grandfather said in a finer tone than I'd ever heard him use when talking to

51

humans. He patted the dogs' heads, then picked up a straw-berry, dipped it in melted chocolate, and consumed it in one bite.

"Grandfather," I began, approaching the table, "you have to pay the ransom."

"I'm thinking of starting a zoo. What do you think of that?"

"You can change the subject, or you can ignore me, but I'll keep talking until you accept the facts. Max needs our help. Please pay the ransom. It's the only way."

Grandfather forked a thick stack of pancakes and plopped them on his plate. "Must we go through this again? It's an utter waste of time, and I have no intention of wasting my money as well." He smeared the pancakes with butter, mounded them with cream, then drowned them in syrup. "What happened to finding Maxwell yourself? I take it that didn't go very well?"

I compressed my lips. "Not with you pitting the police against me."

"I simply told them the facts." He chewed, yet he some-how managed to maintain a smirk.

"At least I found Max's car."

Grandfather lifted his knife in the air. "Ah, ah, ah—not Maxwell's car, *my* car."

I inhaled deeply, smelled the mingling scents of sweet and savory food. "Yes, your car. But that's beside the point. Since we can't find Max, and the police are dragging their feet, we have to pay the ransom or we're gambling with his life."

"Interesting choice of words there, that 'we.' It's not our money, it's mine."

"I know that! That's why I'm here, begging you, please, *please* use it. It's the only chance we have." I took a deep trembling breath but couldn't get enough air. "How can I make you see? I won't be able to live if something happens to Max. He's not just my brother, he's my twin. He's half of me, he—"

"Please don't go getting all emotional. It's bad for the digestion. Not mine, mind you, but Grim's. He has a sensitive stomach, don't you boy?" Grandfather rubbed the dog's ears, and Grim whined pathetically.

I slammed my hand onto the table, making Grandfather's tower of pancakes sway. "You care more about your pets than your own grandson! Don't you realize time is running out? A kidnapper is not going to be patient."

Grandfather shook his head. "I've told you before. This is a waiting game. Soon enough, Maxwell will have had enough of this foolishness and show up on his own."

"He'll show up all right," I said, my voice dropping. "He'll show up dead. And it will be your fault, all because you're stubborn and greedy and cruel." I pointed a finger at him. "You just sit back and play with your trains and feast like a bloated Buddha and dream about new ways to waste your money by building extravagant amusements that no one enjoys—not even you—but I'm not going to watch. If Max isn't here, I've got nothing to stay for. I hope you're satisfied. I'm out of here, and I'm never coming back. Chew on that!" And I swept Grandfather's plate off the table with one angry stroke. The crashing and cracking and clinking made a wonderful racket.

I had wanted to shock Grandfather, who seemed so un-shockable, but even I didn't expect him to react the way he did. First his face turned purple, then blue. His body seemed to quiver. One moment he was seated calmly, the next moment his fork clattered to the table and he clawed at his chest. Grim and Reaper started howling.

"What's the matter?" I cried, instantly repentant. "Are you choking?" But Grandfather couldn't acknowledge me because he fell into a lifeless slump. I felt for a pulse, but didn't think I could find one. I screamed, "Rob! Rob!", simply because I knew no other hired help by name.

Suddenly, Rob was at Grandfather's side. "I'll take over. Call 911."

I dialed and spoke without registering a word, my eyes riveted to Grandfather's limp form. Rob had laid him on the wood floor and was performing CPR.

Please, God, let it work. If he died, I'd be forever haunted by my last words to him.

While I stood uselessly, Grandfather burst to life in a fit of coughing. Rob, on his knees beside him, stopped pumping his chest and helped to steady him. The dogs licked Grandfather's face.

Rob glanced at me. "What happened?"

My lips felt like wax, stuck together coldly. Shame lurked deep inside me, but I refused to acknowledge it.

"I had a heart attack, that's what happened," snapped Grandfather, who tried hoisting himself to a sitting position. He didn't make it all the way. His arm wobbled and turned to Jell-O at the joint. Rob reached out to support him. Grandfather's face had changed from blue to an ashen shade. He turned to me, and I thought I saw fear for the first time in his eyes.

"An ambulance is on its way," I managed to say, my voice sounding meek and contrite.

"A heart attack," Rob muttered, glancing at the table. "Can't say it's a surprise. Your diet would make a pig sick. I'm putting you on a fruit and vegetable regimen."

"You'll do no such thing. The best part of life is eating."

After the ambulance arrived and Grandfather was being transported to his room because he refused to be taken to the hospital, Rob asked me in a lowered tone, "So what's the whole story? Was it just the food, or did something shock him?"

"Yes, something shocked him. Me," I admitted. Then I left the room to follow Grandfather. I wasn't finished with him yet.

―――

Amazing how quickly the doctors and nurses appeared. They flitted about like bothersome moths and advised me to stay out of the way. I told myself I wasn't hungry, but while I waited for them to finish with Grandfather, I crammed down three donuts.

I was licking powdered sugar from my fingertips when I spotted a nurse leaving. I hurried to Grandfather's room and questioned all the doctors and nurses I saw.

"He's had a heart attack. You need to let him rest," they insisted. "Come back tomorrow."

"Let my granddaughter talk to me if she wants," Grandfather said in his most commanding voice. "In private."

Passing under an oak archway, I entered his room. The heavy jade canopy of a four-poster bed was tied back with gold cords, but it was still difficult to locate Grandfather, buried as he was amidst mountains of blankets and pillows.

"I've decided—" He interrupted himself with a fit of coughing.

I located a glass of water among a clutter of medicine bottles and handed it to him.

"I've decided it's time to look into this matter." He thrust the glass back at me. "It's time to take the next step."

The glass was slippery in my hands. "You mean Max?"

"Maxwell."

Hope kindled within me. "So you're going to follow the ransom instructions?" I tried not to sound eager, for fear Grandfather might read it as a sign that I *was* in on some scheme. Instantly, I despised the fact that I had let his contorted way of thinking infect my mind.

"Yes, I'll follow the instructions. Will that satisfy you? Will you calm down now and leave this to me?"

What a relief that would be. Except for one thing. "I want to deliver the money." I knew better than to trust Grandfather. He might only be pretending to concede in order to placate me, not intending to follow through with anything.

"What? And give the kidnapper a chance to get you, too? Don't be absurd."

"I spent all day at the ski hill yesterday, and I was fine." No need to bring up my ankle. "I'm not negotiating." I thrust out my chin. "I'll go to Whitecap Mountain every day this week and guard locker thirty-eight unless you let me deliver the money. I'll stop anyone you bring in to do it."

It was a bogus claim. All the bravery in the world wouldn't make my muscles grow. Grandfather could bring in any guy to overpower me and get the job done. Even Rob could do it. "Have it your way," Grandfather said. "But if you get kidnapped too, don't expect me to bail you out."

I was so relieved, I actually lifted the water glass, which I'd been holding tensely all this time, to my lips. Realizing at the last second that it was Grandfather's, I set it down on the bedside table.

"It will take some time to get matters arranged," Grandfather continued. "I'll call when things are ready." He paused to battle his pillow. "I still don't like this. Do you realize the consequences of giving a kidnapper what he wants? It means crime pays, and he won't think twice about doing it again. It feeds a hunger that can never be satisfied. He'll brag, and other would-be criminals will be motivated. You think you have it hard now? After this, you and Maxwell will be targets for the rest of your lives. You won't be able to step out your front door without a flock of bodyguards." He turned piercing eyes on me. "Is that what you want?"

"It's not about what I want." Getting Max back safely was all that mattered. We could deal with consequences when they came. I almost smiled, this was such a new way for me to be thinking.

I left Grandfather so he could rest, though I doubted that's what he'd do. Finally, I felt as if I'd helped Max. Grandfather had disguised and manipulated the discussion well, but that still didn't change the outcome. For the first time in my life, I had won.

I returned home to wait for Grandfather's call. I met Gwen and Joy in the great room, sitting cross-legged on the Persian rug, painting their nails and laughing like two girls at a slumber party.

"Max still not back?" Gwen asked, pausing in painting her fingernails a daring shade of red.

"I'm beginning to worry," Joy said.

They're still clueless, I realized, feeling a pang of guilt for not informing them sooner. "I have something to tell you," I began, "and I need to sit down."

"Why don't you paint your nails, too?" Gwen squealed. "It would be such an improvement."

"Sorry," I declined, sinking onto the leather sofa, "but no thanks."

Swish, swish went their little brushes. Giggle, giggle. How nice to feel so carefree. I sucked in my breath, about to speak, when Gwen interrupted me.

"Then how about untangling my rosary? It's right there, next to you."

I glanced over at the glass side table to see a messy mass of silver chain and blue beads.

"I'd do it myself," she continued, "but my nails are wet, and besides, you're so good at it."

I plucked up the rosary and began examining it. "You were using this to play with Mitsy again, weren't you?"

"Can I help it if it's her favorite toy?" Gwen shrugged. "Maybe she's a holy cat."

"That's so irreverent. You know you could actually try using this to pray." *Hypocrite. I haven't touched my own rosary in months.*

"I don't need a rosary to pray," Gwen countered. "Listen, I'm praying right now: Saint Anthony, please find Max." She looked at me. "Saint Anthony is the one who finds lost things, right?"

"Right. But Max is not a thing, and he's—"

"Okay." She thought a moment. "Saint Christopher, give Max a safe journey."

I fought to keep my fingers from twisting the rosary into new, impossible knots. "Max is *not* on a journey. That's what I need to talk to you about. He—"

Gwen gave a dramatic sigh. "I'm running out of saints here. Help me out."

I shook my head. "Listen, please. This is serious. I have bad news about Max."

"Pass me the blue moon polish, Mom," Gwen said. "Red's

so last year."

I opened my mouth and the words finally spilled out. "Max was kidnapped."

"Kidnapped!" Gwen and Joy said in unison, actually looking up from their nails.

"That's right. On Friday. We think he was taken from Whitecap Mountain Ski Resort. Grandfather got a ransom note yesterday, and I'm going to deliver the money soon."

"Oh, that's terrible!" Joy exclaimed.

"Horrible," Gwen cried. Then she whispered, "How much money?"

"Gwen!" Joy admonished, but I could read the concerned curiosity in both their features.

"Don't worry." My fingers continued working the beads and chain. "It's only two million. It won't cut into our allowances."

Joy shook her head. "Don't say that, Charlene. We only want Max back safe and sound. Why, he's like a son to me. Do you have any idea how he is?"

"No . . . but I'm hoping this will all be over today and he'll be back before dark. I'll be leaving as soon as I get the call from Grandfather."

"Do you want us to come with you?" Joy asked quietly.

"Thanks, but no." I couldn't imagine keeping a low profile with Joy and Gwen by my side. "It should be simple enough, and it would probably be best to just have one person there."

"I can't believe your grandfather is willing to part with that much money," Gwen persisted.

"He has no choice," I said. "Not if he wants Max back."

"Still, it's not like him. And how do you know you can trust the kidnapper to keep his end of the deal?"

"Hush, Gwen," Joy said, "you've been watching too many movies." But her expression was equally unsettling.

"I'll be in my room if you want me." Pocketing the rosary, I retreated upstairs as fast as possible, escaping the poisonous nail polish fumes and the even more poisonous thoughts running through my head.

———

Alone in my room, I feigned patience as I clipped and filed my nails. This was better than biting them nervously. I even started painting them, which proved how desperate I was for distraction. I never could understand how Gwen, who was so careless with other things, managed to paint super-slick nails and clump-free mascara—all in record time.

My phone rang, making me almost spill my pink polish bottle. As it was, I streaked a nail. I didn't care. I wouldn't have cared if the polish was scarlet and stained my white carpet.

"Grandfather?" I yelped into the phone, not even looking at the screen.

There was an unsettling silence on the other end. My heart filled the hush with thumping beats.

"Definitely not," drawled a female voice. "Is Max around? I'd like to speak to him." The voice sounded like it could belong to a teenager, and I tried to decide whether or not I recognized it.

"He's not here at the moment."

"Do you know when he'll be back?"

"Not exactly . . . He's hard to get ahold of," I said carefully, still not sure who this was. "It would be best if I took a message." When I received no reply, I prompted, "Is that okay?"

I heard a long-suffering sigh. "I guess it will have to be. Tell him Alice McGregor called." She said her name as if she were pronouncing a royal title. "I need to know what time he's picking me up for the New Year's party."

Alice McGregor. The most sought-after girl at school. Guys wanted her; girls wanted to be her. *Congratulations, Max.* "How did you get my number?"

"The tutoring board at school." She said it like it was a joke, and I was sure I heard a smothered giggle. "I wouldn't have called *you* except Max is obviously having phone trouble. I keep getting his voicemail."

59

And obviously no guy would ever ignore a call from you.
"Anything else?" I asked.

"Yes. Tell him to buy me a fresh rose corsage from Tacey's Floral. White roses. And remind him to pick me up in the Jaguar."

I hung up, wondering what it was that everyone thought was so special about Alice McGregor.

Grandfather's call came an hour later. In fifteen minutes, I was on my way to save Max.

One bulging backpack heavy with money. Check.

One roll of nylon string. Check.

One pair of mini scissors. Check.

I was making a list. A mental one only—since I was in the process of driving to the ski resort—but it helped.

One nervous girl in control of the wheel. Check.

Okay, it wasn't helping anymore. I felt anything but in control. I felt alone. Vulnerable. Scared. What if the kidnapper changed his mind? What if I messed up? What if he took it out on Max? What if Grandfather was right, and the kidnapper was only waiting for a chance to snatch me, too? Maybe I should have accepted Joy's offer to come along.

I wished I didn't know the way to the ski resort. Then maybe my thoughts would be taken up with concentrating on the roads and signs.

At last I turned onto a road that was flanked by huge piles of plowed snow and a mountain-shaped billboard. I wound up the hill and turned into the parking lot. The car bumped and rumbled over gravelly snow while I searched for a spot to squeeze into.

The lot teemed with people. The ones who couldn't wait to get on the hill and risk their lives were suiting up out here and taking skis and snowboards off car top carriers. Stepping from my car, I felt out of place with no skis or snowboard. Not that anyone would notice me—unless there was someone here solely for that purpose, someone waiting and watching for me, with no intention of skiing either.

Resisting the urge to study my surroundings and search every face and figure, I hoisted the backpack and headed for the lodge.

Inside, I waited patiently in line. *Do this right,* I ordered myself. *Don't give him any cause to back out of the deal.*

"Locker number thirty-eight?" asked the guy at the desk.

"First time we've ever had a request for a specific number."

"My lucky number," I explained.

Indulging me, he handed over the key.

See? I directed my silent question at the kidnapper. *I'm doing this precisely as you directed. You can have the money. You're welcome to it. Just give Max back.*

I hoped I looked as if I were putting determination into my actions, signaling to anyone watching that I was reliable. I stuffed the pack into the rust-speckled locker littered with gum wrappers. When I glimpsed a tarnished penny stuck to the inside of the locker by a wad of gum, I thought, *You can have that, too.*

The bag almost didn't fit. I punched it into place, then closed and locked the door. Ready to proceed to the next step, I had a horrible thought, a "what if" that had not occurred to me in the car, or even earlier when it should have—the moment Grandfather had handed me the bag.

What if the bag was not filled with money? What if Grandfather was trying to outsmart the kidnapper? I had been so intent on not tampering with anything that it hadn't occurred to me that something might already be compromised.

Using the key, I reopened the locker. I paused with my fingers on the bag's zipper. Glancing over my shoulder at the throng of people, I thought, *This is the worst possible place to do this.* I couldn't risk someone catching a glimpse of a bag full of money, giving them a chance to steal it before the kidnapper could. It was almost hilarious, worrying that the wrong thief might get the money.

I'm not trying to double-cross you, not trying to swipe a few bills for myself, I wanted to explain, because I felt an uncomfortable awareness of someone watching as I took the bag with me to the ladies' room.

Inside the privacy of a stall, I hung the backpack by its leather handle from the hook on the door, which left my hands free to explore the bag's contents. I made a mental note to ask Max why people found it necessary to scribble obscenities in bathroom stalls. *When I see him next. Soon,* I assured myself.

Unzipping the backpack made a tremendous noise in the empty bathroom. Wait—it wasn't empty anymore—the door squeaked open and boot-clad feet plodded into a stall—the stall beside me.

Suddenly I recalled a horrible scene from a movie (Max's pick) in which a guy enters a bathroom stall and someone in the neighboring stall stabs him through the flimsy divide. I forced the image from my mind, but nonetheless made sure to scoot away from my neighbor's stall.

Orderly stacks of bills did indeed lie in rubber-banded piles inside the backpack, and they were not counterfeit, either. I examined each and every stack, removing and holding bills up to the fluorescent light. One thing Grandfather had made sure my education had not lacked was the ability to tell the difference between real and counterfeit money. *Look for blue and red fibers* in *the paper, not just printed* on *it. Find the security thread running vertically. Check the watermark.*

While rifling through a pack of hundreds, I heard a flush, making me jump, and I almost dropped the pack of bills in the toilet. *Get ahold of yourself.*

Rifling through one last pack, I caught a flash of white. Just when I had been feeling admiration for Grandfather for not pulling any tricks, I tugged out a sealed white envelope. A message to the kidnapper?

Of all the audacity. Whatever Grandfather had to say, I knew it couldn't help our chances of getting Max back safely. Without hesitation, I ripped through the old-fashioned seal of melted wax stamped with a "P" for Perigard, and pulled out a thick sheet of gold-embossed stationery. *Impressive. So suitable for a greedy kidnapper.*

Reading the message, however, I soon discovered it was not intended for the kidnapper at all. It was for Max. Grandfather still believed Max was behind everything. I should have known better than to believe my pitiful pleadings had gotten through to him. I should have realized he'd given in too easily. I'd thought maybe the heart attack and fortunate recovery had had something to do with it—maybe given him a change of heart—but I was wrong.

Maxwell, Grandfather wrote:

> *It's been a good game. You won this round. Take the money as your prize. You earned it. Now it's time you returned home to resume your responsibilities. Do this, and we won't discuss this matter any further. With the proper training, I believe you will make an excellent businessman one day. You've proven you have the mind as well as the will for carrying out a daring business venture. We'll consider this a lesson and leave it at that.*

Chapter Seven

I wanted to scream. I wanted to kick something, so I turned and kicked the toilet. It burst to life with a gushing roar. Inspired by the noise, I tore the note to shreds and sprinkled it into the bowl, watching delightedly as the pieces whirled around and around and the gold scraps were swallowed into the depths of the sewers.

So much for Grandfather's attempt to sabotage Max's return. I didn't know how this kidnapper thought, but I was fairly sure he wouldn't have appreciated being taken for a teenager playing a trick.

I went through a laborious scrutiny of the remaining packs of bills until I was satisfied Grandfather had not pulled anymore underhanded stunts. Marching out of the restroom without even washing my hands—a major first for me—I squished the backpack into locker thirty-eight, locked it, and returned to the restroom.

"I can't manage to leave this restroom for more than a few minutes, either," said a woman soaping her hands at the sink. "The moment I see those hills . . ." She shuddered, sprinkling water onto the cracked mirror and onto me. "I feel safer hiding out in here."

Smiling what I hoped was a sympathetic smile, I dove for the far stall. My hand stopped on the handle. The stall was occupied.

"A stall over here is open," the soap woman said.

"I—I think I left something in this one."

The door swung open so suddenly it almost hit me. "No, you didn't," said a woman wearing ski pants of such a bright orange color they looked like a hunting costume. "Unless it's that wad of paper on the floor."

Not answering, I squeezed inside and locked the door. I wrinkled my nose at the smell, like a horrible school lunch that, never having been appetizing in the first place, had been left to go cold and rotten. I tried holding my breath, but that only made each frantic breath of air harder to take.

The things I do for you, Max.

From my coat pocket, I pulled a short length of string and a little pair of rather blunt scissors. I took the tiny locker key from my jeans pocket and threaded the string through it, tied what I hoped was a secure knot and, squatting on the slimy floor, lowered it carefully through the grate of the round drain, then tied the end of the string onto the grate.

Was it inconspicuous? Not really. But then who would bother untying it unless they knew its purpose? Which led me to wonder . . . Why did the kidnapper want it done this way? Wouldn't it have been simpler to make a clean trade—the bag for Max? Perhaps, but not safe for him. This way he didn't have to make a predictable appearance. *And there are no security cameras in a bathroom,* I reminded myself.

The kidnapper wouldn't want any of his actions to look suspicious. In which case, I realized as I turned a spray of water onto my hands, how would he get into the ladies' room to retrieve the key? *I've been assuming the kidnapper is a man, but maybe there's a woman in on this too.* The thought dumbfounded me. My hands were lathered, but they didn't feel clean, and I stayed rubbing my soapy hands under hot water for a long time.

When I emerged, I threaded my way through the boisterous crowd and ended up in the cafeteria. I glanced at the counter, but didn't see Cindy. Though I wasn't hungry, I considered getting a burger so I'd have an excuse to linger. Ironically, the closer I was to the kidnapper, the closer I felt to Max. But what would I do even if I did spot the kidnapper? Tap him on the shoulder and say, "Excuse me, but I did what you directed, so now will you please let Max go?"

As if it would be that simple.

But isn't that what he expected me to believe, that by simply dropping off a backpack, this nightmare would be over?

I'd staked all my hope on the fact that the kidnapper would release Max once he got the money. Now I saw my naiveté with glaring clarity. Why should a criminal keep a promise? It would be easier to kill Max and flee. *I'm not leaving*, I decided. *I'm watching the locker. I'll call the police the moment I see the kidnapper, then I'll follow—*

A finger on my shoulder startled me, and I whirled around.

"Hi! What're you up to?" Cindy grinned from ear to ear and looked past me hopefully. "Is Max here, too?"

"No, he's not. Sorry." I noticed a ketchup stain on her shirt. Like yesterday, she was in uniform, and I studied it thoughtfully. Her forest green shirt and cap featured a rugged Whitecap Mountain logo, and she wore black pants and an apron like a dozen other workers. If I could change into an outfit like that, I'd have a better chance of watching for the kidnapper without him—or her—recognizing me or giving me a second glance. Even if I could just get a cap, it would help shield my hair and face.

"Say, Cindy, do you think you could do me a favor?"

"Sure. What is it?"

"I need to hang out here today, but I kind of need to keep a low profile, blend in, so to speak. What are the chances of your being able to find a uniform for me to wear? One like you've got on."

She glanced down at herself. "I might be able to," she said, a bit dubiously. "I think there are some extras in a back closet, but I'm not sure of the sizes."

"Even if you just get me an apron and cap, that would be a big help."

"Okay, I'll see what I can do." She zipped off, her ponytail flying, and I turned back around to face the locker room.

I shouldn't have taken my eyes off the lockers, I realized. Though my exchange with Cindy had been brief, I was suddenly worried that I might have missed the kidnapper.

Scanning the room's occupants, I observed a mom and a dad helping two kids tug on their boots, a loud group of teenagers, and several other people suiting up or un-suiting. The only person without any ski clothes or equipment was a guy striding from the direction of locker thirty-eight, heading for the exit. Of average build, he wore khaki pants and a bulky black coat with the hood up.

My instincts said to follow him, so I hurried through the locker room, almost tripping over a pair of skis. I pushed open the door and peered in all directions, just catching sight of the man as he entered the parking lot. I broke into a sporadic sprint, attempting to spy on him without getting too close. My hand dove into my pocket and grasped my phone, ready to call the police with a description and license plate number if necessary.

The hooded man glanced over his shoulder, and I ducked behind a car. A shapely woman exiting the car next to me avoided my eyes and trotted away with a nervous quiver. Slowly, I stood back up. The man was opening a car door, and I took a step closer. The car, a sleek black Mercedes, looked familiar.

I immediately knew why. I'd seen it lined up with several other luxury cars, all belonging to Grandfather. My hand released my phone and my lips pinched together angrily. I stalked forward, no longer afraid of being seen. I caught a glimpse of a tan face, and it was enough. "Rob!" I shouted. His head almost turned to look at me, but then ducked as he hopped into the car.

"Don't pretend you didn't hear me!" I reached the car and planted my booted foot inside so he couldn't close the door as he was about to. I pulled his hood back. "What are you doing here? Grandfather sent you, didn't he? Why?"

Rob faced me with no hint of shame. "Sheesh, quit freaking. So what if your grandfather sent me? We're all on the same side."

"Oh yeah?" I narrowed my eyes. "Then why didn't I know about this? Why the sneakiness? Was Grandfather afraid I'd take off with the money myself, or that I was going to join up with Max or something?" Another thought hit me. "Did you come here to steal the money back? That would be just like Grandfather."

While I scanned the interior of the car for the backpack, Rob lifted empty hands and shook his head. "You've got some imagination, Char."

"I asked you before, please don't call me that."

He ran a finger through a film of window vapor. "All your anger's steaming up the car."

I watched in disbelief as he proceeded to draw stick figures in the moisture. "Just answer me straight: Why are you here?"

He traced a cloud of angry steam billowing from the head of a curly-haired stick figure, and I knew very well who his picture depicted. I fought the urge to react.

"Why am I here?" He looked up and smiled. "Simple. This is an important operation. My job's to make sure you did everything you were supposed to."

"So you were checking up on me."

"No, you've got it all wrong. I'm here as your protector, your guardian angel, so to speak. Like a bodyguard." He flexed an arm, but any muscle was hidden by the heavy coat.

"A guardian-angel-bodyguard?" I rolled my eyes. "You've got religion crossed with superheroes."

"My kind of religion."

I shook my head. "I still don't see why this had to be a secret, but it doesn't surprise me. I should have seen it coming." A car door slammed across the way, and I suddenly realized I'd been gone from my post much too long. I wanted to dart back to it, but I didn't want Rob following me. I was glad that he appeared to be leaving, but I had to make sure. "So if your reason for coming here was to protect me, why are you leaving?"

"Who said I'm leaving? I'm just grabbing a smoke." He produced a pack of cigarettes from his coat pocket. "Want one?"

"No way." My frown deepened. "If your reason for coming here was to protect me, leaving for a smoke is a pretty irresponsible thing to do. I'm glad I'm not depending on you."

"Oh, come on." He tapped a cigarette into his palm. "You were just talking to that worker chick. No threat there."

Worried about the time I was wasting, I removed my foot from the car. "You can leave now."

He flicked his lighter and touched the flame to his cigarette. "Thanks, but I'm in no hurry." He spoke around the cigarette. "I think I'll stick around till you leave."

I crossed my arms. "Why do you think I came outside? The ransom's delivered, so what reason do I have to stay? I'm heading to my car right now." I gestured vaguely. "But suit yourself."

He let out a puff of smoke, and it found my face instantly. "Guess there's no reason for me to stay then. See you back at the big house, Char." He gave me something of a salute before closing the door.

I walked slowly in the direction I'd indicated, making my way toward my car so that my words weren't technically a lie, though they were misleading. *Yes, I'm going to my car, but then I'm racing back inside. And I better not have missed the kidnapper because of you, Rob.*

My ears tuned into the sound of an engine as Rob pulled out. I turned slightly and saw him exit the lot.

The moment he was gone, I darted inside. No one stood near locker thirty-eight, and I backed up to keep watch without being too close. Glancing briefly toward the cafeteria, I didn't see Cindy, but figured she'd find me when she got a chance. An offensive odor made its way to my nostrils, and I took a step away from the garbage can on my left.

It made no difference. Perhaps the smell was coming from the restrooms. I glanced in that direction and noticed a hulk of a man with his back to me, hauling a black garbage bag down the hall. His dull clothing looked like a janitor's. *Good, maybe he'll change this garbage can next.*

Only . . . he was walking away, toward an exit. I looked back at locker thirty-eight, then at the rapidly retreating

69

janitor. Something wasn't right. He was only carrying the one garbage bag, and it didn't look as if it contained a full load of trash.

Suddenly, two threads of memory meshed in my mind, two recent conversations regarding janitors at Whitecap Mountain. First, Wayne had told me how he had commented on the smelly garbage to a janitor who did nothing about it. That happened Friday, the day Max was kidnapped. Then yesterday, Saturday, Cindy informed me that there was no day janitor on duty this week.

She could be wrong, of course, or maybe a new janitor had just been hired. But wouldn't the rest of the place be in a cleaner state by now? All the garbage cans I'd seen had been practically overflowing. And why was this guy leaving the building with only one small garbage bag?

It's just the right size to hold a backpack. Blood surged through my veins, and I left the lockers behind to follow the janitor, suddenly convinced he'd just picked up the ransom.

He shouldered the door open and disappeared outside. I shot down the hall, then peeked through the grimy window before slipping on my leather gloves and exiting the same door.

Walking neither too close nor too far away was tricky, much harder than when I'd been shadowing Rob. For one thing, this guy walked faster, and for all his bulk, he was a challenge to keep in sight. He rounded vehicles with no hesitation, plowing across the lot with no care for traffic or pedestrians. As I attempted the same, a van honked at me.

I stumbled out of the way, fearing the janitor turning and spotting me. But he didn't. In fact, he didn't even glance from side to side in a paranoid way, as I imagined a criminal would. He marched on, carrying that black plastic bag slung Santa-like over his shoulder, and never looked back. He finally stopped at a beat up red pickup truck. I watched through two windows of a Ford a few rows away.

If the bag truly contained garbage, I would have expected the guy to sling it into the bed of the truck. Instead, he held onto it possessively as he heaved himself into the driver's seat. At this point, I was convinced I'd found my man. Now I had to make sure not to lose him.

Ducking, I wove a frantic path to my car, hoping I'd be able to catch up to the rusty truck before it left the lot. I had no breath to spare, but my mind managed a hasty prayer as I entered my car. *Please, God, let him lead me to Max.* Snapping my seatbelt together, my stomach fluttered as I wondered just how fast I might end up going.

Come on, come on, I prodded silently as a young couple, arms linked, took their time strolling past the rear of my car. A second after they cleared me, I zipped out of my spot, shifted to drive, and moved forward as fast as I dared.

Catching sight of the pickup turning left out of the lot, I made the same turn a few moments later, onto a sloped road that curved just enough to keep me worried that I was losing the man. Dirty fumes twirled from his exhaust pipe. I pressed my booted foot hard on the accelerator, making my car slip and slide and zigzag forward.

Not taking my eyes from the snow-fringed road, I snaked my hand into my pocket and seized my phone. I tried Donnelly's number, but now when I needed him to, he didn't pick up. I left a brief message, barely pausing for breath as I spoke. "It's me, Charlene. I'm on County Road C right now, trailing an old red pickup, heading north. I think the driver's the kidnapper. I followed him from the ski lodge, he's dressed like a janitor, and I'm almost certain he has the ransom. I hope you get this soon. Send cops, please!"

The truck was getting too far ahead of me.

"Donnelly," I muttered, and dialed 911. I sped up, hoping to read the truck's license plate.

"911, what is your emergency?"

"I think I'm trailing the guy who kidnapped my brother."

The dispatcher began asking detailed questions. She wanted the truck's license number, but I could see now that it had no license, at least not on the rear of the truck.

The driver never used indicators when turning, so my turns

71

were abrupt. I wished I could clamp both hands on the wheel. "What road are you on now?" the dispatcher asked. "Um." I scanned the roadside for a sign. "I don't know anymore. County Road C when we started, but that was a little while ago. We took some turns . . ." Flustered, I let my voice trail off. I'd been so focused on following the truck, that I'd forgotten to watch signs.

"Let me get this straight," the dispatcher said slowly, as if I had all the time in the world. "You haven't been kidnapped. You chose to follow this man. You don't know whether he is a kidnapper or not, you're guessing; and you don't know where you are, but you want me to send help?"

"That's right, more or less." Upset at the lack of urgency in her voice, I added, "I have very good reason to believe this guy's the one responsible for kidnapping my brother." I switched to defending myself. "How could I let him get away? Of course I followed him."

"Well, if I don't know where to," began the dispatcher, and then all I heard was dead air.

"Hello? Can't you trace this call?"

". . . do what we can . . ."

"You're breaking up," I cried, then realized as I swung around a bend, it was, of course, *me* who was breaking up, losing service on these twisting, remote roads.

Remote. I swallowed. *Isolated. Alone with a potential kidnapper.* I clenched my teeth and forced a prayer through them.

My eyes flitted to my gas gauge. I had about a quarter tank left. What if I broke down in the middle of nowhere? How far was this kidnapper planning to go? What if he drove all night? At some point, he was going to wise up to me. *I could turn around. No one could say I didn't try.* My foot pressed on the gas. *Trying is not going to comfort me if Max ends up dead.*

Again, I thumbed Donnelly's number. My phone flashed "no service" and I was tempted to chuck it out the window.

The pines grew tall and tight on each side of the narrow road, so that the sun might as well not have existed. The green

72

branches twisted together, gleefully choking all light. Then the branches began turning ghostly white under falling snow, and I switched on my windshield wipers.

The flakes fell like frozen feathers through the yellow glow of my headlights. I shivered, though my heater blew full blast. It was just me and the truck driving on a gray tattered ribbon of road in a world becoming increasingly obscured by snow. *Why aren't there any other cars?* My anxiety increased. *This guy's going to realize I'm following him, if he hasn't already.* I eased my foot off the gas and slowed down.

The truck's taillights glowed red, then disappeared around a bend. By the time I rounded the same bend, I didn't see the truck on the stretch of road ahead. Fearing I'd lost him, I increased my speed.

My eyes were so focused on the road in front of me, that by the time I saw the truck behind me, it was too late. The hunk of metal bore down on me like a motorized monster. My stomach dropped to my feet and I floored the pedal. Somehow I picked up my phone and punched the buttons. Still no service.

Flicking my eyes to the rearview mirror, I gasped as the truck rammed me. My head slammed back against the headrest. The phone flew from my hand. The car spun and my heart lurched. Too late, my hands fought the wheel in an attempt to correct my sliding tires.

I didn't have time to scream or even breathe before the car thudded to a halt. Whipped by the impact, my neck radiated pain. Belatedly, my heart picked up a panicky rhythm. All I saw out the windshield was a white wall of snow, and despite my fuzzy brain, I realized I'd been forced off the road into an embankment. *He did that on purpose. I've got to get out of here.*

My seatbelt held me tight inside the tilted car. I fumbled with my clumsy gloved hands to unbuckle the belt. Immediately, I fell forward. I twisted my body in the cumbersome bulk of my coat and opened the door. I squished through at an awkward angle, and the rhythmic purr of the wipers reminded me I'd left the car running. Backing up, I saw its nose was buried obstinately in a drift, like an animal in hibernation. The snow that fell in the glow of my taillights seemed tinted with blood. My ears pricked at the sound of another door being opened—the door of the truck behind me.

He's coming after me. Alarm shot through my body and I hurtled into the woods. My heavy boots, the thick snow, and the snaring, snagging underbrush caused me to stumble.

The voice that bellowed after me told me I was not overreacting. "Get back here, girl! It'll only be worse if you run."

I ran faster, and promptly tripped. My mind processed the fact that my little scissors had fallen from my pocket into the snow.

Amidst wicked laughter that was coming much too close, I scrambled to my feet and kept running. The scissors were too small and blunt to be an effective weapon, anyway, even if I did have the courage to use them.

If only it wasn't wintertime. I wouldn't be weighed down by bulky clothing. And the thick lush green foliage of summer would have gone a long way in helping conceal me. Maybe I could have even climbed up a tree and hidden high among the leafy branches. As it was, the stark contrast of naked brown tree trunks against white snow left too much visibility. There were not enough evergreens in this forest, though along the road there had seemed to be so many. At least I was wearing my muted blue coat and not a bright red or yellow one that screamed, "Here I am!"

"I'll catch you eventually, girl," my pursuer yelled. The tree branches chattered as if from fear. "You can't outrun me, because even if I can't see you, I can follow your footprints."

I choked on a curse and turned it into a prayer for more snow. *Snow thick and heavy, snow to hide me like a curtain, snow to fill up my footprints fast as I make them. Snow,* I continued, my mind chilling on this one concept, *snow so pure and white and good, snow so soft and clean and gentle,* my mind chanted inanely. Maybe I was going crazy with fear.

Branches scratched my face, but my skin was so numb with cold I barely felt it. My chest heaved with each breath, and my lungs alternately burned and froze. I was tiring much too quickly. My occasional fitness runs had never prepared me for the intensity of running for my life through a woods of obstacles, inches of snow hindering my feet like wet cement. My boots felt heavier each time I lifted them, but I didn't dare slow or turn around. I had no destination to run to. Just away. Away from the fear of the unknown, of what my pursuer would do if he caught me.

At one point, I thought I heard him yelling again, but if so, it came from a distance. A sliver of relief pierced my frigid thoughts. For the first time, I risked a backward glance. The man was nowhere in sight. By now the snow was falling faster, and concern at the thought of him being able to follow my footprints, faded.

I assessed my situation, wishing I had some point of reference. I was thoroughly lost in a strange woods, with no idea how big it was, or any sense of direction, not with the sun smothered by clouds. I wondered how long the man would continue hunting me. I was acutely aware that he could appear at any time. Maybe he was hiding behind a fat tree trunk. My eyes searched the bare deciduous trees interspersing the snow-clad pines and dry frilly ferns. All I heard now was the happy twittering of winter birds.

If only I had my phone. I pictured it lying uselessly on the floor of my car, were it had probably landed after being jarred from my hand. *It wasn't working anyway,* I told myself, though this was no consolation. What a mess I'd gotten myself into. Grandfather had been right to send Rob to watch out for me, after all. I would gladly swallow my pride to have him and his confidence with me now.

I smacked my hands together. In all fairness, I couldn't blame Grandfather for this one. No one could have foreseen that Miss Responsible would get herself into this grave situation.

Snow continued sifting down. I clasped my cold fingers

together. *You should have worn mittens,* I rebuked myself. *Mittens keep you warmer than gloves.*

I let out a frustrated laugh, but stopped when I heard the echo, so hollow and unnatural, flung back at me as if even the woods didn't want it. *The kidnapper would want it,* I reminded myself, and I bit my lip.

I spun in a circle, but every view promised the same endless stretch of trees and snow. I sighed, mentally flipped a coin, and began walking—doing precisely the opposite of what I'd been taught from kindergarten to do if you get lost, which is to stay in one place till you're found.

"Problem is," I mumbled, "that doesn't do any good when no one's looking for you."

No one, that is, but a freaky kidnapper.

Chapter Eight

*W*ith no destination in sight, I continued plodding through the snow, each lift of my boot an enormous effort. My feet sweltered in their wool socks while my nose prickled in the cold.

My thoughts turned to the basic instinct of self-preservation. Even Max was momentarily forgotten. I needed to find help for myself before I could resume my search for him. If I could find the road, maybe I could flag down a car. The more chilled I became, even hitching a ride with a stranger sounded inviting, especially in a heated vehicle. I trudged on, thinking that if I kept walking, maybe I would come across a house; but realistically, I couldn't imagine anyone living in this creepy woods.

My mind tortured me by recalling the way Max and I, as little kids, used to play Hansel and Gretel in the forests up north with our dad. On those rare vacations, scary thrills had been welcome. Security lay in knowing the game could be ended at any time, and that my family was near.

Unlike now. Quirky thoughts about breadcrumbs and gingerbread houses failed to amuse me. I felt like I was walking through an enchanted forest in which the trees formed a deadly maze. *I may wander in here forever*. At that moment, I determined that no matter how tired I became, I would not lie down to rest. *Because I might never get back up.* I tried not to think about nightfall, which would be coming soon.

I could have looked at my watch to find out how soon, but unburying it from my fat coat sleeve would require energy, and I had none to spare. All energy went into keeping my legs stumbling forward. I lost my footing countless times, collapsing in the snow like a wobbly newborn fawn.

Get up, I ordered myself. *Get up.* As I heaved myself to a standing position for what felt like the fiftieth time, I caught sight of movement beyond the trees several yards away. Was it animal or human? A chill managed to quiver up what I'd assumed was my already frozen spine. Sucking in breath, which shot like ice water through my teeth, I pressed my body up against a tree trunk and watched the figure come closer.

It was a person, but I knew right away from the man's build, that he was not my pursuer. If this man was muscular, it didn't show through his thick flannel coat. He held a five-gallon bucket and a fishing rod in one hand, the bucket bouncing against his leg as he strode through the woods. Instead of continuing in my direction, he swerved to the left and began climbing a slight hill.

Nothing about him seemed threatening, and I didn't have many options, so I called out. The weak voice that came from my throat sounded pitiful. I scrambled forward.

"Hello!" I called again as I struggled up the slope after him. "Wait, please," I panted.

He was just turning around when I slipped and fell, planting my face in the snow. I barely felt the cold on my senseless skin, but I lifted my head and brushed the clinging crystals away. Through icy lashes, I saw the fisherman approaching. My foggy mind told me that the young man had a kind face. A very good-looking kind face.

"Are you okay?" He peered down at me, blinking like he didn't quite believe what he saw. His forehead wrinkled beneath his black stocking hat, which failed to conceal all his brown hair. He offered me his gloved hand. Taking it, I hauled myself to my feet and looked up at him, into eyes that matched the deep brown of his hair. "Are you okay?" he repeated.

"I'm cold. Tired. But fine," I managed between chattering teeth. *And why do I suddenly feel like I'm blushing?*

"You look terrible."

You don't. I blinked. *I'm losing my common sense. So what if he's incredibly handsome? That's really low on my list of importance right now.* But I couldn't stop staring.

His dark eyebrows drew together in concern. "Your face is white and your lips are purple. You must've been wandering out here awhile. You by yourself?"

I let out a weak breath. "I wasn't originally by myself, though that would have been preferable. Some maniac—" I stopped, afraid he'd think I was delusional. I couldn't afford to scare him away. "I really just need to warm up and call for some help. Do you know how to get out of these woods?"

"Sure. I've got a cabin not too far from here. That's where I'm headed. But first—" he squinted at me—"did I hear you right? Something about a maniac?"

I shook my head, causing snow to sprinkle from my hat. "Forget it. It was nothing." My gut told me it was best not to confide in a stranger, no matter how good-looking. If past experience proved anything, he wouldn't believe me anyway. Besides, there was nothing that could be done about the situation until I contacted Donnelly. Even then, I knew not to expect much.

The fisherman shrugged, then lifted the bucket and pole. "I was out on the lake doing some ice fishing. Didn't catch anything worth keeping, though. Come on, I'll help you to the cabin and start a fire so you can warm up."

"That sounds great. Thank you." We walked slowly, and though he offered me his arm, I declined. He had the bucket and pole to carry, and if I focused, I could muster enough energy to walk without stumbling.

While I hardly felt up to it, I made small talk. Mainly asking questions, I learned the name of the closest town was Cedar Hills, a place I'd never heard of before. I also learned that the fisherman's name was Clay Morrow, he was twenty-one, and he lived in a college dorm two hours away, but he liked to come here to fish when he got the chance. I preferred discussing him rather than me, as I didn't want to go into all the crazy details of my current situation. He didn't prod. In fact, he didn't say much of anything besides answering my questions.

We arrived at the small log cabin, and I was disappointed. We were still in what I considered the middle of the woods, with trees surrounding the cabin on every side. A snow blanketed drive sloped down to a rustic road, however, and that was promising. Beside the cabin sat a small blue Geo, and I assumed it was Clay's. Ugly rust bubbles had erupted through the paint on the lower part of the car.

From here the cabin appeared dark, even with bright white flakes clinging to the logs. Hundreds of concentric knots in the wood peered like dark eyes beneath brows of snow, scrutinizing me. The roof was rimmed with a fringe of ice daggers.

I followed Clay up three rickety steps onto the small wooden porch, where he deposited his fishing pole and bucket and then scooped up an armload of firewood from a nearby stack. Shreds of bark peppered the snow. He hugged the wood under one arm while unlocking the door. I watched him enter the dimness, wondering why I suddenly felt so wary of following. But he stood waiting patiently with his arms laden with logs, and I needed shelter and warmth, so I stepped inside.

He closed the squeaky door behind me, then dropped the logs near a dented wood-burning stove, its crooked black pipe stretching to the ceiling. Chunks of snow dropped from my boots onto a thin brown mat. I felt no warmer than I had outside.

"Can I get you something to eat or drink?" he asked as he knelt and opened the door to the stove and arranged some sticks. "We don't have anything fancy, but we do keep the place stocked with canned food. We've got running water, too."

My mind flitted curiously over the "we," then forgot it at the "running water" statement. How could anyone live *without* running water? I sniffed, and even through the cold, I detected a suspicious musty smell, an odor of dirt and dust and mold. Doubting Clay had anything I'd want to eat, particularly from a rusty old can, I responded, "Thanks, but all I really need is a phone."

"A phone?" He crumpled some balls of newspaper and tossed them into the stove's belly. "Sorry, but we don't have one. Up here we rough it. This is your basic hunting cabin, no luxuries, unless you count our old dryer, which hasn't worked for years. I come here to get away from it all, live rustic-like." Without turning to me, he indicated a chair. "Go ahead and have a seat."

I peered suspiciously at the tattered brown chair and brushed it off discreetly before sitting down. I gripped my gloved hands together tightly. "But you do have a cell phone somewhere, right?"

"Somewhere, yeah, but not here. No signal," he offered unhelpfully as he struck a match and lit the crumpled newspaper. Smoke soon puffed out of the stove. He added two small logs, angling them in an inverted "V," before closing the stove door.

While he remained crouched in front of the stove, I scanned the room with a sinking feeling. It was a man's hunting cabin, to be sure. No curtains, no carpet, no tablecloth, and no decorations. Against the same wall as the wood stove stood a narrow bookshelf containing books and a small radio with a ridiculously long antennae, above which hung the mounted head of an unhappy deer. I began counting the points on the antlers. Ten.

Leaning back in my chair, I saw a meager little kitchen with a tiny sink and an olive green fridge, an ugly remnant from the seventies, I assumed. "You have an oven."

"Yeah," Clay conceded, "but we don't usually use it." There was that "we" again. I scanned the rest of the cabin, wondering suddenly if someone else was here right now. I spotted the useless dryer he had mentioned, as well as a trap door in the floor, which probably led to a cellar.

Other than that, I saw, through a partially open door, what looked like a primitive bathroom. There was only one closed door, and I assumed it led to a bedroom. I was surprised to see a small floral wreath hanging on the door. Curious, I noticed it was made of red roses and ivy. Sheer white ribbon twined around it and draped from the bottom in two soft strands. Definitely a feminine touch, but the only one visible. Also definitely out of season. The flowers had to be silk. *Clay's probably married,* I concluded, feeling oddly let-down.

"This is our biggest luxury," he said, flicking on a lantern. "It uses an LED." He set the lantern on the worn table, then sat down in a creaky rocker as far from me as possible. "The room will warm up soon," he said, keeping his eyes on what little bit of the fire could be seen through the stove's door. I was surprised he didn't continue the small talk or press me for details about why I was in the woods.

Shifting uncomfortably, I looked over my shoulder and spotted a beady-eyed fox staring at me from a corner. It stood stiff and dead, forever frozen in stalking position. "Did you shoot that?"

Clay's eyes followed my gaze. "No, my brother did. He's the big hunter; I mainly stick to fishing."

"Oh." Suddenly I felt very aware that I was sitting in this dimly lit cabin with a strange man. I realized how much more comfortable I would feel with another woman here, stranger or not. I even began hoping Clay *was* married.

"Where is your brother?"

"Out hunting, probably. He wasn't here when I arrived, didn't know I was coming. So he'll be surprised to see us." A hint of nervousness seemed to shadow his words.

I swallowed. "I should really be going."

"Already?"

I was sure he sounded relieved.

"You can't be thawed out yet."

"I'm warm enough." I stood. What now? I couldn't call anyone to pick me up, and I didn't want to walk out the door into the vast, cold, snowy void. I'd be no better off than before. *Although I could follow the road, perhaps hitchhike.* I shivered.

"See, you are still cold. Sit back down and we'll figure out how to get you home."

I remained standing. "All I really need is to get to town. I'm sure I could call someone from there." *Why don't you offer to drive me?*

He plucked off his hat and rolled it in his hands. I struggled to keep my lips from twitching into a smile at his endearingly disheveled hair. The fact that he didn't seem to realize how attractive he was only made him more attractive. Finally, he cleared his throat and looked at me. His eyes held uncertainty. "I could give you a ride."

I nodded and smiled. "That would be great, actually. If you don't mind. I'm sorry I'm being so much trouble—"

I flinched as the front door banged open unexpectedly, bringing with it a gust of arctic wind, snow, and a large man gripping a rifle. He filled the doorway. From his hair and deep-set eyes down to his coat and boots, he was nothing but darkness. His goatee gave him a devilish look. I shuddered and glanced at Clay, who appeared slender and weak compared to this guy. If this was the brother he had mentioned, I never would have guessed the relationship.

As if on its own, the door slammed shut behind the beefy man. His boot smashed to the floor, and I realized he'd kicked the door shut. The room almost trembled.

The man barely glanced at me before turning his face to Clay and demanding, "What are you doing here? You told me you couldn't get away this week."

Clay stood up rather clumsily. "What's the big deal, Abner? I got some unexpected days off and thought I'd come do some fishing." He clenched his hat in his hand, knuckles going white. "You've never cared before."

A shadow rippled over Abner's angry features as he stepped closer to Clay. "You've got rotten timing, kid. And since when have I said you could bring guests here?" Abner's eyes jumped to me, and I almost jumped back. I'd never seen such black eyes. His leech-like lips curled. "But it might just work out for the best."

He was speaking to his brother, but the words were meant for me. The voice was terrifyingly familiar. *"I'll catch you eventually, girl."* My breath snagged in my throat as the truth came flying at me with horrific speed—the speed of a charging red pickup driven by an angry hulk of a man.

This man.

Carefully, I shifted my eyes to the cabin's small front window, straining to see through the grimy pane. I made out the shape of a pickup parked under a tree. I couldn't distinguish the color, but I knew with gut-wrenching certainty that it was red and rusty. My heart hammered violently. Sweat poured from my body.

While the two brothers talked, I edged toward the door.

"I'm sorry about bringing the girl here," Clay said in a low voice, as if thinking I couldn't hear him, "but she was lost, freezing . . . I didn't know what else to do. I couldn't leave her out there." He cleared his throat and changed the subject. "So where were you all this time? Hunting?"

"Yeah," Abner said slowly, "hunting."

Trying too hard to sound casual, Clay asked, "Get anything?"

"Sure did. Gave me a real fine chase, too. Almost thought I lost her, but then she made a mistake. A big mistake."

As Clay echoed, "A mistake?", I darted for the door and ran smack into Abner's broad chest. A grip of iron clenched my shoulder as if no coat or clothing padded my skin.

"Yeah, a mistake," Abner sneered. "She trusted you. And now here she is." He gave me a shake that rattled my brain. "A real priceless treasure, this one. Can't say I needed your help, Clay, but I appreciate it all the same."

"Let me go!" I demanded, kicking and striking wildly. In response to my struggling, Abner wrapped his entire thick arm around me and squeezed so I could barely move or breathe.

Clay dropped his hat. His face paled. I tried to keep from passing out by focusing on the freckles that appeared on his nose.

"What the heck, Abner? What are you doing? I—she—Abner, she can't breathe!"

"Not your concern."

My eyes pleaded for help. In response, Clay lunged toward Abner.

Barely moving, Abner lifted his rifle. I watched dizzily as the butt of the rifle struck Clay's head with a *thwack*. He staggered back and dropped to the floor with a groan. "You know better than to mess with me, boy. You got yourself into this, so you're gonna have to put up with it. From now on, you do things my way."

Clay put a hand to his forehead and looked up slowly. Blood trickled down his temple like a red tear drop. Fear showed in his eyes.

Thanks for trying, swam through my murky thoughts.

A moment later, Abner sent me hurtling across the room. I knocked into Clay, and we both went sprawling. When Clay climbed to his feet, he pulled me up as well. Then we both stared down the barrel of Abner's rifle.

"Look Abner, I just want to know what's going on." Clay wiped the blood from his face and turned to me. "Who are you?"

Rubbing my shoulder, I shook my head. "Nobody."

"Nobody." Abner repeated the word, pleasure dripping from his voice. "How ironic. Hilarious, even." He let out an alarming laugh that made me shrink inside myself. "I comb the woods for you, and you come to me."

"You're crazy." I took a deep breath. "You smash into my car, run me off the road, and chase me through the woods, all for tailgating you? Talk about road rage." I held up my hands. "Just let me out of here now, and I won't report this."

Again, the unnerving laugh. "I'm no fool, girl. I know exactly who you are and why you were following me. That was your big mistake, by the way. If you hadn't followed me, I never would have run you off the road. Maybe if I caught you in the woods, I wouldn't have recognized you because I would've smacked you around too quick. But now that I've seen you clearly, you don't stand a chance. That arrogant Perigard face is unmistakable."

He paused, and then I heard it, exactly as I had on the

phone, the evil whisper: "Hello, Charlene."

I swallowed.

He chuckled. "Sound familiar? It's thanks to you I discovered that phone on your brother. If you hadn't called, I might not have found it and got rid of it in time."

I strangled a moan. "Fine. So you know who I am. Then you know why I followed you. Where's Max? He'd better be all right."

Clay attempted to intervene with a question of some sort, but Abner saw it coming and silenced him with a sharp, "Shut it, boy. Think hard about whose side you're on."

Clay's eyes narrowed, but he closed his mouth.

Still aiming the rifle, Abner addressed me. "And don't be thinking about turning to my little brother for help. He knows where his loyalty lies. He's got too much at stake to risk, and he knows it. Not that he could take me if he tried. He just demonstrated that very well."

Abner grinned, showing stained teeth. "He'll make the right choice. He knows I can whoop him worse than our good ol' dad used to. But you were asking about your brother, weren't you? You want to know how he's faring? Well then, why don't we go pay him a little visit?"

He waved his rifle. "That way. March. You too, Clay."

I didn't have far to walk: Through the little kitchen, past the wreathed door, and past the narrow bathroom. I ended up facing a log wall. The rusty, chipped dryer—surprisingly large—sat in the corner to my right, and there was nowhere left to go.

I'm facing a wall. My stomach plunged. *He's going to shoot me now.*

Chapter Nine

*Q*uit staring at the wall like an idiot and turn around," Abner ordered.

My neck stiffened. *I'd rather be shot in the back.*

But Abner's tone compelled obedience. Slowly, savoring what might be my last breaths, I pivoted to face him. Clay stood to my left, near the dryer, and I noticed his ears flamed red.

Abner still held the rifle aimed at us. *Surely he wouldn't shoot his own brother.* I couldn't fathom such a horrendous action, not when I was here for the sole purpose of rescuing my own brother. I bit my lip and waited, my eyes moving from the rifle to Abner's high forehead and lank, greasy hair.

"See those keys?" He indicated a row of three keys dangling from a wooden duck-shaped key rack hanging on the wall to my right. "Get the middle one."

Obeying, I slid the key from the hook. Two keys remained on the rack. *What do these unlock? Torture chambers?*

"Clay, move away from the dryer," Abner barked. "Girl, open the dryer."

I gaped stupidly, trying to make sense of this. Abner had said we were going to see Max, but—what in the world did a dryer have to do with anything? He prodded me with the rifle. "Go on."

Curious despite myself, I pried at the edge of the dryer door. I gulped down a sickening urge to laugh. *What, is Max being kept prisoner inside of here? A dryer—a hide-and-seek spot for toddlers, not teens. A dryer—a place where socks get lost, not people.* The metal door seemed stuck, but suddenly swung open on squeaky hinges. Leaning down, I saw that the interior was empty, the metal finish scuffed. Yet it was the back of the dryer that drew my attention, a large round metal door, like a portal, secured with a padlock.

"What the—" Clay began.

Abner cut him off. "Unlock it, girl."

So I climbed awkwardly into the dryer. My boots protruded as I knelt uncomfortably on the curved metal. I fumbled in the dimness of my own shadow to fit the key in the padlock, but once I lined it up, it slipped in easily. I turned it, heard a click, and the padlock snapped open.

"Toss the key back out here."

I did as Abner said, and the key clattered to the floor. I watched Clay pick it up and, as if he wanted to prevent Abner from ordering him to do it, promptly hung it back on the hook.

"Now push the door open," Abner told me.

I splayed my gloved fingers and pressed the metal. It swung back easily into thick blackness, and I drew back instinctively, fearing a fall. I swallowed, dreading Abner's next demand.

It came swiftly. "Climb down. There's a rope ladder hanging from the opening. You can use that," he added, as if offering a luxury.

Imagining all sorts of horrors, I whispered, "But I don't know what's down there."

"Do it, or I'll throw you down."

Without thinking, I made the sign of the cross, surprising myself that the action came so naturally. Then I turned and lowered my legs into the seemingly bottomless pit. A fierce coldness clutched at my legs as I searched gingerly with my clumsy boots to find the rope ladder. I couldn't help thinking how ironic it was to be entering this frigid environment from a dryer, the abode of warm fluffy towels, woolen socks, and cozy sweatshirts. My toes sank onto a taught rope, and I braced myself for the blind climb down.

Yet I lingered with my head in the dim light, not wanting to leave it, afraid I'd never see light again. Apparently satisfied that I was doing as told, Abner addressed Clay. "Your turn."

"Abner, no."

From my low view, I saw Clay take a step back, but I couldn't see his expression.

"Sorry, kid." Abner sounded anything but sorry. "You brought this on yourself. Maybe next time you'll think twice before crossing me." He jabbed Clay with the rifle until he ducked into the dryer.

I moved down the ladder to make room for him and tried not to panic at the swaying of the rope. *How much farther?* I wondered as I descended, and yet—I feared reaching the bottom. I tried not to imagine what I'd find, wanting to find my brother, yet fearing what condition he might be in.

I hadn't realized that rope could creak, but this one did. I looked up to see Clay had stopped climbing down. "Abner," he called, "you can't expect me to be on your side if you don't explain any of this. I don't have a clue what's going on." I assumed that the brave confrontational tone of his voice came from the fact that he was no longer standing within arm's reach of Abner.

The rifle appeared, pointing down from the opening. "You never were very bright, were you, Clay?" Abner began speaking very slowly, as if to a moron. "It's very simple. I kidnapped this girl's twin brother, Max Perigard. Don't tell me you haven't heard of the famous, disgustingly wealthy Perigards?"

"Kidnapped," Clay broke in. "Man, Abner, that's—"

"Don't interrupt," Abner growled. "Obviously, I'm smart enough not to get caught. In fact, I picked up the ransom today, and that's when the girl decided to try and follow me. Like I said before, big mistake. Now that I've got her to take care of, old man Perigard is gonna have to pay double."

The rifle wavered slightly. "I never intended for you to get involved in this. I purposely planned the kidnapping for a week when I knew you couldn't make it here—so your time in the hole is your own fault. Think about that while I go count my money."

With a clunk, the door slammed shut, and we were plunged into utter darkness.

Above me, Clay cursed.

I almost joined in. Then I thought, *Why make it more like hell than it already is?* I resumed my descent into the black pit.

"He descended into hell," my mind chanted, snagging a line from the Apostle's Creed, *"the third day He rose again from the dead . . ."*

A prayer, but I felt no consolation.

I'd thought I was cold before, but the coldness I felt now rattled through my body and threatened to shatter my bones. I was thankful I hadn't shed my winter gear in the cabin.

At last I felt solid ground beneath my boots. Dirt-packed ground, I figured from the rough, uneven lay of it as I inched forward carefully, my arms outstretched. The waiting silence made the back of my neck prickle, despite my scarf.

"Max?" I called into the nothingness. "Max?" I intended it to come out sounding confident, not as this weak whisper. "Max?"

No response.

My gloved fingertips brushed a wall, also solid earth, I assumed, and I followed it several feet till I came to a far corner. My boot struck a firm, yet yielding, form. My heart leapt into my throat, choking my words. "Max, is that you?" I yanked off a glove and felt the form—shoulders, neck, head—definitely a person. But the skin on the face—so clammy and cold. "He's frozen, he's dead!" I cried, a rush of emotion devastating me.

Suddenly, the body shifted. I heard a low groan, then, "Char?"

I knew that voice. "Max, you're alive!"

"Sleeping," he mumbled. "Guess I'm still dreaming."

I felt his head bob under my hand. "No, Max! This is real. Wake up!" He always had been an infuriatingly sound sleeper.

There was a scrabbling sound and my hand fell as he stood. "Char, is that you?"

"Yes."

"What in blazes are you doing here? Don't tell me that creep got you, too." A string of curses made me shy away, but only for a second. I wrapped my arms around him and hugged until he pushed me away. "Cut it out, Char."

"I can't help it. I've been so worried about you—and searching for you, and—oh, I just wish I could see you." I opened my eyes as wide as possible, but there was no adjusting to this literal black hole. I thought about how when lights go out in cartoon shows, eyes shine in the dark. But it wasn't like that at all. I couldn't see a thing.

"Here, maybe this will help." The voice startled me. I heard a click. A light came on, and I glanced over my shoulder. I'd forgotten about Clay. He stood behind me, holding a thin, small flashlight. "It was in my coat pocket," he explained, almost apologetically, his breath coming out in a visible mist.

Max's scruffy face hardened. His shadowed eyes narrowed as he pulled me protectively to his side and scrutinized Clay. "Who are you?" he demanded, making a threatening fist.

"Whoa, buddy." Light bounced off the uneven walls as Clay spread his hands defensively. "I'm not looking for a fight. I'm down here same as you—not by choice."

My body tensed. He had obviously avoided mentioning the fact that he was the kidnapper's brother.

"Char?" Max's voice came out strong, but huskier than it should have. He broke into a hacking cough, and my worries heightened.

"You don't look good, Max. We've got to get out of here. There must be some way—"

"Done it, tried it. Hopeless. Tell me how you ended up here. I'm guessing Grandfather didn't pay the ransom?"

I rubbed my forehead. "Not at first. He thought this was a joke, some kind of stunt you were pulling for money and attention."

Max growled. "Stupid old man."

I hastened to explain, as briefly as possible, how I had

trailed Abner, who ran me off the road and chased me into the woods. I finished with an indication toward Clay. "He found me in the woods and brought me to this cabin—we didn't know it belonged to a kidnapper." I also avoided mentioning the fact that Clay was related to our captor. Why did I feel the need to protect him? I must have felt indebted by his earlier attempt to save me. "Abner forced us down here at rifle-point. Now tell me your story."

Max grimaced. "It's a lame one." His nostril's flared. "I still can't believe he got me that way. I was at the ski hill—just finished an awesome day of snowboarding—and I went to use the restroom. While I was in there, a janitor came in. I didn't think anything of it, but the next thing I knew, I was waking up in a reeking garbage can, bouncing around in the back of a locked truck bed. The guy must have used chloroform to knock me out, then smuggled me out of the restroom like garbage. Too easy," he said resentfully.

"So we get to this isolated cabin, and when he opens the truck bed, I jump him." Max worked his jaw. "I'm still feeling it, but I'd fight him again. It's our only chance."

I glanced at Clay, who averted his eyes. *Coward* came to mind before I refocused on Max. He looked different, so grim and tired. I was almost sorry I woke him. "You look like you need to rest."

He gave a bitter laugh. "All I do down here is 'rest.' I'd rather stay awake and at least know I'm alive."

He observed my crestfallen look and softened his tone. "Sorry, Char. You know I'm not angry at you. I'm just going crazy thinking about that maniac—what he did to me, what he did to you . . . what he might do next."

We became silent. I noticed that Clay still held the flashlight as if he didn't know what to do with it. Like me and Max, he wore a coat, but unlike us, he didn't have a hat or gloves. I walked over to him. "Here, let me take that light. You can warm your hands in your pockets."

He responded with a slight nod before surrendering the metallic blue flashlight.

"And thanks for trying to help me earlier, by the way," I added.

Again, a barely detectable nod, as if ashamed of his efforts and knowing that "trying" meant not succeeding. "This is messed up, big time," he muttered. "I can't believe Abner's doing this."

"Believe it," I said shortly. "He's a monster."

Clay's lips parted, as if about to speak, perhaps even protest, when a sound came from above that made me look up. On impulse, I switched off the light. The metal door swung open, and Abner's ugly face appeared, mottled with shadows. "Clay? Get up here."

Wow, it sure didn't take him long to miss his brother.

Clay hurried to the ladder like an obedient dog answering his master's call.

"Why do you think the creep wants him?" Max asked once Clay was gone and the door closed.

"Because—" I caught myself. "Who knows?" Looking at Max, I tried to gauge how worried he was. As his twin, I could usually read him, but not now. The mere days we'd spent apart suddenly felt like months, months that had created a chasm between us. "At least we have the flashlight." I began shining it around our prison for a better look.

The dugout room was a rough rectangle of approximately ten feet long and eight feet wide. *I wonder how long this took to make. Abner must have been planning this for a long time.* This disturbed me much more than thinking that the kidnapping had been impromptu, because this enhanced the fact that we were facing not just a criminal, but an evil mind that calculated fiendish long-term plans. Shining my light upward, I was surprised to see our dirt roof stretched no more than ten feet from the floor. The climb down here had felt so much longer.

I clicked off the light when I heard the door opening once more. I didn't want Abner to discover, and thus confiscate, the flashlight. He stuck in his head and I wondered briefly where Clay was. "Get up here, boy," Abner yelled down, obviously referring to Max.

Max glowered, but he stalked forward, confiding in me, "The only reason I'm going is because I want to. 'Up there' is one step closer to freedom." He touched my shoulder. "Stay strong. I'll be back for you."

I fought against the tremble in my jaw. *I only just found you, and now you're leaving me. What if I never see you again? What if Abner's summoning us up, one by one, to be executed?*

Left alone, doubts and fears assaulted me. I didn't even hear the door open the next time.

"Your turn, girl."

Turn for what? I lifted my eyes to Abner's grim face, and shuddered. My insides churned as I climbed. *This makes no sense. He only just locked me down here.*

I emerged from the dryer to face the expected rifle barrel. Abner pressed the metal into my back and directed me to the cabin's main room, where I saw three aluminum folding chairs lined up facing the wood-burning stove. Clay sat in the first, Max in the second.

Their arms were drawn back behind them, and white nylon rope stretched tight across their chests, pinning their arms. The same rope wound tight around their legs and ankles. No gags plugged their mouths, but they didn't speak. Their lips were set in firm lines, their eyes angry slits. I wondered briefly, pointlessly, if they realized how similar their expressions were.

The third chair was empty.

"Have a seat, girl," Abner ordered.

My eyes roamed the room, desperately searching for a way out. I spotted the ransom backpack sitting on the table.

"When I tell you something, you listen the first time." Abner shoved me onto the chair and dropped a lasso around me, tightening the rope before winding it countless times around my chest and arms. He set his rifle on the table so he could bind my wrists. He tied my legs next, then my ankles, and when he was finished, I had no circulation.

He planted his large self in front of the wood stove. "I'm sure you're wondering why I brought you all up here," he began formally, as if this were a school presentation instead of a torture session. He reached over, grabbed the backpack from the table, and held the lumpy sack by one strap. "This is why." He pushed the bag in my face, then unzipped it so I was facing a pile of green bills. "Looks like a lot of money, hey?" I nodded, not knowing how else to respond.

"Well, it's not!" He grabbed a fist of bills, opened the wood stove, and chucked them into the fire. The paper caught instantly, flaming high. "It's worthless! Fake! Counterfeit! Useless paper." He leaned close to my face, his own face blotchy red. "Did you know that all along?"

My eyes burned in the smoky air and widened at the sight of his bloodshot eyeballs. "No," I breathed. "That can't be right. They are real—I checked them myself right before putting the bag in the locker." I blinked rapidly as I ran back through the day, searching for an explanation. "Rob," I said, the truth dawning. "He followed me. I didn't realize it, but he must have switched the money." *When I was talking to Cindy.*

But then why had there been a note to Max in the real money? In case Rob didn't get it switched in time? And how had he managed it? *Grandfather probably makes sure his henchmen know how to pick locks.*

My head spun in confusion. Where had Rob stashed the real stuff? He hadn't had a bag of any kind. I groaned, recalling his big coat. He hadn't needed a bag, not with a roomy, many-pocketed coat.

"Who's Rob?" Abner demanded. I cringed as he clasped my chin with his coarse-skinned fingers. "Tell me the truth or I'll tear out your tongue."

"He works for my grandfather." I clenched my teeth briefly. "Grandfather must have come up with the plan and told Rob to follow me and swap the money out after I delivered it."

Anger sparked in Abner's eyes, but I felt it spark in my own eyes as well. Because of Grandfather's lack of trust in me and Max, we were going to suffer. More than we already had. "That so? How very unfortunate for you." Abner squeezed my chin with barbaric intensity. "Because he's not the only one with a plan."

"You don't understand." I forced my diaphragm to work. "My grandfather isn't defying you. He just doesn't believe this is a real kidnapping—"

"He will soon enough. That's why you're up here." Abner released my chin and cracked his thick knuckles. "It's time to give the fool some proof. Undeniable, visible, serious proof." He chuckled briefly. His eyes roamed from me to Max, back and forth for what felt like eternity, before finally settling on Max.

Max returned Abner's stare with cold stillness. Only a muscle near his jaw twitched.

Abner glanced back at me. "Don't feel left out. If this proof doesn't convince the old man, it'll be your turn next."

"Abner," Clay spoke up, "you have to stop—"

"Did I ask for your input?"

Clay shook his head.

"Then don't give it. Your job is to watch, listen, and learn. Got it?"

"No, I don't get it!" Clay strained against his ropes. "This is crazy. How can you treat them like this? And me? You're not a monster, Abner, I know you're not. You're my brother, you—"

"I'm going to have to gag you if you don't shut up."

Clay closed his mouth.

Abner moved into the kitchen for a moment, opened a drawer, and returned with a pair of sharp steel cutters. The curved rusty blades looked strong enough to snap through thick tree branches.

I drew in a loud breath. Suddenly all I heard was breathing: Clay breathing shallowly, Max breathing quickly, and Abner breathing deeply, wetly, like a salivating animal anticipating a kill.

He set the pruning tool on the floor, in plain sight as if to mock us, then crouched to remove Max's boot. It took some time to maneuver the boot out from the snug ropes and pull it from Max's foot, but when Abner accomplished that, he stripped off Max's sock.

The obviousness of what was coming next hit me, and I started pleading and crying like a child. "No! Please, don't hurt my brother. It's not his fault our grandfather messed up. Please, think of another way. We could call him, or write to him—we'll say anything you want—or you could send him something. I mean something like—like—my watch, or my hair. My hair! That would work as proof, I promise. Please, please!"

"Stop it, Char," Max snapped, his face set like stone. "Don't give him the satisfaction."

Abner chuckled and spoke to Max. "Think you're pretty tough, huh? You'll change your mind by the time I'm through."

With that, he lifted the cutters. He snipped the air contemplatively a few times, as if practicing, and the blades made a *whisk, whisk,* sound. Then he took a firm hold of Max's ankle and pointed the blades from toe to toe, chanting, "Eenie meenie miney moe." He stopped at the toe next to the little one.

Even though Max tried whipping his foot away and wiggling his toes crazily, he couldn't avoid the cutters.

The sharp blades closed around his toe, and I closed my eyes.

Chapter Ten

Max's howl of pain was so excruciating, so loud, I prayed that someone, somewhere, would hear it and send help. I barely realized that I'd joined in, with screams so intense they lacerated my throat.

A crash startled me, and when I opened my eyes, I peered through a bleary film of tears. It was just as well. There was nothing I wanted to see. Abner stood calmly wiping the cutter blades on his shirt, leaving a streak of blood across the blue checkered flannel. Max writhed in pain—as much as his bonds allowed—but on the floor now. He must have toppled the chair by struggling so violently, and thus caused the crash I'd heard.

Abner proceeded to ignore the loud, painful scene, and methodically packed the "evidence" for Grandfather in a small box lined with cotton balls. Clay watched it all mutely, his face white. Max had moved on from screaming to cursing.

I agreed with every curse I heard. God had abandoned us. What was there left to do but curse?

"I think I managed to break you," Abner said, sounding very satisfied as he stood over Max, whose prone form was no longer writhing, but wilted, as if all energy had drained from him. He couldn't right himself from his awkward, chair-bound position, and I saw with horror that his cheek was pressed in a pool of his own blood. My gaze flicked quickly to his foot. Blood still flowed.

"You have to wrap his foot," I sobbed. "Can't you see how much blood he's losing? You got what you wanted, now help him, please!"

Abner rubbed his goatee. "Guess I don't need him dying

on me just yet." He cut Max's ropes, then approached me with the cutters. "Since you love him so much, I'll let you do the honors." He snipped me free from my bonds and gave me a roll of bandage, and I leapt to Max's side, peeling off my gloves. My bare hands became bloody in an instant, and I didn't care. All that mattered was ceasing the constant red current.

After tying off the bandage, I moved Max's head from the pooling blood and wiped his face as best I could. "He passed out," I whispered, and felt his neck for a pulse, fearing the worst. The artery still pumped strongly, despite the ashen shade of his face. "We need to get him to a bed and prop his foot up."

Abner laughed. "What do you think this is, a hospital? You're not putting him on any bed."

"Fine," I countered, lifting Max's foot and holding it up, "a couch then." But I quickly remembered that there was no couch in the cabin.

"I'll tell you what will be good for him," Abner said smugly. "The cold. Nothing constricts blood vessels like the cold, so you can just head on back down to your hole."

Panic fluttered in my breast. "But he's unconscious. He can't climb down."

"We can always drop him."

I swallowed a retort and suggested, "You could carry him down," but even as I spoke, I knew it would never happen. How I wished I was a man with muscles to easily handle Max's one-hundred-sixty pounds.

"I'll do it," spoke a voice, and I turned to see Clay, whose eyes neither looked at me nor Abner, but focused on some point beyond us, some distant speck on the logs.

Abner laughed. "You think you're that strong? Fine, give it a try. There's nothing to lose. But first," his tone grew serious, "you've got to answer one thing for me, boy, and you'd better answer right." The cutters still in hand, he fingered a blade as his eyes drilled Clay's. "You with me, or against me?"

"You can't expect—"

"I can, and I do." Abner pressed the steel points to Clay's chest. "You're bound to me, whether you like it or not, by flesh and blood. There's honor in that. You stick with me, and I can promise you plenty. Money, for one thing. Your life, for another. Make your choice."

Clay's Adam's apple bobbed as he swallowed. Perhaps he felt my eyes on him, because he shifted his gaze my way.

"No, boy." Abner let the blades creep up to Clay's throat. "Don't go looking for guidance from her. She's nothing. She'd as soon see you stabbed to death."

I shook my head, but Clay's eyes were no longer on me; they were on the blades prodding his throat. My arms ached from holding Max's leg up. I wished Clay would spit in Abner's face.

"This is your chance to be a man," Abner continued, "wielding the power, calling the shots. So what's it gonna be?"

Still no answer.

"I'm losing patience," Abner hissed.

The blades pressed, and Clay flinched. "All right," he said grudgingly, "I'm with you."

Abner removed the blades from Clay's neck. "You've made your decision," he said with the finality of a judge passing sentence. "There's no going back. The consequences would be deadly." Rifle in hand once more, he used the cutters and set Clay free from the chair.

I watched with pounding heart. Yes, Abner held the rifle, but it wasn't aimed. It was the perfect time for Clay to go for it, to grab the cutters, to sock Abner, to try something. Anything.

But he didn't.

My head drooped. Clay had made his decision about whose side he was on, and no matter how pressured he'd been, it appeared he meant it. He was now the enemy.

Yet I let him heave Max over his shoulder and lug him toward the prison hole, because I had no choice. I was forced to enter the hole first, but then I shone the flashlight up to make Clay's journey easier, for Max's sake. Clay moved slowly down the rope ladder, but the fact that he managed to perform the awkward feat without dropping Max amazed me despite myself. Finally he laid Max on the cold dirt floor, and left.

While I fretted at Max's side, Clay returned from above with a pillow. He began to put it under Max's thickly bandaged foot, but I swiped it from him and did it myself.

Clay hesitated, then spoke quietly. "I'm sorry, you know. But you were there. You've got to see I had no choice—"

"You had a choice," I said stiffly, speaking to the shadows. "It wasn't an easy one, but it was still a choice."

"I'm still really on your side." His tone begged me to understand. "Think about it. What good am I locked down here? At least this way, I can help. I'll try to get some things to make it better for you and your brother. Some food, water, blankets, painkillers—"

"But not freedom. Not a doctor. Not the police. Correct?" The silence told me all I needed to know. "We don't want anything from you or your brother." I laid my hand on Max's forehead. "You're both criminals now."

There was a pause before Clay said, "Fine."

He was so far from the hero I yearned for, that I couldn't stand to even look at him as he turned and walked away, climbed up the ladder, and left me for the world above.

—⌁—

I felt as if I were keeping vigil at a corpse's side. I felt I should pray, but bitter anger and hurt ate away at my heart and soul, so that I was incapable of any act of faith. I was an empty shell. If Max died, I would die, too. I didn't know how, but I knew I would.

The flashlight stood up like a candle from where I'd balanced the narrow handle on a level spot of ground. This and my dark, earthen surroundings only enhanced the tomb-like atmosphere. I kept my fingertips on Max's pulse, and this was my one hope, because I continued to feel the movement of his life-blood throbbing steadily.

Eventually, he stirred. I leaned over him and studied his face. "Max," I whispered, "can you hear me?"

He blew out his breath and even while I wrinkled my nose at the stale odor, I rejoiced to see he was coming to.

"Water," he mumbled, and he licked his chapped lips.

I squeezed his hand. "I'm sorry, Max, I don't have any water."

He groaned and opened his eyes. Eyes pooled with pain. I watched the realization dawn on him as he lifted his head slightly and looked around. "Back in here," he said flatly, letting his head fall back down on the cold floor.

"I'd rather be in here than up there with that savage," I said viciously. My voice softened as I added, "You were very brave."

He grunted. "No, I wasn't. And I don't want to be. I just want out of this hellhole." His eyes rolled back in his head, and he winced.

"Does it hurt a lot?"

"No, Char. It feels great. You should try getting your toe hacked off sometime."

A muffled sob escaped my throat.

"Sorry, that was uncalled for." He sighed. "I'm not really thinking straight right now."

"Don't apologize. It was a stupid question."

He rose up on his forearms and slid back a little, struggling to prop himself against the wall. I automatically moved and adjusted the pillow so it kept his bandaged foot elevated. Then I sat next to him, hugging my knees and trying not to think about anything.

Instead, I wondered about Clay, and his intention to bring us water, food, blankets, and painkillers. I wished now that I hadn't reacted the way I had, for Max's sake. *He could really use those things.* But it had been a long time since Clay left. I doubted he'd be back tonight, if at all.

"Where'd the pillow come from?" Max asked, as if noticing it for the first time.

102

"Clay brought it."

This seemed to trigger something in Max's memory. "Clay," he repeated, his eyes tightening. "He made us think he was a victim, but he's really in on this. I thought he was just some random fisherman who was in the wrong place at the wrong time, but he's really Abner's brother."

I didn't say anything, just stared at my knees.

"Char?" His tone was sharp. "You knew all along, didn't you?"

At that moment, I hated twin intuition.

"Yes, but—"

"The kidnapper's brother, Char?" His voice rose. "The kidnapper's freakin' brother! Why didn't you tell me?" His fist flashed through the air. "I could've taken him easily when he was down here before. Pummeled him to a pulp."

"Max, please. That wouldn't have done any good."

"Would've been worth a shot. And it sure would've felt good." He turned his eyes on me accusingly. "Why the heck were you protecting him?"

"Max, I'm sorry." I couldn't bear to have him angry at me. Tears gathered in my eyes and trembled on my lashes. "I really thought he was on our side. He did help me, he—"

"Man, talk about naive."

"How do you think you got down here?" I asked defensively. "If it weren't for Clay, Abner would've thrown you down here. Clay carried you on his back; he didn't have to do that."

"Okay, so if he's really a victim like us, where is he now? Why isn't he down here, too?"

I was silent, weighing my answer. But there was only one way to say it. "He joined Abner. Abner threatened him, made him—I know," I hurried on, because I could tell what Max was thinking, "that's no excuse. I agree with you. Clay's clearly not on our side."

"Clearly."

As I sat there in utter discomfort, I began to realize that I'd been smelling a foul odor for quite some time now. I wrinkled my nose. "What's that awful smell?"

Max gave me a hard stare. "That, dear Char, is our toilet. Sorry to break it to you, but this place doesn't exactly come with plumbing."

I plucked up the flashlight and swung it around the room, illuminating a large green bucket in the far corner that I had failed to see on my previous sweep through of our prison. I cringed, all my senses assaulted at the realization that I needed to use the bucket. Plodding over to it, I clicked off the flashlight.

Then I, a self-admitted clean freak, was reduced to squatting over a reeking, stagnating toilet bucket, in frigid temperatures, while my brother sat nearby.

And what will we do when the bucket's full? Better not think that far ahead. Hopefully, we won't be here anymore.

Negatively, my mind added: *We'll probably be dead.*

───

Max was not a pleasant companion. I couldn't blame him, not under our circumstances and with him in such unrelenting pain. The minutes dragged by, and I wished sleep would claim him, or me—or, preferably, both of us—but rest had never felt more impossible. Thirst plagued me. My tongue felt thick, dry, cottony, and it stuck to the roof of my mouth. *A person dies after about three days without water,* my mind warned me.

At the same time, I kept fantasizing about a soft mattress, thick quilts, and fluffy pillows. This alternated with my food fantasies. All I'd eaten today was three donuts, not ideal survival food. And just envisioning Grandfather's heavily laden table caused me to drool and fume with anger. His brunch feast now seemed so long ago.

I rubbed my forehead. *How did so much wretchedness get crammed into one day?*

According to my watch, it was now 10 p.m.

I rested my head back, then instantly removed it. Too late. The cold, clammy earthen wall had already sucked what little warmth I'd had left. But I wanted to rest my pounding head so badly. I finally leaned it forward on my knees.

Knees. Knees are for praying. God . . . was all I could manage. Did that even count as a prayer? Was my mind freezing up, so I could barely form a prayer? Or did I just not want to? Was I giving in to despair?

Suddenly, the metal door to our prison clanged open, and I braced myself for more Abner torture.

But it was only Clay. He climbed down with two plastic grocery sacks in hand and approached us tentatively. I glanced at Max, who was glaring at him. Clay cleared his throat before crouching down, keeping his distance from us both. "I brought you some stuff." He pulled two worn blankets from one bag.

Unable to help myself, I reached forward and snatched them, immediately dropping one on Max before wrapping myself in the other, although it was rather thin and musty smelling.

From the remaining bag, Clay produced two plastic water bottles and two cans of baked beans. "Sorry about the mess," he said as he handed them to us, "but I had to open the cans before coming down." A silverware handle protruded from each can and some of the contents had slopped over the sides. "You'd better eat fast. Abner's timing me, and I have to bring the cans and spoons back up."

What, so we don't try to kill ourselves with them? I began gulping down the beans and hoped Max wouldn't be too stubborn to do the same. We needed any nourishment we could get.

"These are for you." Clay set a small paper cup near Max. "Painkillers." Apparently feeling the need to explain himself, he went on. "I would have come sooner, but Abner made me clean up the mess . . ." He let the sentence trail off, probably realizing how tactless his words were.

"Oh? He made you?" I said acidly. "I thought joining up with him was supposed to give you the power of 'calling the shots.' "

Ignoring me, he continued trying to justify himself. "Then

105

I had to help him get rid of your car, and after that we dropped the—uh—package in a drop box so it'll go out to your grandfather first thing. You'll probably be out of here before you know it. Maybe even tomorrow," he said brightly. Too brightly. His hand rubbed the back of his neck. "Anyway, I just want you both to know that I'm looking out for you and doing what I can—"

"Save it." Max's voice oozed disgust. "We're not buying your crap. You're looking out for your own skin, and that's it."

"No," he retorted. "I just don't see the need to go looking for trouble. I've tried standing up to Abner. It didn't accomplish anything, and it cost me. He's bigger and stronger, and he can deck me no problem. Sorry, but I'm not looking to get killed."

"Stop whining," Max said scathingly. "You're a sorry excuse for a man. You've got nothing we want to hear, and we've got nothing to say to you; and if I wasn't out of commission right now, I'd beat you myself."

Clay worked his jaw silently and waited for us to finish eating. Then, gathering the cans, spoons, and bags, he left without another word.

Max gulped down his painkillers with a swig of water. I took a deep drink as well, but also tried to be conservative, as I doubted Clay would be back.

———

10:30 p.m. I pressed my lips together and wished they weren't so chapped. At home, I used lip balm constantly. Max called it an addiction. Sometimes I carried ChapStick in my pocket. Thinking this, I ungloved my hand and reached into my jeans pocket hopefully. Sure enough, I felt the smooth tube. And something else, something beaded. Along with the ChapStick, I pulled out, to my surprise, a rosary. But it didn't belong to me. I studied the blue beads closer, then recalled Gwen asking me to untangle this rosary earlier today. It felt like weeks ago.

I was ridiculously thankful for the ChapStick and the relief it brought as I spread the waxy stuff thickly on my rough lips. After repocketing the lip balm, I fingered the rosary contemplatively. It felt good in my hand.

"Haven't seen one of those in a while," Max commented. "Wouldn't it be nice if life was that simple: Say a prayer, and all's good." His derogatory attitude reminded me of my own, yet I cringed at it.

I gripped the little crucifix and found myself saying, "I do believe that God can get us out of this. If He wants to. That's the two-million-dollar-question: Will He? Kind of like Grandfather." I bit my tongue, hoping that hadn't been blasphemy. *I'm a perfect illustration of fallen human nature: Forget God when things are good; blame Him when things go bad.*

Out loud, I said, "I haven't prayed much since Mom and Dad died. I guess because Grandfather always prodded me to 'pray for their souls.' I didn't want to think of them as souls, without bodies. And all those times he forced us to go to confession . . ."

"No kidding. Grandfather's enough to turn anyone off religion."

I rolled the smooth elongated beads in my fingers, musing. Could I blame it all on Grandfather? Not really. There always seemed to be a reason not to pray. Not enough time. Too many distractions. And, most of all, lack of desire. But now . . . all I had was time.

"It wouldn't hurt to ask Him to help us," I said quietly. "God, I mean."

"What, you actually want to pray?"

"It wouldn't hurt," I repeated. "Just one Rosary. Will you join me?"

"Fine," Max grumbled. "If I'm lucky it'll put me to sleep."

I crossed myself and began. Technically, I thought, we should pray the Joyful Mysteries, as it was still a Sunday in the Christmas Season, but that seemed highly out of place here. The Sorrowful Mysteries would be much more fitting, I decided grimly.

Our voices droned unenthusiastically in the darkness.

". . . now and at the hour of our death, Amen" took on a whole new meaning. Any moment could very well be our hour of death.

I noticed that the little flashlight stood before us like a vigil candle, casting a comforting—or eerie—glow, depending how I looked at it. As I peered around our bare room, I studied the earthen walls with all their ridges and shadows. For quite a long time, I stared at the farthest wall, until I began to believe that I saw a cross. I blinked my weary eyes and refocused them, expecting the cross to vanish.

But no, it was no trick of my eyes. There really was something like the shape of a cross scraped roughly into the dirt of the back wall. Only, it wasn't quite right. The longest part of the cross, the vertical part, stretched too long at the top and too short at the bottom, basically forming more of an upside-down cross than anything.

My eyes bleared, and my voice finished praying. Next to me, Max breathed a deep rhythm of sleep. I yawned, crawled forward for the flashlight, laid down with my blanket, and snapped off the light.

The cross disappeared.

Chapter Eleven

"Escape is our only chance," I told Max for the one-hundredth time, as if saying it would help us come up with a plan. It was my second day of captivity, and to make matters worse, we'd been given no water or food yet today.

"Hey, I'm all for it," Max said. I heard him hobbling carefully around the pitch black room, testing his damaged foot and attempting to warm his muscles. We'd decided to turn the flashlight on only when necessary, as we wanted to preserve the battery. Knowing we had some way of dispelling the oppressive darkness was an immense comfort, not one we wanted to relinquish.

Standing, I shed my blanket and flexed my stiff legs before making my way carefully around the room, feeling the dirt walls.

I removed a glove and scratched at the wall. A few semi-frozen dirt flakes gathered under my nails. "We could dig out."

"With what?"

I thought hard. Our fingers would be numb and bleeding before we dug five inches. "With spoons, maybe . . . No wonder Clay took them from us." I sighed and thought harder. "The door, then." I climbed the ladder and examined the metal portal for a crack or a hinge or something to work at.

"Even the key wouldn't do you any good, not with the padlock on the outside," Max said. "I'm telling you, I'd like to see Houdini try to get out of this one."

"Shh." I'd begun to hear muffled voices through the door. I thought I'd heard Clay shouting, and caught the words, "bring them food." So maybe he would be back. I pressed my ear against the cold metal. I heard no more distinguishable words, but a plan began to form. It wasn't ingenious and it wasn't foolproof. It was risky and maybe even stupid. But was it worth a shot? Definitely.

I spoke down the length of the ladder. "We'll just have to get one of the kidnappers to let us out."

"Sure, that'll be easy."

"Seriously, if Clay comes down again, we should make a move. Do you think you could tackle him?"

Max snorted, and I imagined the are-you-kidding-me? look on his face.

"Okay, so here's the plan," and as I described it to my skeptical twin, he became a little less skeptical.

So that we'd be ready, he and I traded shifts listening at the door. Most of the time there was nothing to hear but the insane hum of silence. Every once in a while I'd say, "Max?" or he'd say, "Char?" just to reassure ourselves that we weren't alone.

When the silence became too strained, we prayed a Rosary. "We might as well make this a novena," I said, using the little metal crucifix to scrape a mark in the dirt wall to keep track of the days. "Just in case we're in here that long."

"So we pray for nine days straight, then we're miraculously set free? Is that how it works?"

I had to smile. "Something like that."

"You know what would taste awesome right now?" Max didn't wait for an answer. "Eggnog. Thick, creamy eggnog. I'd eat it in a mixing bowl full of chocolate cereal."

"Sounds utterly weird and disgusting," I said from my perch at the top of the rope ladder. "I'd go for soup. Hot clam chowder in a bread bowl, like the kind we had on the pier in San Francisco."

"With Mom and Dad? I remember that California trip. Alcatraz was cool."

Trust Max to admire a prison when he was stuck in one

himself.

"I liked the old mission in Carmel. Remember the chapel?" Fuzzy scenes of colorful gardens under blue sky, a tiered fountain, and warm sand-toned stucco buildings grew clear in my memory. The sense of comfort that came with sitting in a pew with a parent on each side and feeling Someone all-powerful watching over us and loving us, had been incomparable.

Max and I dropped off into silence . . . or perhaps prayer.

The next day I finally heard the long-awaited sound of the key clinking in the lock. I sprang to the ground and scurried to the far wall. My energy was surprisingly high for someone who was starving. "Get into position, Max." I clicked on the flashlight and stood it up like a candle. Warped shadows mingled with the weak light.

Max lay down on his blanket beside the wall farthest from the door. He stayed deathly still while the metal portal opened. I sank into the shadows beside him, putting my hand on his forehead, and watched surreptitiously as the figure climbed down.

Relief filled me when I saw that our visitor was Clay, not Abner. So far so good. He toted a small bag, in which I assumed was food and water. When he was about a foot from the ground, he dropped the bundle and began climbing back up.

"Clay," I called out. "Wait, please."

He paused on the ladder.

"Something's very wrong. I'm worried about Max. Will you take a look at him, please?" I let a slight tremble enter my voice. It did the trick.

He dropped from the ladder and walked our way. Above him, the door still stood open.

"I hope you have time to do this," I said worriedly. "Abner's not timing you again, is he?"

"No," Clay said shortly.

"Really? Why not?"

"He's out chopping wood."

Perfect.

"I don't know what good I can do," he said, kneeling beside Max. "But you're right, he doesn't look good."

"Maybe you could listen to his breathing. It seems kind of shallow."

He leaned in, and right on cue, Max clamped strong arms over him.

"What the—" Clay swore and struggled, but Max's grip didn't fail.

"Give us your keys." Max growled as he flipped with a quick roll, pinning Clay down.

Grunting, he responded, "What keys?"

Max struck Clay's face—a move we hadn't discussed—and I flinched. Nonetheless, the violence was effective.

Clay's expression hardened. "In my coat pocket."

I promptly fished out the key.

"I said 'keys,' plural." Max drew his fist back. "Where's your car key?"

"I don't have it. I don't even know where it is. Abner took it," Clay added with something close to embarrassment. I allowed myself a twinge of pity for the way he was being roughed up by both us and Abner. *But it's his own fault.*

"You'd better not be lying." With all his weight pinning Clay down, Max searched his other pockets, but this revealed no key, so we had no choice but to accept Clay's explanation.

"Get moving, Char." Max began binding Clay's wrists behind him with the rosary, which was long enough to double-wrap, strengthening it so it wouldn't break. We had tested it earlier. "I'll be waiting."

I shot up the ladder with the one key in hand, hoping everything else would turn out the way we'd planned. I'd go for the police and bring them back. We'd discussed, at some length, the possibility of Max fleeing with me, but ultimately decided against it. I could move stealthier and faster alone. Max's wounded foot would be too much of a risk. So he would sit tight, guarding Clay, waiting for me to bring the police.

I tried to close the portal without the usual clink, but it wasn't possible. No matter that Clay had said Abner was out chopping firewood, I was still nervous that he lurked inside, close by, ready to recapture me. I snapped the padlock into place and pocketed the key. At least now Max was safe from Abner.

Outside the dryer, I looked up at the key rack and, as expected, saw no keys.

But they've got to be somewhere. Listening, I heard a distant rhythmic thud. Assured that Abner was still chopping wood, I decided I could devote a moment to searching his room for car keys. Maybe I'd even find a gun.

I pushed open the wreathed door and stepped onto an ugly gray carpet which was stained darkly in multiple spots. A double bed filled most of the room, and a camouflage sleeping bag lay on the floor. I opened a closet door and searched inside a pair of mud-caked hiking boots, cracked sneakers, and stinky slippers. No keys. I rifled through the few shirts and pants on hangers, checking the pockets. No keys.

Moving to the bed, I felt under the pillow and inside the pillowcase. Still nothing. An alarm clock sat on a bedside table, but that was all.

Wood chopping sounds still rang out reassuringly, so I turned my attention to the small walnut dresser. This would be the most logical place, I told myself, but grimaced at the thought of pawing through Abner's underwear drawer.

I started with the top drawer, pushing aside socks and t-shirts and boxer shorts. *How does he even do laundry, with no washer and no working dryer? Better not think about it. The brute probably never washes his clothes.* My fingers wanted to recoil, but I forced myself to continue searching. I reached to the very back of the drawer and found a long black taper candle. Weird, but not useful.

In the second drawer, I rifled through shirts. *How many checkered flannels does he need? And they all look the same.* Something clunked against the side of the drawer, and I pulled out a silver-framed photo of a raven-haired beauty in a lacy wedding dress. She reminded me of Audrey Hepburn. Finding the lovely picture creeped me out. Who was she? Another victim Abner had kidnapped, or was currently stalking?

Finally, I hurried through the contents of the last drawer, a hodgepodge assortment of nails, rubber bands, duct tape, bullets, and a large wad of tissue paper. Poking the tissue, I realized it surrounded something hard and metallic. A gun?

I unrolled it carefully and was left holding a gold chalice flecked with red, ruby-like stones. Were they real? And what in the world was someone like Abner doing with such a beautiful treasure? *He probably stole it.* Frowning, I re-wrapped it, closed the drawer, and hurried from the room, afraid for a moment that the chopping had stopped. But no, it started up again.

I couldn't waste any more time in here. If it came down to it, I'd rather face Abner outside than in the confines of the cabin.

On my way through the kitchen, I grabbed a butcher knife. Just in case.

Turning my attention to the importance of the moment, I crept out the front door and down the steps, scanning carefully for Abner. The resonating thwacking of an ax on wood made me stiffen as I realized it came from the direction of the parked truck and car.

Why couldn't he have gone deep into the woods to do his wood cutting? That's how it's done in Hansel and Gretel. Why was real life never like a fairy tale? *Except for the bad parts. The evil, torture parts.*

As I approached the corner of the cabin, and the vehicles, I spotted Abner among the trees. His back was to me, at least. The way he swung the ax, so fiercely, did not so much make him look strong, as ruthless. The sound of splintering wood suddenly reminded me of splintering bone.

I slunk toward Clay's car with the slim hope that maybe the keys were inside. I prayed for it to be so, but of course it was not. So I moved stealthily to Abner's truck and mounted the step to peer through the window. No keys in the ignition or on the seat.

Suddenly, the chopping stopped, and I shrank down, ducking, then crawling beneath the truck, gripping my knife. I looked at the snowy ground, then up at the belly of the truck. And there, stuck magnetically to the metal above, sat a black plastic key case. My mind registered the sound of ax blows once more, and I triumphantly slid a key from the container. *Yes! It has to be a spare for the truck.*

Now, of course, I still had to get into the truck without Abner spotting me, and drive away before he could reach me. There was no way I could stop him from being alerted the moment I turned the key. At least by then, however, I'd be safely locked inside.

My hand shook as I struggled to fit the key in the door, but somehow I did it. Then I hoisted myself into the seat. I brushed away a pack of cigarettes, a Budweiser can, and a popcorn bag. The smell of melted butter mingled wretchedly with smoke and beer.

Another thing I hadn't counted on: I couldn't see out the front window, which was a frosty pane of ice. *This isn't happening.* I closed my eyes briefly. How was I ever going to scrape the windshield without Abner discovering me? For that matter, what was I going to scrape it with?

I glanced back at Abner, the pile of split wood growing around his chopping block. He seemed totally absorbed. I was just going to have to trust that he was.

I found a scraper under the passenger seat, set my knife down, then eased open the door and slipped to the ground. Standing on tiptoe—hard to do in boots—I scratched at the front window, clearing flakes of ice till my muscles ached.

Good enough. But I couldn't resist quickly scraping the side mirror. Throwing one final glance at Abner, I jumped back into the truck, locked the doors, and turned the key.

The truck roared to life with a wrath that suited the moment. I pressed the gas. The truck rumbled, then shuddered and bounced as I steered it down through the steep pine-bordered path which served as the driveway.

I'd never driven anything so enormous. I felt like I was on an over-sized, out-of-control sled. Trying to stay inside the narrow path between trees was terrifying, but my ride didn't last long. My eyes flew to the rearview mirror just in time to see Abner leap into the truck bed. Brandishing his ax, he charged, smashing through the rear window. I threw my hands up to shield my head and neck from flying glass, but it didn't work. Shards pierced my right cheek.

The truck pitched forward and rammed into a snow bank. I tried to scramble from the truck, but Abner dove into the front seat beside me, making it impossible to reach my knife. He no longer held the ax, but I was still horrified. His hands were weapons enough. With one beefy palm, he jammed me against the seat. With the other, he drew back and struck my face.

My teeth rattled and I was afraid they'd fall out. My cheek stung as if attacked by a million bees. Intense pain radiated through my head, and I wondered if it was possible to become brain-damaged from a slap.

Like a fierce giant with eyes flashing, Abner snarled in my face, and I tried not to breathe. I was barely in control of my senses, and for some reason, my foot pressed the pedal, but the truck's tires only spun while the motor sputtered and growled feebly.

He grabbed me by my hair, ignoring my cries, and yanked me from the truck. I almost called out for help. *Jesus Christ, protect me!*

I knew there was so much more I should pray, but the alarm of the situation choked me. Abner dragged me up the cabin steps while I stumbled and tripped, each move creating searing pain at my scalp.

Even inside, he didn't loosen his hold. He shook me a few times, causing an instant, deep headache, before ramming me against the dryer, knocking all breath out of me.

"Where's Clay?"

My eyes widened, confronted by such a close, repelling view of Abner's face and mouth. It looked like someone had used their fingers to push his eyes deep into his head. Maybe he'd done it himself. He was capable of anything.

I realized I was stuttering, and I drew a deep breath to start over. "He—he's in the hole."

The sharp tug on my hair told me he wanted more of an explanation. I wet my lips. "He came down to give us some food, and—and we tricked him. Max pinned him down. I escaped."

"Escaped?" Abner raised a tangled eyebrow. "No. The one thing you most definitely did not do—and will never do—is escape. Where's the key?"

I didn't answer immediately, and it cost me another hair-ripping pull.

"Don't play ignorant. I know you've got it. Unlock the prison door, or I'll search you for it."

I hastily extracted the key from my coat pocket. He finally released my hair, but replaced the pain with new torment as he shoved me into the dryer, smashing my limbs and creating what felt like fifty bruises. I couldn't unlock the portal fast enough or reach the ladder quick enough. The hole suddenly seemed like a safe-haven. As long as Abner didn't follow me in. *God, no. Please, not that.*

In darkness, I tumbled from the ladder, falling the last couple of feet and landing on what felt like cold concrete. I remained there, sinking into a defeated, pitiful heap. Max snapped on the flashlight and I was vaguely aware of his sharp intake of breath.

"Listen up!" Abner bellowed down. "You're making me angry, and believe me, that's a serious mistake. There are many things worse than death, and I won't hesitate to use 'em all. Got it?"

Without waiting for an answer, he continued. "Clay? You're as stupid as they come. You climbed in there alone, unarmed? What did you expect? And I did not give you permission to unlock that door. So since you wanted to visit them so badly, you can stay with them."

"Abner, I—"

"Stupid kid, pleading will only get you locked up longer, so shut it." The malice in Abner's voice intensified. "You all just enjoy your time together. And if you feel like knocking each other around, have at it." The door slammed shut, leaving behind remnants of an angry echo and three very disturbed prisoners.

———

Max came to my side and laid a hand on my shoulder while I shuddered and sobbed. At last, I contained myself. I mustered the strength to lift my head, rub my nose, and relate in halting phrases what had happened. I wondered if he blamed me for botching the job, but I was too weary and beaten to care. I pressed my still stinging cheek to the frigid dirt wall, and it began to numb the pain.

Clay sat quietly against the opposite wall, which seemed very far away, almost like I was looking down a tunnel. He was obviously bound with his wrists behind him, because his arms were drawn back and his shoulders pulled awkwardly—quite an uncomfortable way to sit.

Perhaps he saw me looking at him and hoped to gain sympathy. His eyes met mine wearily. "You really think this is necessary?" He strained against his bonds. "What's this rosary made of, anyway? Iron? Come on, untie me. I'm not going to fight anyone."

"That's for sure," Max scoffed. "You are definitely not a fighter. I bet you've never stood up to anyone in your life."

Clay's tone bristled. "Don't talk to me about my life. You know nothing about it."

Max hooted. "Lucky me. I'm sure it's a real sob story."

Sensing this tense sparring of words could continue for hours—something I was not up to, particularly with a pounding headache—I put in, "Maybe we should all just shut up."

Max and Clay glared at each other but, surprisingly, said no more. I wondered if we should turn off the flashlight, but couldn't bear the thought of being submerged into blackness.

The silence lasted about one minute. I was the one who

broke it. Noticing the bag from Clay still lay where he had dropped it, about a foot from where I sat, I pulled it toward me. The bag crinkled, and I saw two peanut butter sandwiches and two bottles of water inside. My stomach growled loud enough for everyone to hear.

Max and I each took a sandwich and claimed a bottle of water. I chewed hungrily and tried to forget Clay. *He hasn't been parched and starving since yesterday.* Still, it seemed rather rude to eat and drink in front of him, offering him nothing, particularly when he was the one who had brought us the stuff.

My sandwich didn't taste nearly as good as I thought it would. When it was gone, I began to yawn.

Max turned to me. "Why don't you go ahead and lie down, get some sleep. You've been through a lot. I'll stay awake and guard him." Max indicated Clay with a thrust of his stubbly chin. "I don't want us both falling asleep."

"Yeah, I might come over there and breathe on you," Clay muttered. "What a lot of damage that would do."

"Your brother's right about one thing," Max said evenly. "You're a stupid kid, and you should keep your mouth shut."

"I'm older than you, kid."

"You sure don't act it. You probably still cry for your mommy every night."

A look of fury swept over Clay's face. In the strange shadows, he looked frightening. He jumped to his feet and charged across the room at Max.

Max leapt up and met him with a blow aimed at Clay's head, but Clay dodged it. Then Clay kicked Max and nearly knocked him off his feet. For a moment, it seemed the fight could go either way, until Max landed a fist to Clay's stomach, and he fell to the ground.

Max dusted his hands triumphantly and turned to join me, when Clay sprang up unexpectedly and rammed Max to the dirt.

"Stop it!" I cried.

They ignored me, scuffling and kicking until finally Max

slammed Clay against the wall. Clay slid down to a sitting position and stayed there, breathing heavily.

"That'll teach you to mess with me," Max said.

"Real fair fight," Clay countered as Max walked away. "Let's try it evenly matched—without my hands tied—and see how far you get."

Max swung back to face Clay, but I dashed over and tugged Max's arm. "No, please stop. Both of you. Why make this situation more horrible than it already is? That's what Abner wants—us to torture each other. Don't you see? We'll never get out of this if all we do is fight."

Neither Max nor Clay spoke, but they didn't resume battle, and Max returned with me to our side of the room.

"I really want to go to sleep," I said wearily, "but it will be impossible with you two going back and forth. Do you think you can restrain yourselves?"

"Fine," Max said grudgingly. He darted a glance at Clay. "But we're obviously not going to untie you."

"Suit yourself. You're obviously afraid."

"Obvious, nothing. I'm just looking out for my sister."

"Guys, please." I groaned, crawled onto my blanket, and collapsed. If any more arguing ensued, I was dead to it.

Chapter Twelve

*H*e fell asleep," Max announced as soon as I woke up. I flipped on the flashlight and looked across the room to see Clay's head slumped awkwardly against his shoulder, his eyes closed. Listening, I heard deep breathing.

"He couldn't take it," Max said. "He couldn't outlast me, and I bet it's been longer since I slept than it has been for him."

I shook my head. "Are you still at it? Does everything have to be a contest?"

"If you were trapped down here with some catty girl, maybe you'd know how I feel."

I sighed. "Well, I'm awake now, so you should get some sleep. Maybe it will improve your disposition," I added. "I'm sure we still have quite a few hours left to spend in Clay's company before his brother calls him back for some kind of grunt work, so let's just bear with it, all right? We should be spending our energy on figuring out another way to escape."

"My unrelenting sister. You never give up."

For some reason, Max's words unsettled me, and I pondered them after he fell asleep. There had been plenty of times in my life when I'd given up. I searched through my memory. I'd enjoyed painting when I was younger, especially watercolors. They were a challenge, but I persisted, spending hours on getting the wash of a sky just right. At ten years old, I even decided to paint a picture for Grandfather. I spent a week of after-school free time creating what I thought was an enchanting watercolor scene of Gardburg. Grandfather only laughed when I gave it to him, saying, "At least now I know not to waste money sending you to art school."

I'd had some deluded idea that he would hang the painting

in his new art gallery. Instead, he probably threw it out, as I never saw it again. I'd tossed my paints in the trash and hadn't touched a brush since.

Grandfather. The very word grated in my mind, conjuring up resentment and hurt, more so because it was supposed to be such a comforting, loving word. I'd given up on him, to be sure. I'd given up on him caring about me, and I'd given up on him paying the ransom or coming to our rescue.

Even if the ransom was paid, I doubted it would do me and Max any good, not after all I'd come to see of Abner's cruelty. Besides, only a stupid kidnapper would endanger himself by freeing us when we could identify him. *No, Abner won't let us go, even if just to pay us back for the trouble we've given him. Each day we sit in captivity brings us closer to death.*

As each day does anyway.

Thoroughly depressed, I fell deeper in thought. On the grand scale of things, there was the question of God. I'd given up on Him many times, usually when I was hurt and feeling abandoned, like after each of my parents died.

Basically, I'd given up on being happy. But maybe that was connected to the God factor. I recalled my religious instructions about how God is the only One Who can make us happy. *But then why does He send so much misery?*

The answer came immediately: *It's a test, a challenge.* I rubbed my face. *But I can't take anymore. Academic tests, sure, but this spiritual stuff . . . It's all so gloomy and oppressive, like God's just waiting for us to mess up.*

My headache came back as I recalled nightmares I'd had, from a young age, of the End of the World, chastisements, God's wrath. I'd heard Grandfather warn of these things too many times.

"What are you thinking about?" Clay's voice startled me. I looked up to see him awake and watching me, his curiosity evident.

I flushed and wondered how transparent my emotions had been. I didn't relish the thought of him analyzing me as some form of entertainment.

"What were you thinking about?" he persisted.

"The past," I said shortly. *Max would tell me not to talk to him.* The thought annoyed me slightly. Who was Max to order me around? If anything, I should be giving the orders, since I was older. By two minutes.

"Yeah? Your past couldn't have been that bad, growing up all rich and pampered."

I shot back with, "Remember you told Max that he doesn't know anything about your life? Well, you know nothing about mine. So don't judge. Having money isn't a free ticket to happiness."

"But it helps."

"You think so?" I had half a mind to rouse Max so he would shut Clay up. "You think if you and Abner get the ransom and take off with it to some other country, you'll be happy?"

"A heck of a lot happier than I am now." He frowned. "I'm not saying I want any part of this kidnapping or ransom money, but we've been over that. Let's not talk about it."

"Let's not talk at all," I snapped.

Tension-filled moments plodded by. He strained against his bonds, muttering, "Stupid rosary."

"Stop trying to break it. I don't want it wrecked." In fact, I still hadn't prayed a Rosary yet today, and if I was going to keep up with the novena, I'd prefer to have the rosary back.

He gave a short laugh. "Don't break it? You should have thought about that before using it like handcuffs. Isn't that kind of what you Catholics would consider irreverent, any-way?"

"God would understand."

Clay scoffed. "Isn't that what we all say to justify our-selves? Not that I give any credence to God or what He thinks."

In too much of a spiritual jumble myself to preach about God, I redirected the subject. "I'm sure if you'd just calm down, Max will eventually release you."

"I am calm," Clay said evenly. "And what's to stop you

from releasing me? Not afraid of your brother, are you?"

"Don't think you can goad me into freeing you. It won't work. And look who's talking about being afraid of their brother. Wow."

He glowered.

I continued. "If Abner's always been like this, I can't imagine why you'd come out here seeking his company." I tossed my tangled curls as best I could, considering they were confined by a wool hat. "I think I'd go live on the opposite side of the world from him."

A ghost of a grin touched Clay's face. For the first time, I noticed a dried smear of blood and a bruise on his jaw. Probably courtesy of Max.

"Abner hasn't always been like this. But I didn't make the trip out here because I missed him. No. I needed to get away, take a break, relax." He glanced at the dirt ceiling. "Yeah, that turned out real well."

"What was so bad that you had to get away?" I asked skeptically.

"Oh, life in general. Out in the wilderness, things like school, jobs, relationships—they don't matter."

"I see. Some girl dumped you, is that it?"

I wasn't sure in the dimness, but his face seemed to redden. That, or it darkened. "No, that's not it. I lost my job, is all. A job as a night stocker in a grocery store. How sorry is that?"

"It's honest work. So what happened?"

"I fell asleep on the job. Finals week. I didn't have the time to sleep between school, work, and visiting my ma."

"Visiting your mom?" Surprise touched my voice. "That's nice."

"No, it's not. I hate it."

"What a terrible thing to say!"

He sent me a slanted look. "I hate it because she's dying. She's got cancer, and I can see it sucking the life out of her. You want to know one of the issues I've got with God? My ma is as holy as can be, but what does she get? Stuck with a horrible husband, two worthless sons, and now she's diseased and dying in pain. What kind of God would let that happen? Not any kind of God I want to believe in."

Uncomfortable, I shifted on my blanket. *My mother died of a fatal disease, too.* "Is she in a hospital?"

"No, but probably within a year."

The dragging on, the not knowing . . . yes, it's torture. I lowered my gaze.

He gave a hollow laugh. "You know what she wanted to name me? Tarcisius, after some stupid saint."

I searched my mind for the story and recalled that it was about a young boy of the third century. He had served Mass in the catacombs and was beaten to death while trying to protect the Blessed Sacrament.

"I'm lucky my dad intervened," Clay continued. "I would have been called 'Tarcisius the sissy,' for sure. Ma meant well, but man, talk about trying too hard."

"So what's your middle name?"

He scowled.

The corner of my mouth quirked. "Tarcisius is your middle name, isn't it? Don't be bitter. Saint Tarcisius was a very courageous guy."

Clay's scowl remained.

"Tell me more about your mother."

Slowly, his grim look receded, replaced by grief. "She used to be so alive, so beautiful. I've got a picture of her in my wallet."

The way he said it made me think he was going to take it out and look at it. And despite myself, I was curious to see it. I wondered if she resembled him or Abner in any way. "Can I see?" I asked hesitantly.

"Like I said, it's in my wallet. I can't get to it, remember?"

Right, the bound wrists. Well, I certainly wasn't going to go digging in his pockets. I was silent for a minute. "I think I could untie you now."

"Yeah? What will your brother say?"

"I don't care." I pushed stray curls from my face. "Just

125

promise you won't pick a fight with him."

"Fine, I promise."

"Move closer to the light so I can see what I'm doing. I've got a feeling this rosary's going to be a challenge to untangle."

He did as I asked, and after picking carefully at the beaded chain, twisting and untwisting, I eventually managed to remove the rosary, still in one piece. I placed it in my pocket as he removed his wallet.

"Here she is," he said, almost reverently. I peered at the small square picture. It showed a smiling young woman of petite features and delicate bone structure, wearing a string of pearls around her neck.

For a split second, I thought of my own mother and her pearl necklace. Pink pearls, a gift from my dad. How I'd admired that necklace as a child. She'd let me try it on once. I touched the hollow of my throat, remembering. *I wonder whatever happened to that necklace.*

Clay cleared his throat, and I saw he was looking at me oddly. I returned my focus to the photo of his mom. Her brown hair was the same color as his, but ruffled softly around her shoulders. Peering very closely, I could just make out a few freckles.

"I can see a resemblance to you, but definitely not Abner."

He closed his wallet and tucked it away. "Yeah, he looks more like our dad, who was kind of a beastly guy. He didn't deserve my ma. She did everything for him. For us. A home-cooked meal every night. Awesome desserts. I can almost taste her pistachio cream cake . . ." His mouth set itself in a rigid line.

"She said she'd always wanted a lot of kids, a house full of laughter . . . But what she got was far from it." He paused. "I guess it turned out for the best that she only had two kids. The world couldn't handle anymore Abners, hey?" He laughed shortly.

"But like I said, he wasn't always this way. He was very protective of me as a kid, though there's ten years between us. When I was seven, he saved me from a fire when our house burned down. It got our dad, though." Another pause.

"Ma, fortunately, was at church at the time. If you look at Abner's hands, you'll see burn scars. So you see, since then, I've always felt I owe him, and I've got to stand by him, overlook his shortcomings."

"Shortcomings?" I snorted. "I'd classify them more severely than that."

"Either way, he's still my brother. He's defended me through the years. In high school, there was this one girl I wanted to date for the longest time. When she broke up with her boy-friend, I got my chance. Turned out she was just using me to make him jealous. It worked, all right. He beat me up. Then Abner put him in the hospital." He shrugged. "After that, I was known as 'the monster's brother.' "

"He is a monster. And I wouldn't imagine that incident made you too popular." I arched an eyebrow.

"I've never cared about being popular. Neither has Abner, and he was certainly never popular with women. But then he met Lydia."

I almost choked. "Don't tell me he's actually dated a woman. Who in their right mind would go out with him? I mean—"

"Like I said, he was a different person." Clay's voice held a touch of annoyance. "He met Lydia by accident. Not to sound corny, but it's actually a good story. He was driving along and saw some guy snatching this lady's purse. So he stopped his car, took off after the guy, and tackled him."

"So the criminal catches the criminal."

He folded his arms across his chest. "If you don't want me to tell it, I won't. We can just go back to our respective walls and let time drag."

"Sorry. This does help pass the time. Please don't stop."

He eyed me and went on. "So he brings the lady back her purse, and they get to talking, and it turns out they were heading to the same bookstore, so Abner gave her a ride. And that was how it all began. They fell in love and got married a year later."

"Married?" My mouth fell open as I tried to fathom this. Abner, a bridegroom? Abner, a lover? I shuddered. Finally I managed, "Is this Lydia very pretty, with dark hair, and a face like Audrey Hepburn?"

"What, the old movie star?"

"Yes." I waited tensely for his answer.

"Yeah, I guess so."

She must be the woman in the photo in Abner's drawer.

"She was real nice, and she was good for Abner."

" 'Was?' What happened?" I felt a sudden sense of dread. "She died, didn't she?"

He shook his head. "No, nothing that tragic, though she might as well have, as far as how Abner took it. See, they had a big blowout after he lost his job, and she left him. He hasn't been the same since. Bitter, angry, just plain mean. He moved out here and kind of went into brooding seclusion."

And began plotting a kidnapping. Doesn't make much sense. "So did he build this cabin himself?"

"No, this place has been in my family for years. Used as a vacation getaway."

Or a criminal hideout.

"My dad brought us here a few times for fishing and hunting." He stared distantly at the wall. "I remember this one time, when I was six, he locked me in the cellar overnight."

"By accident?"

"On purpose. Like I said, he wasn't an ideal dad. Some of his personality must have rubbed off on Abner."

Or maybe it's bad blood, and it transforms you at a certain age. Though I had to admit, I couldn't picture Clay turning into an Abner. Then again, I didn't really know him.

"So what did you do that was so bad it landed you in the cellar?"

He grunted. "I didn't want to stick a worm on a hook. My dad went into this rage about not having a wimp for a son, then he locked me down there. I still hate that cellar. This place isn't much better," he muttered.

I recalled the trapdoor I'd seen in the kitchen floor, and

frowned. "If this cabin already had a cellar, why didn't Abner lock us in there instead of going to all the trouble of digging this place?"

"Beats me." Clay thought a moment. "Maybe because he stores stuff in there. Or maybe he thought it would be too easy to escape from."

"Char?" Max's voice startled me, and I flinched as if I'd been caught doing something wrong. He marched to my side. "What are you doing over here with him?"

"Max, calm down. We're just talking, passing time."

"Why are his hands free?"

"I wanted my rosary."

"Stupid girl. Am I going to have to stay awake constantly to keep an eye on you as well? Don't you know this guy's bad news?"

He didn't even wait for my answer, but pulled me away as he hollered at Clay, "Stay away from my sister, got it? She doesn't know a thing when it comes to creeps like you. But I do, and I'll be watching you."

Both guys looked like they wanted nothing more than to fight, but each was waiting for the other to start it. Maybe Clay remembered the promise he'd given me, because he remained silent and still.

I, on the other hand, turned to Max and said frostily, "Thanks for the vote of confidence, little brother." He hated when I called him that.

Unfitting as it felt, I drew out my rosary, indignation radiating from me. "We still have to pray today if we're going to keep up with the novena."

Launching into the Apostle's Creed, I didn't expect Max to join in, but he did, though I think he spent the entire five decades glaring at Clay.

When we were done, I made my tally scratch in the wall.

Clay shook his head. "Religion is just another form of captivity."

—--

129

By the next morning—at least, morning according to my watch, since we had no natural light to judge the time by—we were all sleep-deprived and out of sorts. Max and I were bickering about whether or not to turn off the flashlight, and Clay was pacing the floor.

"Fine, I'll tell you what we should do with the flashlight," Max said. "Use it as a weapon. I'm gonna climb up the ladder, and the moment Abner sticks his ugly mug in here, I'll club his brains out."

I was about to scoff, "The flashlight's way too small," when Clay piped up.

"You think I'd let you do that to my brother?"

Max jutted his jaw. "I'd like to see you try to stop me."

"Seriously, Clay," I snapped, "quit trying to make excuses for Abner. This is a matter of survival; we've got to kill him before he kills us."

"He wouldn't do that," Clay retorted, but I saw a flicker of doubt cross his face. "He's my brother."

" 'He's my brother,' 'he's my brother,' " I repeated, exasperated. "You're like a broken record. So what if you're related? He's no brother to anyone. He acts more like a tyrannical father, the way he orders you around and talks down to you. He even disciplines you, for goodness' sake. He's always calling you 'boy' or 'kid,' and you're how old? Twenty-one?"

"Shut up," Clay snarled.

Any walls that had crumbled down between us yesterday, rebuilt themselves in an instant.

Minutes dragged by. With nothing else to do, I bounced numbers around in my head, figured some math problems, and counted how many hours I'd been held prisoner. And as I tallied the time, I realized something. "It's New Year's Eve today."

"Big freakin' deal," Max said. "What are we supposed to do about it? Throw a party? Get wasted? I wish."

"I wish you would, too. At least then maybe you'd fall

asleep and quit being so mean." *I'm beginning to wonder why I ever went searching for you.*

I thought of Cindy from the ski hill, drinking root beer floats with her dad and watching *The Three Stooges.* Sounded like heaven.

What I wouldn't give for one more moment with my dad. I'd never even said goodbye to him when he left that tragic day. Skydiving. Why did he always have to go looking for excitement? Why couldn't he be content with what he had? It was the same with Max. Always searching for the next crazy thrill.

I looked at Max's sour expression and something inside me snapped. "Why'd you ever have to go snowboarding, Max? Why couldn't you have just stayed home for once?"

His eyes sizzled. "Like you? A hermit? A social outcast? Don't blame me for this. I never asked you to come looking for me."

I didn't answer, but something inside me withered.

Moments passed.

A suspicion that had been plaguing me for days, a painful truth that I didn't want to face, finally erupted from my lips. "You really were going to run away that night after snowboarding, weren't you?"

His silence confirmed it.

"You were, and you didn't even tell me, didn't care that I'd be worried sick." I tried to contain the hurt leaking from my voice. "But Wayne knew. That's why he wasn't worried when I told him you were missing."

He sighed. "I tried to tell you, Char. I would have kept trying. I didn't plan it ahead of time, but things just lined up. I was so ticked off at Grandfather. Then when we were snowboarding and Wayne told me about a cheap rental room he'd heard about, I called the guy and he said I could move in that night. Once I decided, I tried calling you like ten times—"

"Six," I cut in. "You called six times, and you didn't leave a message."

"You know I don't leave messages. I wanted to tell you

where I would be, and I didn't want that recorded. Wayne didn't want you to know anything at all, but I wouldn't do that to you, Char. You know that."

I almost cursed Wayne and his hand in all this. "Why didn't he at least go with you? Make sure you got there okay?"

"Seriously, Char? What am I, seven?" He shook his head. "You can't blame Wayne. We drove separately, and he had to get home. And he didn't tell you where he thought I was because he wouldn't have wanted to risk Grandfather finding out. Wayne's loyal; he didn't want to blow my cover."

I huffed. "So why was your top-secret magic notebook gone if you didn't plan the whole thing ahead of time?"

"My top-secret—how the heck do you know about that?" Indignation sputtered from his lips.

"Come on, Max. Under the mattress? *Not* the best hiding place. What are you, seven?"

He muttered something about snoopy sisters before saying, "I lent the notebook to Wayne. If we're going to have a magic act together someday, we've gotta be on the same page."

I nodded, done with the conversation. A pitiful heaviness fell on my soul as my twin intuition told me Max and I were thinking the same thing: "Someday" was probably never going to come.

During a long stretch of silence, I saw that Max had actually fallen asleep. I relaxed slightly, and found myself wishing I could talk with Clay the way we had yesterday, to pass the time and turn my thoughts in some direction other than insanity.

But when Clay suddenly spoke up from across the room, it gave me no relief. "I wish I never came down here. But I knew you were hungry and thirsty, so I brought you food and water. Then I tried to help you, and what did you do? You attacked me."

"Go on," I said, "get all your grousing out while Max is

asleep."

"Fine. I wish I never laid eyes on you. You've brought me nothing but trouble. And if you hadn't lured me yesterday with your lies about Max being sickly, I wouldn't be stuck down here now."

I kept my eyes focused on the dirt wall, kept my jaw stiff, and didn't reply. *You're not going to make me feel guilty. You're a coward and a jerk.*

Moments later, there was a clang, and Abner opened the prison door. "Clay," he called, his deep voice reverberating through the hole.

I was surprised when Clay remained silent and didn't jump up and run to his brother.

"Clay," Abner bellowed, "I know you heard me. Don't make me call you again." This time, the echo was painful. Amazingly, Max didn't stir from his deep sleep.

I watched Clay's scowl turn to a grimace. He suddenly reminded me of a cornered animal. Not a fierce one, but a gentle one. *Quit it, Charlene.* I yanked myself back to cold reality. *Don't pity him. He chose this.*

"If you ever want to see the light of day again, boy, you'd better get up here now."

Clay's hands clasped the back of his head.

"You've got till the count of ten," Abner proclaimed. "One. Two. Three."

Clay shifted uncomfortably, seeming to battle within himself.

"Four. Five."

His eyes turned to mine, as if seeking advice.

I slid my eyes away.

"Six. Seven."

Dropping his hands, Clay stood.

"Eight."

He trudged to the base of the ladder and gripped a rung.

"Nine."

"I'm coming," Clay shouted, with attitude.

Hairs rose on the back of my neck. I couldn't help trembling as I watched him move closer to the top, closer to Abner.

Abner's silence as Clay crawled out, surprised me. No barrage of angry words. And yet . . . I pictured a snake, coiled and ready to strike.

Something made me move to the bottom of the ladder. I just caught Abner's voice saying, with creepy calmness, "You like to test me, don't you?"

Hearing no response, I climbed up a rung.

"You only get this many chances because you're my brother." Abner's voice grew louder the higher I climbed. Below, I saw Max stirring.

"You're my brother," Abner repeated, "yet you fail to appreciate the fact. Your ungratefulness is appalling."

"Char," Max said, "what are you—"

"Shh!" I pulled myself up another rung, my gloves slipping on the stiff ropes.

Abner was still talking. "You can't forget whose side you're on. Got it?"

My ears were strained by a long stretch of silence. Then, suddenly, I heard a wicked *whack.*

"Got it?" Abner paused. "I don't think you do." Another pause, then his voice came ominously soft: "Close and lock the door."

The door clanked shut as I scrambled up to put my ear against it. My heart pounded in my ears, but not so loudly that I couldn't make out the sound of fists smacking flesh.

God, let it be Clay hitting Abner. But as I pressed my forehead against the cool metal, I knew it wasn't so. Waves of nausea swept up my throat. Abner was thrashing Clay.

And it's my fault.

I made myself listen to every blow, every thud, but not once did I hear Clay cry out. It seemed to be forever until the brutal sounds stopped. Then I heard Abner's gruff voice, though the words were muffled.

Numbly, I slunk down the ladder to relate the events to

Max, who was waiting curiously at the base of the ladder.

He enjoyed the story. "Serves the jerk right." He smacked his fist into his palm. "I hope they kill each other!"

"Max!"

"Come on, Char. Don't tell me you don't want Abner dead."

"Of course I do—it's just—"

"Oh, I see," he said darkly. "You don't want cutesy-boy Clay to get hurt. Boy, he's got you fooled. What a sucker I've got for a twin. For someone who's supposed to be so smart, you sure—"

"No, Max, it's not that." I rubbed my forehead. "I'm thinking logically. If they kill each other, we'd never get out of here. At least—no one would find us until it's too late."

"Good point," he admitted. "I take it back, then. You're still smart."

"Thanks," I said in a small voice, feeling no better.

"And Char? I'm sorry for the things I said earlier . . ." He looked uncomfortable. "You know, about you being a hermit and all . . ."

"I know. I'm sorry, too."

Chapter Thirteen

*A*s my bare fingers clawed against the earthen wall, the dirt flaked easier under my nails, and a tremor of hope and excitement rippled through me. "Max. Max, wake up." Of course, I had to shove him around for a full minute before I succeeded in forcing him awake. He was obviously catching up on the shut-eye he'd missed when Clay was with us.

"Whatcha want?" he mumbled.

"Max, listen. You're going to be glad I was talking to Clay yesterday, because it turns out he gave me a valuable piece of information. I didn't realize its importance till now, but it just might help us escape."

He sat up on his blanket, blinking. "Yeah?"

I pointed at the long wall across from us. "Behind that wall is a cellar. All we need to do is dig through. Judging from where I remember the cellar door being located, compared to the dryer, this wall can't be more than two or three feet thick."

"Wonderful, won't take us more than a couple years to scrape through." He began to slump back down. "I thought we covered this already. The walls are practically frozen."

"The *outside* walls are," I corrected him, "the walls that don't connect to a room. We tried those and assumed they were all the same, but they're not."

"Really?" Max stood and followed me to the wall against the cellar. He removed his glove and scraped at the dirt. "I don't know," he said dubiously. "Feels just as hard to me."

"It's not," I insisted. "The dirt yields a little easier. I know it's only a slight difference, but it *is* a difference."

Max let out his breath, his hope clearly deflating. "We still can't dig through that with our bare hands."

"True. But if we could get something—something like a spoon, or a metal bowl—I don't think the job would take us more than a few days."

He crossed his arms. "Okay. What then? Say we dig through? What's to say we can get out of the cellar?"

"I remember seeing the door, and it's wood. I'm sure we could break through it, even if it is locked, which I doubt."

He nodded slowly. "That still leaves us with the problem of a digging tool. Even if they bring us more food, you know they won't let us keep any spoons."

"I know." I pinched the bridge of my nose. "That's the one glitch. But maybe an opportunity will come up. It doesn't have to be a spoon, just something hard and durable . . ." Saying this, I strode over to our flashlight and picked it up. I brought it to the wall and tried scraping the dirt with it.

"Don't break it," Max said.

I stopped. "This won't work anyway. It's too blunt."

"What about that rosary you've got? You're always scraping marks into the wall with the crucifix. That's metal."

"Yes, but that's to make one little mark, not to dig with." Still, it was a valid suggestion. I gave it a shot, but in the end, it was simply too small to be effective. I groaned. "I wish I wore big, heavy earrings like Gwen. She has a pair that look like metal disks. I bet those would work like shovels, and we'd each have one."

"Like you said, maybe an opportunity will come up."

I knew Max didn't think one would, but I appreciated his effort to comfort me, all the same.

About an hour later, Abner summoned me upstairs. As I climbed out of the dryer, I wasn't surprised to see he had a handgun trained on me. I blinked in the unnaturally bright overhead light and wondered uneasily where Clay was.

"I'm running out of patience," Abner began. "I went to check for the ransom earlier today, and it's still not there."

I felt blood drain from my face. *He's going to hack off my toe.*

"Now, now, no need to jump to conclusions. What I'm asking is very reasonable: I want a New Year's Eve feast." He smacked his lips disgustingly. "So you better be able to cook a decent lasagna, because if I like it, you get to keep all your fingers. Don't, I let you choose which one you lose." He grinned. "Think you can handle that?"

You don't cook *lasagna, you* bake *it,* my mind quibbled while I curled my fingers into my palms protectively. "Sure I can handle that," I tried to keep my voice from shaking, "as long as you've got the ingredients."

The expression on his face gave me a sinking feeling.

"Come now, I'm sure a smart Perigard like you can figure something out."

"I can't create something out of nothing."

Abner merely responded, "The kitchen is yours." He prodded me forward with the gun, and as we passed the closed bedroom door, I wondered about the floral wreath. It had to be Lydia's. I could understand the old photo stuffed away in a drawer, but if he was so bitter about his wife leaving him, why did he let the wreath still hang in full view?

He saw my gaze on the door and remarked, "Clay's in there sleeping off a beating."

Remembering the brutal sounds I'd heard hours earlier, I wondered if he would ever wake up.

I faced the kitchen on rubber knees and drew in a deep breath, hesitant to open the fridge and cupboards. Abner was obviously trying to give me an impossible task, like in a fairy tale when a fair maiden is commanded to spin straw into gold. He wanted me to fail so he could carry out his dastardly threat. Well, I might not have been a fair maiden, but I liked to think I had a fairly decent brain. I'd figure out some solution.

Abner crossed the small living room and fiddled with the dials of the radio while still keeping an eye, and the gun, on me. A beer can sat on the bookshelf. Warmth seeped through my coat and thawed my cheeks, and I assumed the wood stove was burning strong. I removed my hat, scarf, gloves, and coat, and I felt ten pounds lighter. Then I smoothed my hands on my jeans and got to work.

A quick glance through the squeaky cupboards revealed a major lack of ingredients, as well as a sprinkling of mouse droppings. Trying not to cringe, I began accumulating canned tomatoes, Italian dressing, a chunk of rock-hard white cheese, and a bottle of ketchup. "No lasagna noodles!" I exclaimed, almost ready to give up. Then I glanced at Abner, sitting in the ragged rocking chair, gun in one hand, beer can in another. His eyes speared mine and glinted, making my gaze jump back to the cupboard.

He must have turned the radio on to some easy-listening station, because I caught strains of soft music and gentle lyrics. *A highly unfitting soundtrack for this cabin of nightmares.* The music did nothing to soothe me, as such songs normally would.

While I inspected the cheese for mold, Abner said, "Girl, bring me another beer."

I begrudgingly separated another can from the large collection in the fridge and brought it to him. He popped the top immediately and began guzzling.

Back in the kitchen, I made a point of observing the trap door to the cellar, but casually, from a distance. The door was actually two doors that closed like shutters, each one with a raised handle made for a wooden slat to be slid through as a bolt. But this one was not bolted, I noted with satisfaction. And the wood was thin, probably flimsy.

I heard a groan as the bedroom door opened. Clay emerged, rubbing his mussed hair. "Here I am, the human punching bag." He gave a feeble grin, stretching his split, puffy lip.

I tried not to stare, but he looked terrible, especially in the revealing electric light. His face was more bruises than not, one eye was swollen shut, and blood stained his shirt. He was in no condition to tackle Abner or escape for help, so I told myself it was time to stop holding him up to such expectations. Messed up as he looked, I was relieved to see he wasn't worse.

He lowered his voice. "What are you doing up here?" His

tone sounded worried.

"Making dinner. And I've got to get it just right, or it'll cost me a finger. Abner's conditions."

He glanced in Abner's direction.

I whispered, "He actually seems really absorbed in the music. I guess I should be glad, but it creeps me out."

"Don't let it." Clay's voice was equally hushed. "He's just dwelling on the past. Music like this reminds him of Lydia, I think. He gets like this sometimes, especially when he's got a couple of beers in him, but don't be fooled, he's still alert."

"Clay!" Abner barked. "Let her do her work. Come sit over here where I can keep an eye on you."

Clay made a face—quite horrid, considering his face was already disfigured—and trudged away to the tune of Louis Armstrong's "What a Wonderful World."

The only meat I could find was a hunk of frozen venison wrapped in plastic. I set the reddish-brown chunk in a bowl of warm water, then returned to the problem of no lasagna noodles. I couldn't make them, not without eggs. Determined to find a solution, I recalled a time I'd made a Mexican Lasagna, which actually used flour tortillas instead of noodles. *Tortillas use simple ingredients. Flour, salt, water, oil . . .* Yes, this just might work.

I mixed a crumbly dough, then worked it into a dense, flexible ball, which I then divided into six smaller balls. I flattened them between my palms, then found a rolling pin to finish the job. It didn't take me long to fry each tortilla in a skillet.

While the radio trilled on with "Love of a Lifetime," I poked the blob of meat and found it sufficiently thawed. Since it wasn't ground, I'd have to chop it finely. I plopped it on a cutting board and pressed a butcher knife into it. The oozing red juices made me think of blood. I couldn't help imagining getting my finger cut off. I swallowed. The venison's fleshy smell gagged me, and suddenly, I knew I was about to heave.

"I don't feel good." I retreated to the bathroom just in time to wretch over the toilet. Not that I had anything in my stomach to throw up.

Eventually I managed to close the door and lock it, then prop myself over the sink. I stared at my pale face in the mirror, wishing I could stay in the bathroom forever, or at least until I figured out a plan. My freckles stood out like cinnamon on cream. My hair was matted tangles.

I opened the medicine cabinet, more so that I wouldn't have to see my reflection than to look for something to ease my sickness. My eyes roamed the shelves. A bright pink bottle of Pepto-Bismol stood out from the white and orange plastic medicine containers. I rinsed a little cup—trying not to think about what it may have contained at one time, because that would only feed my sickness—poured the thick liquid, and gulped it down, scattering droplets into the sink in the process.

I closed my eyes and realized my head was pounding. But my heart was pounding harder. Shoving the medicine bottles back into the cabinet, I knocked over a couple. *What do they need all these for? Oh yeah, to dull pain after Abner mutilates someone. Wonder how strong this stuff is?*

I peered closer, studying the different labels and searching my mind for information from health or chemistry textbooks that might give me an edge. Besides the typical aspirin, Tylenol, and cough syrup, I found some stuff that, from the cautionary description, looked promising. I tore a sheet of toilet paper and dumped several tablets into it, barely catching one before it rolled onto the floor. After wadding up my little package, I shoved it into my jeans pocket.

Taking a deep breath, I opened the bathroom door, stepped out, and was instantly confronted with Abner. "What were you doing in there for so long?"

"I was sick. I threw up. Would you rather I did it in the lasagna pan?"

"I heard you in the medicine cabinet."

"I took some Pepto-Bismol. Go see for yourself—I spilled some in the sink." Silently, I thanked God that I hadn't rinsed it down.

Abner's eyes searched mine. With my shoulders thrust

back and my head lifted, I stared back defiantly, telling him I had nothing to hide. The dark skin of his face stretched tight as rubber over his skull, except for under his eyes, where it hung in two purple pouches. He looked like he never got any sleep. "Get back to work." He grabbed a fistful of my sweat-shirt and he hauled me back to the kitchen.

Once he was resettled in his rocking chair, I held my breath and finished dicing the venison. Then I dumped it into a fry pan and let it sizzle till it was brown. But my mind was no longer on the lasagna. Thankful for the kitchen counter, which hid my lower half from view, I drew the tablets from my pocket and set them on the Formica. I used the rolling pin to crush them into a fairly fine powder, which I brushed carefully into a small measuring cup. My heart beat loudly, above the sound of the radio saxophone. I drew out plates and silverware and, choosing carefully, white frosted glasses. With my back shielding my actions, I poured the powder into two glasses.

After sliding the lasagna into the oven and setting my watch for forty-five minutes, I opened a couple cans of fruit and mixed a fruit salad for dessert. Then I set the table with plates and silverware. But I still had forty minutes to kill. I walked into the living room to face Abner. "The lasagna has to cook for a while."

"Then sit down and wait."

I eyed the bookshelf. "Can I at least read a book?"

"No. You can sit and listen to the music."

I thought Clay was sleeping, but as I was about to sink to the wood floor, he opened his one good eye. "You don't have to sit on the floor." He stood slowly, offering his seat.

"That's okay," I resisted. "I can grab one of the folding chairs."

"No, don't do that. I'll use one of those." Which he promptly did. I wondered if he was remembering being tied to it, as I recalled very vividly, and I sank gladly into his aban-doned chair, which was soft and warm.

I stared into the fire for what felt like eternity, feeling more awkward than frightened, with the incongruous love songs still playing. In another time and place, I could have enjoyed sitting by crackling flames and listening to slow music, but not in this company. Each song was out of place, and I was too aware of Abner's steely eyes on me, as well as the sinister single eye of his gun.

"Hey, Charlene?" Clay's voice obscured the current heart-tugging lyrics.

"Yeah?" I met his eye and waited.

He tapped his fingers on his jeans. "I just wanted to apologize for some of the things I said, you know, earlier, in the hole. I shouldn't have said what I did, and I'm sorry."

Did he expect an apology in return? All I said was, "Okay." I doubted I'd hear him apologize to Max. Mostly, I was surprised he'd spoken in front of Abner, whom I expected to start berating him. Instead, Abner remained silent. The radio now played "Glory of Love" by Peter Cetera. The strange way Abner kept looking back and forth at me and Clay, like he was plotting something, made my skin crawl. Clay didn't seem to notice.

It was one of the longest forty minutes of my life. Thanks to Abner, an entire batch of love songs was destroyed, and I never wanted to hear them again. In fact, if I ever escaped this kidnapping situation and lived to get married, I decided I'd ban music at my wedding.

On the first beep of my watch, I scrambled up to pull the lasagna out of the oven. I set the steaming pan on a hot pad on the table, then returned to the kitchen and opened the fridge. "I'm assuming you want beer with dinner?" I said, sounding slightly annoyed as I lifted a can. Abner gave a gruff acknowl-edgement, so I popped the tab and poured the beer into the two waiting glasses. I panicked a moment as the powder floated and swirled obviously, but then it subsided and the foam on the beer and the frost of the glass camouflaged it. I poured myself a glass of water.

At last, Abner turned off the radio. I set the glasses and fruit salad on the table, and sat down.

"Smells good," Clay said as he practically hobbled to the table.

Abner said nothing, merely tucked his gun in his pants and ambled over.

While Abner and Clay began serving themselves, I made the sign of the cross and bowed my head briefly.

When I looked back up, Abner's eyes bore into me like black worms. "What a reverent expression of faith." He elbowed Clay, making him wince. "Try it, boy, and the truth will set you free. Maybe it'll even heal your wounds. See how well it works for Little Miss Saint Girl? See how free she is, sitting here with us, a couple of wicked sinners?" Abner let out a harsh guffaw and raised his beer.

Drink it, drink it, drink it.

He didn't drink it. He paused with the glass almost to his lips. "Why'd you put it in glasses?"

I shrugged and met his eyes bravely. "I just thought this would be a little more civilized, that's all."

"That's what you thought, is it?" His upper lip curled. "I think you thought a whole lot more than that. In fact, I think your little brain is trying to be clever again. Don't you know that gets you into trouble?"

He slid his glass to me, sloshing beer over the rim. "Drink it."

"No thanks."

"It's not a request."

I pressed my lips together and shook my head. Clay, who had been watching us uncertainly, eyed his own beer warily.

"That's right, Clay. Don't drink it. She's up to her tricks again."

"What are you talking about?" I tried not to sound flustered. "You think I tampered with your beer? What could I have possibly done? And how? You saw me pour it into the glasses." I lifted my nose. "I just don't like beer, and I won't drink it."

"I could force you to," Abner said, "but I have a better idea. I know someone who's probably dying for a drink." He

144

turned to Clay. "Get her brother up here."

With a helpless expression, Clay rose from the table, returning two minutes later with Max by his side.

"Join us for a New Year's Eve feast," Abner said congenially, motioning to a kitchen chair with his gun. "Your sister made it."

Max didn't need to be asked twice; his stomach ruled him. My heart fluttered. *I should warn him about the beer—but that would be as good as admitting my guilt.* I willed him to tune into my thoughts, but he sat readily, his eyes feasting on the lasagna.

"Have a beer." Abner shoved the glass toward him. Max seized it and drank readily. He shoveled in lasagna, then started on the fruit salad, his spoon clanking against the bowl, jarring my nerves.

There was hardly room for all of us to eat at the small round table without bumping elbows. Cozy as this could have been if we were a family, the seating arrangement was a recipe for indigestion. I sat with Max to my left, Clay to my right, and Abner across from me. Seeing how he cut his food into precise pieces and chewed thoughtfully—instead of scarfing it down like an animal, as I'd imagined he would—was more than I cared to know about him.

The sound of chewing and drinking was too close to my ears. I didn't know what to do with my eyes besides stare at my plate or glance at Max. Wolfing down his food, he was no help.

"This is good." Clay reached for more. "If you can do this with venison, I wonder what you could do with all the fish we catch in summer."

"No chance of finding out. We'll be rid of her long before then. One way or another." Abner's grin showed a stringy morsel of meat stuck between his teeth.

By the time the meal was finished, Max had slumped into a drugged sleep, his head on his arm on the table, and he was snoring.

"Didn't tamper with the drinks, eh?" Abner spoke in a low

voice. "You passed the lasagna test, but you had to ruin it for yourself with the drinks."

I began clearing dishes simply to escape the table.

"Clay, go haul the kid back down into the hole."

"But—"

"Don't argue. You lugged him once before, so you can do it again."

I finished stacking plates beside the sink, telling myself if I was useful and quiet, perhaps Abner would forget about retribution. I searched through all the cupboards, but couldn't find any dish soap.

"There's soap on the sink ledge," Abner replied to my query.

"That's a bar of hand soap." Dehydrated, cracked, and ancient. "I mean liquid detergent dish soap."

"Don't have it. Don't need it. Soap's soap. I'm afraid we're not as fancy 'round here as you're used to, royal maiden."

Clenching my teeth, I filled the sink. The flaking yellow soap did nothing to fight the grease. I used all my muscle power to scrub the lasagna pan.

So I had been caught drugging the beer. What would the consequences be? I caught my reflection in the slick black windowpane above the sink, and I looked scared to death.

I shuddered, my submerged hands creating undercurrents in the filthy, lukewarm water. *Water filled with silverware,* I reminded myself, my mind perking up. *Forks, knives, and spoons.* Shifting my eyes carefully, I chose my timing and carefully slipped a knife into the waistband of my jeans, on the right side, for easy access. I concealed two spoons on the other side, for digging.

By the time I was done drying the dishes, my hands were parched and wrinkled. My skin felt foreign, not like skin at all, but like a pair of rough gloves glued to my hands. I found myself wishing for hand lotion, but was jerked from this thought as Abner suddenly towered over me.

"You just don't learn, do you, girl?"

I yelped as he grabbed me and pulled the cutlery from my waistband, grazing my skin with the knife as he did so.

"I see everything you do." He twisted my arm backwards so painfully, I gasped.

My voice came out in a whisper. "God, please."

"What was that? Praying again, are you? You really think God can save you? Since when? Has He ever intervened before? Of course not. He's a deaf God. What a fool you are to keep turning to Him. A fool, like all Catholics."

I was vaguely aware of Clay, sitting in the brown living room chair, his eyes on us. But when the pain in my arm made stars flash before my eyes, I forgot him.

"Since you're such a religion lover, why don't I take a page out of the Good Book," Abner sneered so close to my ear that I felt the warm dampness of his breath, "and we'll see what you think of your God then."

Chapter Fourteen

*U*nder Abner's evil eye, I was forced to fill a plastic basin of warm water and bring it into the living room, along with a washcloth. My heart hammered crazily. Abner sat in the brown chair, which Clay had vacated in exchange for hovering nervously near the rocker.

What next?

Abner held the gun steadily on me as he stretched his legs. "Take off my boots."

I blinked stupidly.

"You heard me. Take off my boots."

My pride buckled at the thought of kneeling down for the task, but I forced myself, telling myself this wasn't that bad, and I could still refuse whatever came next.

And get myself killed.

The laces were crusty, the knots complicated. I picked at them till my fingernails hurt. Once I got them loosened, I pulled the heavy boots off quickly.

"Now the socks."

I wrinkled my nose at the foul, salty rotten odor that hit me the moment I stripped the first black sock from Abner's foot. I actually saw dirt stuck to his skin, and curling, thick dark hairs. Yellowed toenails sprouted from angular toes. *If I throw up on your feet, it serves you right.*

"What are you waiting for? Wash them."

Swallowing hard, I rung out the washcloth and began scrubbing, trying not to think about the task as I performed it. The water in the basin quickly darkened into a murky soup. I held my breath.

At last, no more grime remained. The worst was over. The

end was in sight. This was actually nothing compared to getting a finger hacked off. My breath trickled out in wispy relief.

"Now dry my feet," Abner directed.

"But . . . I don't have a towel." I made as if to rise and get one, but he forced me back down with a crack of the gun on my shoulder. Laughter rattled from his throat. "Don't tell me you haven't been reading your Bible like a good Catholic girl? Because if you had, you would be well acquainted with this entire scene."

My frantic thoughts skittered in all directions, trying to understand, but then he began quoting, and it became all too clear.

" 'Mary therefore took a pound of ointment . . . of great price, and anointed the feet of Jesus and wiped his feet with her hair.' " Abner paused to grin. "That's the gospel according to Saint John, chapter twelve, verse three. Sorry I don't have any rich ointment for you to use, but don't let that stop you."

My throat tightened. *"Wiped his feet with her hair."* My ribs tightened. My entire body tightened, then recoiled. I put two stunned hands to my head, as if to protect my hair. Yes, it was not in salon condition at the moment, but still—if I touched this monster's feet with my hair, I would have to shave it all off.

"Do it," he ordered.

My scalp itched and crawled and prickled with horror as I bent my head low over his foul feet, now so close to my face. My chestnut curls tumbled over his toes and ankles, and my hair—once my crowning beauty, my pride, my source of vanity—became a filthy mop.

When at last Abner sighed and said, "That's enough," I raised my head so quickly I became dizzy with the rush of blood. I saw Clay, still hovering in the background, and shot him a glare. Whether he was wounded or not, I disdained him for standing by, watching, and doing nothing to help me. That his efforts wouldn't have been effective didn't matter. He should have tried.

Feeling thoroughly wretched and dehumanized, I was

allowed to gather my winter things and return to the hole. I descended into darkness feeling utterly forsaken by God. How could He allow such profane ridicule? *No, don't think like that. It's what Abner wants.* To which my anguished heart cried: *But Abner always gets what he wants.*

And the truth was, I wasn't so incensed by the thought of how Abner offended God, as I was over how he'd offended me. I huddled near Max's still slumbering form and wished for the escape of his drugged sleep, the comfort of nothingness, oblivion, as I wallowed in misery. *How does that evil man even know the Bible well enough to mock it in such a twisted way? He even had the verses memorized.*

But I didn't want to think about Abner anymore. With a mad surge of anger, I snatched up my dirty blanket and rubbed it fiercely over my head, till it felt my hair would all fall out. But in the end, this only made me want to avoid touching the blanket as well, and I groaned in despair. The evil taint of Abner was spreading, infecting everything. He was right. I was a fool to think I could ever escape.

"Max?" I tapped his cheek, hoping he would stir. I was worried about the strength of the drug he had ingested with the beer. When he didn't move, I picked up the flashlight and aimed it at his eyelids. "Max, please wake up." I repeated the process of poking his face and shining the light at his eyes for a long time. Eventually, he responded.

"I don't feel good," he groaned, rolling over.

"I'm sorry, Max," and I told him about my plan that had gone awry. I chose to skip the details of my humiliating episode with Abner, as I didn't want to relive it. Instead, I focused on my silverware failure. "I didn't even manage to swipe a spoon, and it was the perfect chance. I'm sure we won't get another one."

"It *was* the perfect chance."

Thanks for rubbing it in, but then I realized he didn't sound disappointed. I looked at him curiously, and he wiggled his eyebrows.

"It was a chance I made the most of," he said, producing a shiny spoon from his coat pocket and raising it dramatically, triumphantly, in the air like a prized sword.

"Max, that's great! But how? How did you manage—"

"Come on, Char. Have you forgotten I'm an expert magician?" The spoon vanished from sight with a flick of his wrist. He waved his hands mysteriously. "Sleight-of-hand is one of the most basic tools of the profession. No self-respecting magician can remain kidnapped. It's very bad for the reputation." He hiccupped.

I laughed and hugged him. "You're awesome!"

We set to work immediately. That is, one of us dug with the spoon, while the other one held the flashlight. When one got tired, we switched. We prayed while working, and thus we ushered in the New Year full of hope.

—

"What's the first thing you're going to do when we're free?" I asked Max as I dug. I reveled in the joy of wording it that way: *"when we're free,"* as if it were a certainty. I'd never thanked God for something in my life as much as I now thanked Him for this spoon.

"The first thing I'd do?" Max repeated. "That's a no-brainer. Report the psycho kidnappers to the police."

"Yeah, well, besides the very obvious, I mean." My arm muscles burned and my wrists ached, but I worked feverishly at the hard dirt wall.

"Okay." He thought a moment. "I'd go to Taco Bell and order everything on the menu."

My stomach growled cruelly. "You can count me in on that, and when we're done, we're cleaning out the nearest ice cream joint."

"Girls," he scoffed.

"But what I really can't wait to do is soak in a long, hot bath—using every type of bubble bath and soap in the mansion. And you know the stash Gwen has; there won't be

151

anyone in the world cleaner than me. And," I added, "I'm going to wash my hair with an entire bottle of shampoo and let it sit for two hours before I rinse it."

———

Despite our eager efforts, we didn't get very far in relation to how much time we spent digging. But that was okay. All we had was time. At least, until time ran out . . . and when that would be, we had no way of knowing. I supposed each day that the ransom failed to arrive would make Abner angrier.

How right I was.

About 4 p.m. on New Year's Day, we heard the familiar, dreaded clang of the dryer door opening above us. We immediately clicked off our light and crept away from the site of our digging project. Perhaps if we were very quiet, Abner wouldn't disturb us. *Or,* I thought hopefully, *maybe he's dropping off some food or water.*

"Girl, get up here."

No, not me again! But I smothered the thought even as my hand went to my throat. I would not wish Abner on Max, even if it did mean sparing myself. And Max was stronger than me. He could dig while I was gone. *And when I get back—*I swallowed—*if I get back, we'll be closer to escape.*

I emerged nervously from the dryer, stood up, and did a double-take. A massive man draped in a black robe stood before me. A heavy hood and a black ski mask hid his face. From the size of him, the voice, and the steely glint of his eyes, I assumed it to be Abner—but then again, the voice didn't sound quite right. He spoke near my face, a grim "Welcome."

I smelled an overpowering stench of beer on his breath, and that's when I knew: *It is Abner, and he's drunk.*

Drunk, but still very much in command. He looked like a messenger of death. *Or death itself.* His talon fingers pressed into my shoulder. The wide drape of his sleeve didn't conceal his gun completely.

"Into the living room," he ordered.

In the living room, the lighting was very dim. I spotted

Clay in the shadows, tied to the rocking chair. He wouldn't meet my eyes. Then I spotted the metal folding chair placed before the wood stove, and a torrent of blood rushed to my ears.

"Sit," Abner commanded. He raised his arm, and the flowing black material slid back slightly to show the gun in full view, aimed alternately at me and Clay. Once I was seated, Abner sliced a rope and freed Clay. "Tie her up."

Under Abner's guidance, he did. I ended up with rope wrapped around me from shoulder to ankle, cinching one arm uncomfortably behind my back and pressing the other arm against my side. Rope constricted my wrist, but my hand poked out at an odd angle so that my palm faced up. I stared at my hand anxiously. It was my right one, so useful, so perfect, with all five fingers.

"All right, boy." Abner waved the gun. "Roll it."

I looked up to see Clay holding a small outdated video camera, just in time to see the red "record" light blink on. I struggled to swallow. *This is definitely not good.*

Abner spoke to the camera in a very low, slow raspy voice. "Greetings, Mr. Perigard. It has now been five days since you received the first ransom note, three since you received Max's special package . . . and you've still failed to meet my reasonable demands. I warned you about involving the police, but you ignored me. Big mistake, old man. This is your last chance, your last warning." He paused.

"Perhaps your cold heart is not swayed by your grandson. Therefore, this time, I'm going to use your granddaughter." Abner made a sweeping gesture toward me. I imagined Clay zooming in for a close-up of my wretched face, and I hated him.

Abner continued. "Perhaps your granddaughter's screams will persuade you to finally cooperate. If not, this is the last you will ever see of her. And now . . . on with the show." He opened the stove door and stuck some kind of black iron in it, probably a poker, I thought queasily. The fire crackled and sparked orange and gold, dancing and writhing with snakelike forms. I tried not to think about what was coming. I wished I could turn my brain off.

Then Abner circled around me, chanting eerily. At first I thought he was just making nonsense noises, but then I caught a few words . . . some kind of language. Yes, I recognized it: Latin. Latin, the universal language of the Church. But how did he know it . . . and why, why would he use it? Another form of mockery, perhaps?

I attempted twisting in my bonds, but Clay had pulled the ropes too tight. Abner reached for the poker. No, it wasn't exactly a poker, I realized. The end was bent, but straight; the whole thing looked like an "L." And the bottom part glowed red-hot.

He brought it toward me, eyeing my hand. I knew what would happen an instant before it did, and I screamed. He pressed the hot iron deep into my palm, the burning tool sizzling and eating my flesh in one searing wave of pain too intense to be called merely pain. Agony. Excruciating. Lasting forever. The pain couldn't have been worse if my palm was being slashed with razors.

The repelling odor of burning skin filled the air.

At last, he lifted the branding iron. But he merely rotated it and pushed it back on my palm for another round of torture. I screamed again, and then I cursed. I cursed Abner, I cursed Grandfather, and I cursed God.

I knew Abner was grinning behind his ski mask.

And even when it was over, it was not over. The pain continued, soaring to new heights, plunging to new depths, rippling and rolling and scratching and tearing. Lacerating my senses. Wounding my very soul.

How, I wondered, *how do I not die from this?* White light flashed in my head. Black spots appeared. I almost passed out—hoped I would—but was not granted such luxury, as the pain kept yanking me back to reality. The reality of torment.

At some point, I became aware that Clay had dropped the video camera. More than that, he was fighting with Abner, or trying to. Abner seemed to be holding him off easily with one arm.

"Are you completely insane?" Clay's voice held horror. "You *are* a monster!"

Abner dropped the iron, and it clanged to the floor. "And you're a weak kid who can't stand the sight of pain. That's where the power is. You still don't get it, do you? I'll do whatever it takes to make the old man pay."

"It's not worth it," Clay cried. "It's just money. Just dang money!"

Abner gripped him by both shoulders. I dazedly wondered where the gun had gotten to. Abner had probably pocketed it in the billowy depths of his robe. "That's right," he sneered, "you still think this is all about money. What a fool. Of course it's not. It's about revenge." He drew out the last word with obvious pleasure.

Clay swung punches, thudding Abner's chest. In return, Abner simply drew back and, with a smashing fist, knocked him out cold. I watched him crumple to the floor through wet, blurry eyes. *No one is ever going to save me.*

Abner turned his venous red eyes on me.

"You're a devil," I cried. "Why don't you just kill me now and be done with it?"

"That's just it, my dear. I'm not ready to be done." He cracked his knuckles. "A slow torture is a so much more satisfying revenge." He let out a little sigh.

"Revenge," I repeated, my spine curling. "Revenge for what? I've never done a thing to you—neither has Max. We never even knew you existed until—"

"True," Abner broke in, "you didn't know me. But your grandfather did. I worked for him, on his oil rigs, and I was good at my job—the best. Then one day, for no reason at all, the old geezer decides to fire me. So the way I figure it, your grandfather owes me quite a bit of money—call it lost wages, if you will. But the revenge?" His eyes narrowed into snake-like slits. "That's for taking my wife."

Your wife? My mind felt fuzzy. Clay had said Abner's wife had left him. I clenched my teeth, still resisting the pain in my hand. Obviously there was more to the story than Clay knew. *So again, we're paying for Grandfather's sins.*

I blinked my leaky eyes and looked at my hand for the first time since the branding, astonished to find a cross shape burned into my palm.

"Like it?" Abner asked. "I thought you would. You and your sign of the cross. Now you're marked as a Catholic forever, whether you want to be one or not!" He roared with laughter as if this were the funniest joke in the world.

I couldn't even move my fingers without the pain of my palm increasing. I was back in the prison hole, and after gaping at my branded hand with the flashlight, Max finished dragging the latest happenings from me.

"I'll pulverize him. Someday. Somehow. We'll see him dead," Max promised. "Then we'll go to his grave and burn it. If he has a headstone, we'll blast it apart. We'll blast his bones apart and throw them in a sewer."

I reveled in the hateful words, but they didn't comfort me. "He'll burn in hell, but we probably will too," I said despairingly.

Max peered at me. "We could pray," he offered. "Would that help you feel better?"

"No. Why would it?" My voice was scathing. All I could think of was the pain, and how I couldn't escape it. "How can I pray when I have no faith left?"

He was quiet a moment. "Maybe that's what helps us have faith," he suggested, as if it were a revolutionary thought, "praying when we don't feel like it."

"Don't preach to me," I snapped.

He clicked off the flashlight. I heard him stalk away, each stomp of his foot exacerbating his wound, I was sure.

Jesus suffered a lot more than either one of us, my soul admonished me.

I clenched my left fist and glared into the darkness, the black, smothering blindness.

A scraping sound told me Max had begun digging for freedom once more.

The dryer door opened.

I'm not going up. He'll have to drag me up. I'd rather stay down here and die of thirst. I held my palm pressed against the cold dirt wall, absorbing the chill, attempting to counteract the still-flaming pain.

But it was Clay, and he came down with a bag and a bobbing flashlight. I noticed how Max sat with his back jammed against the wall opposite me, covering our escape project. Clay headed straight for me. "I brought you some food and water, and some salve for your burn."

"What, you're awake already?" I asked sarcastically. "You were probably faking it all along. Coward."

He worked his jaw, and his eye twitched. His face still looked terrible, and I knew I wasn't being entirely fair. Abner had given him a hard blow. Still, Clay had taken part in the torture from the start.

"Look, I'm sorry I didn't jump in sooner. I honestly didn't know he was going to do that to you—I had no idea."

"You had no idea? That makes it worse. He could have done anything. *Anything!* It could have been far worse. And you would have let it happen."

He dropped the bag and raked his hands through his hair. "I want to stop him—every second of the day—but I don't know how. God, I don't know how!"

"So what do you do all the time you're up there with him? He can't be watching you every second."

"Yes he can. And when he's not—when he's sleeping—I'm handcuffed in the bedroom. That's where I was when he went to check for the ransom. He came home furious, convinced there were undercover cops at the hill."

"So what did you think he was going to do when he had you tie me up and film me? Seriously? Are you that stupid?"

Redness climbed up his neck and he looked ashamed. "I

only thought he'd maybe taunt you a bit."

"Taunt me? When he cut off Max's toe?"

"Yes." His voice was emphatic. "The Abner I know would never treat a woman that way. I don't understand—"

"The Abner you know," I scoffed. "You obviously don't know him at all."

"Believe me, I do now." He bared his teeth. I was surprised he still had them all. "I'm on your side; I just don't know how to help you, other than this." He kicked the bag. "Lame attempts after the fact, I know. Not good enough."

"It's not. So don't do me any favors."

He swung around, searching the shadows as if just remembering Max's presence. But Clay was safe for now. Max wouldn't risk our project being discovered. In fact, I saw Max's eyes were closed as he feigned sleep.

Turning back to me, Clay spoke firmly. "Let's quit wasting time and get your burn taken care of. You know how hard it was for me to convince Abner to let me down here with this stuff?"

"Oh cry me a river."

He pried my hand from the wall.

I tried to pull away. "Real tough you are now. Now, when it doesn't matter."

Ignoring my resistance, he clamped my wrist, uncapped the tube of salve, and squeezed a dab on the center of my wound. Then he used one finger to spread it gently over the rawness.

I braced myself for stinging pain, and it came, but I refused to yelp out. I bit my lip instead. A hacking cough broke my composure, and I cursed the cold. "Like living in a freakin' freezer."

He replaced the cap and pocketed the tube. "I could try to get you some more blankets."

"Like I said, don't do me any favors. I'd rather freeze to death than take your charity."

"Fair enough." He turned to leave. "But I'll see what I can do."

Chapter Fifteen

"You could have helped me out, Max," I tossed across the darkness. "Said something. Clay is such a jerk."

"You've got some pretty hefty standards for the guy. He's only human. Cut him some slack."

I was taken aback. "How in the world can you say that? All you've been wanting to do is deck him."

"And I did deck him. So did Abner. More than once. The guy's a mess. Sheesh, I'm not saying I like the moron; I'm just saying he's in a tough spot."

"He's a pushover," I insisted, "letting Abner run his life."

"Sort of like you."

"Me!"

"Sure. The way he is with Abner—it's kinda like you and Grandfather."

His words rankled my stomach. "Don't be absurd."

"I'm just saying—"

"Well don't," I shot back. "Just dig. Even though it's probably a waste of time."

"Man, Char, you're one negative crank."

Don't I have the right to be? Shuddering in the dark, I tried to ignore my pulsing palm. I heard Max return to digging, and I was left with my own hateful company.

And I hated it.

The portal door opened again so soon, I assumed it was Clay returning with more blankets. I couldn't have been more wrong. I swallowed my last bite of dry sandwich and took a quick swig of water as Abner beamed a flashlight down and found me. "I hear you've been complaining down here. About the cold?"

I remained mute and didn't look up.

"Well, I'll just have to do something about that for you. I can't have you freezing to death before I'm through with you, now can I? You want some heat, how 'bout a fire? Here's the matches, and here's the fuel."

A heavy thud made me jump as something hit the dirt a few feet from me. The spotlight of Abner's flashlight revealed two very unusual objects. I edged closer for a better look. "A Bible," I breathed, "and a crucifix. What—"

"You want some heat? Light 'em up and let 'em burn," he said with wrath.

At that moment, I knew my animosity toward God was not substantial. I recoiled from the mere thought of holding a match to the sacred pages and the holy form of Jesus Christ crucified. In fact, I scrambled forward and gave each a tender kiss.

I felt my eyes kindling as I looked up at Abner. "You're wicked."

He laughed, and the sound echoed through the hole. Again, Max sat pressed against the dirt wall, merely observing. I traced the golden cross on the cover of the Bible, then opened it slowly. A dusty smell met my nose. My gaze went to a name inscribed in black ink on the blank first page: Abner Morrow.

Abner owns a Bible.

Observing the delicate, tissue-like pages, I wondered again about him. He was so evil, and yet . . . I kept coming across these religious connections. Why did he own a Bible and a crucifix? He'd quoted the Bible to me, and I'd heard him chant Latin almost like a priest. I looked up through the flashlight's glare to the dark silhouette of his face. None of this made sense, unless, unless . . . "Were you once a Catholic?"

I expected him to crack up, or spit in my face at the very mention of such a ludicrous thing, but instead, he answered steadily, "Does that surprise you? That someone could know your precious religion and not embrace it for life? You're beyond naive, girl. In fact, you probably think you're going to die a martyr and be canonized."

His satin-smooth tone turned to sandpaper. "There was a time when I thought like that, too. A young boy drunk on zeal. I suppose it's easy to get that way when your mother's a brainwashed Catholic. Let's just say, life made me change my way of thinking. It did please her, though, when I entered the seminary."

I inhaled sharply.

"That's right. Me, in the seminary, on the path of righteousness. Startling, isn't it? I was there for two years, studying intensely. Who knows, I may have gone all the way." His voice softened ever-so-slightly. "But then, on a visit home, I met Lydia. She was a non-Catholic, not even Christian. From the moment we decided to get married, God cursed me." Anger returned to his voice, and I thought I detected a slight drunken slur.

"On our way to the courthouse, we were almost killed in an accident. Then the sky—in an instant—turned black, darkened like doomsday with a thunderstorm so vicious I haven't seen the likes of it since. Lightning ripping the sky, rain slashing, branches flying. We married anyway. And God's hated me ever since, for choosing a woman over Him. And I hate Him back."

Abner spat, and I was glad I wasn't standing in the line of fire. "God, always on a power trip. For years, He kept trying to tear us apart. Finally, He succeeded." Abner swore. "Even after she left me, I prayed. I made one last desperate plea to your deaf God, but He did nothing. So I turned to the other side."

I gasped as everything clicked into place.

Abner continued ranting. "God hasn't answered your prayers either, has He? Of course not. I'll tell you who has power to make things happen to you: Not some God, but me. Me . . . and Satan."

I hastily crossed myself. "How could someone who was going to be a priest—"

"Ah, but I *am* a priest—a real one—a priest of darkness." His voice dropped so low, I almost didn't catch the hoarse whisper. "I'm going to make you wish you had burned that Bible."

The door clanged shut, and the darkness that dropped over me made me shudder.

"Okay," Max finally spoke up. "That was seriously weird."

"Weird isn't the right word." I clutched my arms about myself and tried to stop trembling. Suddenly, I saw with horrible clarity what blaming God could lead to: Denying God, hating God, thinking you were your own God. *Dear Jesus Christ, I need You. I always have. Help me, please.* I felt in the darkness for the Bible and crucifix and moved them over to my blanket just before the door reopened.

Abner ordered Clay down the ladder, and I waited with foreboding for his latest scheme to be revealed.

"Max," Abner barked, and it was the first time I'd heard him use Max's name. "I've got special plans for these two, and they don't include you. So you can either get up here now, or I'll come down for you. If you choose the latter, I promise it won't be pleasant."

Max stunned me by heading for the ladder immediately. I soon surmised that he did so only to lessen Abner's chances of discovering our digging project. Max and Abner disappeared from sight. While I waited for what would come next, Clay said, "Man, I'm sorry I ever said anything to him about the blankets. It sure sparked something."

Something. Something terrible. I worried and prayed for myself, I fretted and prayed for Max—unsure of whom to be more afraid for. I even said a quick prayer for Clay.

When Abner returned, he actually heaved himself onto the rope ladder. My heart constricted when I saw he was once again wearing the black robe. *A devil robe.* He descended one-handed, the other hand carrying two lighted black taper candles in a brass holder, the flames waving and flickering and casting eerie, fragmented shadows through our prison. On the ground, he tied the ladder up out of both my and Clay's reach. So while the door above remained temptingly open, there was no way for us to reach it. Abner wouldn't even have to tie us up to torture us. There was nowhere to run in the confines of this hole.

Without realizing it, I had backed against the farthest wall. I turned to face it now, and looking up, I swallowed. There it was, the upside-down cross, scraped into the dirt, that I had first noticed days ago. It was obviously courtesy of Abner, who had prepared this evil place. It was all so clear now.

I heard someone breathing near me, and turned to see Clay on my right. Was he sticking close to me to protect me? Most likely, he simply wanted to be as far from Abner as possible.

Abner set the candles down and stood in the middle of the floor, his hood casting his face in shadow, only his prominent nose protruding clearly. I watched him draw a small double-edged dagger from a pocket of his robe, the silver blade glinting. He fingered the tip speculatively.

"I'm sure you're both wondering what I'm doing down here. Let me enlighten you." He looked specifically at me. "Girl, you scoff at my powers. You think they don't compare to your God's. I'm here to show you differently, with a little ceremony involving you and my brother. It's really nothing to be frightened of. I'm simply going to marry you."

The shock gave me courage to speak. "You can't!" I sputtered. "You can't marry two people against their will. Even a priest doesn't have that power." I scrambled for the definition of marriage. "Marriage is a sacrament, given freely by two people to each other, in the sight of God. What you're proposing—a marriage of force—it's not valid!"

The corner of his lip lifted. "In the upper world, perhaps. Down here in the darkness, it's a different world." His words came out in a guttural slur. "I make the laws."

"Abner, you're drunk," Clay attempted. "This is crazy. You don't know what you're saying."

"On the contrary. I know very well what I'm saying, and

even better, what I'm going to do." He pointed at Clay with the dagger. "You should be thanking me, boy. I told you if you stuck with me, I could promise you plenty. Marry the Little Miss Saint Girl. You can turn her into Mrs. Deadly Sinner." He laughed at his lame joke.

"Where's Max?" I asked suddenly. "What did you do to him?"

"He's fine. Cuffed in the bedroom. I needed to get him out of the way. Because after the wedding," Abner grinned wickedly, "comes the wedding night."

"Abner—"

"Silence!" He narrowed his eyes at Clay. "No more interruptions. You will both remain where you are and do as I say. I won't hesitate to use this knife on either one of you." He drew himself to his full height, seeming a giant in the confines of this hovel. "I will now begin." He reached one hand into a pocket and produced a dainty silver bell, which he rang. The metallic noise filled the room with a menacing cacophony.

"*In Nomine Dei Nostri Satanas*," he began in a raspy yet reverent tone as he used his dagger to trace a shape in the dirt wall beside him. His chant became a combination of English and Latin, and I heard "Lucifer," "forces of Hell," and "dark blessings," cringing at each one. The shape he drew took form as a pentagram, an upside-down star.

Again, he reached for something hidden within his black robe. This time, I recognized the object he brought out. It was a golden chalice studded with red stones, the same chalice I'd come across during my search through his drawers. I wished now that I'd smashed it or at least battered it until it was unusable. He lifted it with a disturbing solemnity and began invoking "the four crowned princes of Hell."

I shut my eyes and willed my ears to block out the hideous words. Mentally, I prayed the St. Michael prayer, over and over. In the past, I'd never taken much time to pray it. I didn't think it was that important. Satan, demons, evil forces—they had all seemed so obscure and unreal, nothing I would ever encounter in real life.

Now I pleaded for my life . . . *Be our protection against the wickedness and snares of the devil. May God rebuke him we humbly pray . . .*

"We come together in the name of . . . " Abner's voice broke into my head. ". . . to join Clayton Morrow and Charlene Perigard in marriage."

I countered his words . . . *by the power of God, cast into hell Satan and all the evil forces who prowl about the world, seeking the ruin of souls . . .*

Sensing movement near me, I opened my eyes. The man who was Abner looked darker, his eyes more frightening, as he used the dagger to slice the air in front of me and Clay, forming an invisible circle around us.

My eyes, riveted with terror, refused to close as Abner stood before us, staring at us with wild, yet dead, eyes. "Do you, Clayton Morrow, agree to take Charlene Perigard as your wife?" The dagger moved closer to Clay's throat, until it touched it.

"Do you?" Abner's voice blazed demonically.

Silence.

"Do you?"

"Yes," Clay finally said.

Then it was my turn. The dagger pricked my throat. "Do you, Charlene Perigard, agree to take Clayton Morrow as your husband?"

I swallowed, and the movement caused the blade to scrape my skin.

"Say, 'I do,' " Abner growled.

I wanted to answer no, but I knew I didn't have to. God knew this was a sacrilegious sham, no marriage in His sight. That was all that mattered. And yet, I couldn't say yes. It would be like saying yes to the Devil. So I answered, "No."

Abner pressed the blade more firmly against my throat, and repeated the question. This time, I couldn't speak, as the metal edge cut into my skin, and Abner answered for me. "She does."

Gasping, I threw a hand to my throat, pressing against the

sting, afraid to look at my glove, afraid it would be soaked with blood. But I was still breathing; I was still alive. *It must be a shallow cut,* I tried to comfort myself. I pulled my scarf higher and wrapped it tight, bandage-like, around my throat. Clay seemed like a zombie next to me, and I wondered if he'd even caught what Abner had done to me.

"And now," Abner breathed, "the rings."

I expected his hand to plunge into the depths of his robe once more and extract some evil looking bands, perhaps made from twisted black metal, but instead he grabbed my left hand and pulled off the glove. Seizing my ring finger, he quickly sliced around the base of it with the dagger. It was over before I truly comprehended it, and I was left staring at the seeping warm blood forming a thick crimson ring around my finger.

The pain struck me, but I clamped my teeth on my tongue. Clay hollered loud enough for the both of us as Abner did the same thing to his ring finger. Then Abner grabbed our hands and brought Clay's bleeding finger down on top of mine, pressing them together for a long moment.

"Your blood has mingled; you are bound together by blood forever," Abner said solemnly. "In the name of . . ."

My ears rang.

". . . I pronounce you husband and wife. Hail Satan!" Abner's voice boomed. He went off into a long, undecipherable chant, one I had no desire to decipher. I observed the dark handle of his dagger, and it looked like a hissing black snake, the body hunched in half, the tail and tongue curling over the blade.

"Hail Satan!"

He rang the bell again, then spoke to me, his eyes flashing. "And this, my dear sister-in-law, is true power."

I clutched my wounded finger and remained mute.

"Congratulations to you both," he rasped, wiping the dagger on the sleeve of his robe, then tucking away the chalice and bell in his pockets. "I would wish you a long and happy life together, but that would be rather pointless, wouldn't it? Clay, enjoy her while you can."

166

Abner turned coal eyes on me. "This all started because you whined about the cold. Now you can just use your body heat to keep warm. I'll leave the candles for you."

He pointed the dagger at his brother and spoke roughly. "For once, be a man. I've seen the way you look at Little Miss Saint Girl. Find out how good she is, or tomorrow it's my turn."

With that foul order hanging in the air, he retreated to the rope ladder, released it, climbed up, and locked the door behind him, leaving us alone.

Alone.

Alone with Clay, whom I could not trust because he was ruled by his fear of Abner.

Clay, who had just said "yes" in the evil ceremony.

I darted away to my blanket. Like his brother, Clay did not believe in God's power. He followed no moral rules. So what would stop him from fulfilling Abner's command?

He turned to look at me with strange, dark eyes.

I snatched up the crucifix and held it in front of me like a shield. It was sturdy wood. I could use it as a weapon if I needed to.

He took a step in my direction.

"Stay away!"

Another step. "Charlene, please. I have to—"

A clunk, and we were plunged into darkness. The candles. He'd knocked them over as he walked toward me. By accident? Or on purpose?

I heard a footstep. Too close to me.

Sucking in my breath, I lifted the crucifix.

Just as I was about to swing, he caught my wrists, gripped them tight.

He's stronger than me. Tears sprang to my eyes.

I can't stop him.

Chapter Sixteen

*P*lease, Charlene, calm down." Clay's grip didn't loosen. "I'm not going to hurt you."

Struggling, I panted, "Then let me go. And get away from me."

"Listen, that cut's deep, it's pouring blood—"

"I don't care." I'd completely forgotten about my finger. "I don't even feel it anymore."

"You're in shock. I've got to wrap it." He heaved a breath. "Look, I'm going to release you. Just don't bash my head in with that cross, okay?"

Despite the fact that I didn't answer, he removed his hands from my arms. I kept my grip on the crucifix, though I used the back of one hand to swipe away my tears.

"Where's that flashlight?" he asked. "Can you find it and turn it on?"

I found it easily and gladly snapped it on. The minuscule light was better than nothing.

"I didn't mean to knock the candles over." He approached me again. "I'm not exactly free from shock, either, you know. That was one messed up—"

He broke off his sentence as I pressed my back against the wall and hoisted the crucifix like a baseball bat.

Annoyance crossed his face. "What's with you? I'm in this nightmare same as you. That whole wedding thing—" He cut himself off with a muttered curse. "That's why you want to knock me out. You think I'm going to—" His eyes sparked. "You really think I'd do that?"

"Quite possibly." I adjusted my footing. "I have no reason to trust you."

He shook his head, looking like he wanted to spew more curses. "None of the times I've stood up for you have meant a thing, have they? Effort doesn't count, only success. Why don't you get real, girl? I can't work miracles."

"Don't call me 'girl,' " I practically growled. Abner had called me that too many times.

"Fine. Charlene. You said it yourself, Abner's a monster. So how do you expect me to defeat him? He takes me down, every time." He tilted his face toward the light. "Isn't my ugly mug proof enough for you? A physical fight isn't the answer." He worked his jaw. "He's a Goliath, but I'm no David."

"I never said you were."

"Good. I'm also no rapist. Got it?" As he spoke, he seized the edge of my blanket and tore a strip from it with a horrendous ripping sound. He tore another strip, then wrapped one of them around his oozing red finger, bandaging it crudely.

He leveled his gaze at me. "Will you let me bandage your finger?"

Grudgingly, I extended my hand. While he bound my finger tightly, I saw blood already soaking through his own bandage. Perhaps seeing this, he wrapped my wound more thoroughly, until my entire finger was covered, fat and useless.

"Now let me check your throat," he said, a bit more softly. Trying not to wince, I watched his bruised face as he peaked under my scarf. His eyes told me nothing, but a slight dip of his brow worried me.

"You'll be fine. It's shallow. Most of the bleeding's stopped. Let me rewrap it."

When he finished, he turned and retreated to the opposite wall, where Max had been digging. To my relief, he sat down without looking at the superficial hole. "There. Sorry I can't move any farther away." He closed his eyes.

I listened to my still wild heartbeat, thinking, *It's going to be a very long night.* I looked down at my finger. A pattern of red seeped through the bandage, spidering out in all directions. My gaze then fell on the Bible, and relief swept me. Finally, something to read. There was no better way to pass time than reading, apart from talking. And I most certainly did not feel like talking.

I opened the Bible at random, thinking, *My eyes are going to land on the perfect, applicable verse to comfort me.*

But no, it didn't work that way. So I flipped pages and searched for verses I liked, ones such as in Psalms, chapter ninety: *". . . and under his wings thou shalt trust. His truth shall compass thee with a shield: thou shalt not be afraid of the terror of the night."*

The terror of the night.

Yes, I thought, *that's what this is. Never-ending terror of the night.*

Then I found myself searching for the story of David and Goliath. I located it in Kings, and read with interest, envisioning Abner as the giant and Clay as David. But before I finished reading, a thought hit me, and I spoke without thinking. "Were you Catholic once, too?"

Looking up, I saw Clay's eyes were still closed. I had forgotten he was sleeping. My gaze dropped and I returned to reading.

"Yes," he answered unexpectedly. I looked up to see he had opened his eyes. "What makes you ask?"

I touched the Bible. "Your reference to David and Goliath. That and—" I hesitated— "I guess the fact that if Abner grew up as a Catholic, I thought you probably did too. Were both your parents Catholic?"

"Yes, but my ma was the only one who went to church regularly." He crossed his arms. "Go ahead. Ask. I know you want to. Why'd I abandon the faith, right?"

I felt my face flush. "You don't have to talk about it."

He shrugged. "Might as well. Nothing else to do." He stared past me. "With a ma like mine, you'd think I'd have the best chance in the world of turning out right. But you've got to figure my dad into the equation, too." He cleared his throat. "You already heard the abridged version of this story. Here's the full version.

"It was a Friday in June. I was seven. My dad came home from work, drunk, and began roughing up my ma. Abner joined in, trying to defend her. Yeah, Abner—can you believe it? He was seventeen at the time, made it a fairly good fight, but still, my dad won. He was a big, strong guy. Ma escaped and went to Mass. That was always her solace. Pray, go to Mass. Never call the cops."

He ran a hand over his rough chin. "She thought I was gone at a friend's house, but I wasn't. If she'd known that, she would have taken me with her. My dad caught sight of me, and I guess he still had some anger to work off, 'cause he started in on me. My ma had taught me from a very young age not to resist. To take it, and turn instead to God, to pray things like, 'My God, my fortress, my refuge, deliver me.' " His voice scoffed. "It didn't work.

"This time, though, it wasn't too long before my dad passed out on his bed. So I'm lying there on the ground, looking up at my ma's little Blessed Virgin altar—the Mary statue and vigil candle—and stupid kid that I was, what did I do? I lit the candle and said a prayer for my ma, and even my dad." He paused. "That was the last time I ever made the sign of the cross."

I tried to picture him as a little boy and saw a thin kid with unruly hair, a face that would have been cute but for the traces of sorrow, the shadows of fear.

"Afterwards, I left the room and went to bed. Next I knew, I was waking up to smoke. Thick, choking smoke. The house was on fire. I thought I was a goner for sure, but then, who comes crawling through the smoke to find me?"

I held my breath.

"Abner. Abner dragged me out just in time. He saved my life. When the fire department arrived, it was too late. They couldn't rescue my dad."

His throat worked. I could tell he was trying to recount the story in a detached manner, as if it no longer affected him, but it obviously did.

"The cause of the fire was a candle," he said woodenly.

171

"The vigil candle. What an answer to a prayer, hey? I thought I'd blown the thing out, but obviously I forgot." He spread his hands. "So there you have it. I killed my own dad and I lost the faith at age seven. Seven! Most Catholic kids are barely preparing for First Communion at that age. They're fresh with innocence, hope, and zeal. Not me. Those things died in me that night."

He lowered his eyelids. "My ma missed my dad, despite all his faults. Of course she told me she didn't blame me for the fire, but she never looked at me the same after it happened. I tried to stay Catholic, tried to please her, but it just never worked. Maybe because deep down, I was glad that my dad was gone. I'd have these nightmares of him, though. He'd appear at the foot of my bed, burning like an inferno, cursing, screaming at me that it was my fault he was dead, and I was going to burn with him in hell." He chuckled stiffly. "Every once in a while, I still have that dream."

I shivered and cast a quick glance through the shadows, as if expecting a burning phantasm to appear.

Clay raked a hand through his hair and the brown strands stood up in all directions. "So I lost God, lost my parents . . . all in one night. All I had was Abner, and now he's gone too." He peered up at the dirt ceiling. "Sometimes I think he should have just left me in that burning house."

I bit my lip. "God obviously had other plans for you."

"Plans? Like what? To live like an atheist and be pushed around by my older brother for the rest of my life? To watch my ma die in agony?"

"God—"

"Cut the God talk. I don't have patience for Him. Where was He when my ma was sobbing herself to sleep for years? Where was He when I was trembling in fear of my dad's fists? Where was He when I was lying on the floor in pain after a beating, crying my eyes out?"

"He was there," I whispered, "crying with you."

"Bull."

"I'm sorry if—"

He held up his hand. "Don't," he said harshly. "I see that look in your eyes. Don't pity me." He drew his back up stiffly against the wall. "I only told you because you wanted to know why I left your precious religion. Now you know, let's change the subject."

"Fine."

But apparently, neither one of us had anything else to talk about. We fell into a brooding silence, and though I kept staring down at the still-open Bible, I couldn't read it. My vision was blurry.

At some point I realized Clay had turned his body so he was facing away from me, facing the wall. Feeling powerless, I watched him discover the metal spoon that Max had half immersed in a pile of dirt. My heart faltered a moment, then picked up its pace as Clay took the spoon and, with no questions, began digging where Max had left off.

I observed him silently for a long time before I crossed the room to see he had already made noticeable progress. His forehead glistened as if he was actually working up a sweat. I watched him for a few minutes, then asked something that had been on my mind. "Why didn't you tell me Abner used to be in the seminary? Back when you were giving me his life story?"

"Force of habit," he grunted, still working. "Abner never brings it up. And it's been so long, I tend to forget. He was a different person back then."

I nodded slowly and was quiet a few more moments before saying, "Thanks for digging. It's a long, slow process, isn't it?"

He nodded.

"I hope Abner doesn't find out. You won't—"

He whirled and chucked the spoon across the room, startling me. "No, I won't tell Abner! Seriously, Charlene— you think I'd do all this work just to turn around and tell him?"

I backed away from the anger snapping in his eyes. His

173

gruff voice resembled Abner's, and it sent alarm shooting through my veins. I retreated to my blanket, picked up the crucifix, and set it in my lap.

Blinking rapidly, I was glad for the dark. "That's not what I meant." *I was going to say you won't ever know how much your help means to us.* But I couldn't say that now. I took a deep breath and let it out in a rush. "You didn't let me finish."

His features turned contrite. Thankfully, he didn't ask me what I'd meant to say.

"I'm sorry I overreacted." He spoke sadly. "Abner's just getting to me. You don't know all that he's threatened, the things he'd do. Not just to me, but to others. My ma. You." He sighed and crossed the room. I almost thought he was going to sit down beside me, but he simply retrieved the spoon and went back to work.

———

According to my watch, it was four in the morning on Friday, January second. Neither Clay nor I had slept all night. Clay had quit digging about an hour ago. He admitted it would take at least another day of digging before we could break through.

So we sat on opposite walls, trying not to look at each other. Neither one of us put our heads down. I was tired, dead tired. But my mind wouldn't let me sleep.

"There's one very important thing that we still haven't discussed," Clay spoke up, "and that's what we're going to do when Abner comes back. He doesn't make idle threats. And I know I don't need to remind you what he threatened."

Somehow, my blood ran colder than it already was. "He'll have no way of knowing," I practically croaked.

"He'll know." Clay shook his head. "Even if I lie, he'll know. He's always been able to tell when I'm lying. Any ideas?"

"He'll have to kill me first," I whispered.

"What?" The tone of his voice told me he had heard perfectly.

"I said he'll have to kill me first. He'll have his gun. I'll fight him, scratch him, rip his hair—anything to make him mad enough to kill me."

"No."

"Yes. It's the only way out for me."

"I won't let it come to that."

Right. You'll stop him, like you've done before. But I kept my mouth closed, suddenly aware that I was living the last hours of my life.

"The crucifix," he said. "We can use that as a weapon."

I didn't envision it working, not against the gun, but agreed anyway.

"Hide it behind your back," he continued, "while I try to reason with him."

Reason? With Abner? I swallowed a wan laugh.

"It may not come to it," Clay said, "but if it does, I'll attack him. Then you can join in. Together, we just might take him."

My front teeth pressed into my bottom lip. "But when he comes down, he'll tie the ladder up so we can't reach it. Like before. What good is taking Abner down if we can't get out of here?"

He let out a long breath, thinking. "The hole. We finish digging through to the cellar and escape that way."

A new thought worried me. "If Abner comes down here, he's likely going to see the hole right away and know what we've been up to. It's so much more obvious now."

We were silent while we mulled over this new complication. Suddenly, Clay began tossing armfuls of dirt back into the cavity. "I'm just filling it loosely. With the shadows, I don't think he'll notice it. But it'll be easy enough to toss this stuff back out when he's gone."

I eyed the spot critically. "Maybe it will work."

He glanced over his shoulder. "Let's both move to the base of the ladder, against that wall. Then when he comes down, he'll focus on us right away and turn his back to the rest of the room."

"Good idea." I moved immediately, bringing the crucifix.

While Clay finished with the dirt, our light blinked out. "Uh-oh." I felt blindly for the small flashlight. "Batteries must be dead," I concluded after several attempts to turn the light back on.

"We should keep it dark down here anyway for when Abner comes. The less light, the better if we don't want him to spot the hole."

"True." I shivered. I felt so much more vulnerable in the pitch blackness. Closing my eyes, I imagined sunlight and blue skies. Warmth.

"But until then, we could always light those candles." Clay fumbled in the dark, searching for them.

"Do you have matches?"

"No, but didn't Abner toss some down with the Bible and crucifix? They've got to be around here somewhere." But after searching on hands and knees for several minutes, we both gave up.

I brushed dirt from my hands. "Maybe Abner snatched them back on his way out."

"Must have."

We made our way slowly, by feel, to the wall near the ladder, trying not to bump into each other. Then we settled back to wait for Abner.

———

My head rested against a firm shoulder, my face lay close to warmth and a musky male scent. I snapped my head up, ripping myself from the fog of sleep, alarmed to realize I'd been slumbering against Clay. I edged away from him, hoping he was sleeping and that he hadn't been aware the entire time.

Time. *What time is it?* My watch pulsed away, strapped against my wrist, but I had no heart to check it. Death would come to claim me soon. What more did I need to know?

Nearby, Clay breathed steadily. The rhythm was deep, reassuring, bringing to mind that brief moment between sleep and reality when I had nestled against him and felt safe, secure.

But I would have no more moments like that. I was awake now. Facing death. I sniffed back the pressure of tears, blinked away the prickling in my eyes. Fought the rising sorrow in my throat.

"Charlene?" Clay's voice came through the darkness, hushed, but not sleepy. Had he been awake all along? I tried to steady my trembling breath.

"Charlene," he repeated, "are you crying?"

I didn't want to lie, yet I didn't want to admit my weakness. "I don't know . . ." I gave a small laugh. "I'm being stupid. It's just—there's so much I haven't done. I've never written a poem. I've never read *Gone with the Wind*." A wave of remorse crashed over me. *Never been in love, never kissed a man. And now I never will.*

I swallowed. "I always thought someday I'd have a family of my own. Kids. I'd be a white-haired grandmother in a rocking chair, with all the time I wanted to read the classics and write poems. But now . . . I know someday isn't going to come." Hot tears flowed down my cheeks and dripped off my chin.

"Don't talk like that. You'll have plenty of time to do those things."

I shook my head, scattering tears. "No. There's no point in fooling myself. This is it for me, I know it. When Abner comes down—"

"No." Clay's voice was gruff. "No. We have a plan. He won't hurt you. I won't let him."

A small sob escaped my lips.

I felt a touch on my shoulder, barely perceptible through my thick coat. "I know you don't think much of my protection, but I swear I won't let him hurt you again. You'll be okay. Please, Charlene, don't cry."

"I'm sorry." I choked on another sob. "I want to be brave. I want to believe you, but please don't pretend for my sake. I need to face this. There's no point in deluding myself." A vision flitted tauntingly past me, an image of a yellow clapboard house with white shutters and a lush lawn. But no white picket fence. A fence would be too confining. *Like a cage.*

In the backyard, a chubby toddler tossed a ball in front of a colorful flower garden, while a baby lay cooing on a soft blanket. As I gazed longingly at the vision, it faded to blackness.

"So many things I haven't done," I murmured. "And despite all my talk about God . . . I'm afraid to die."

"You aren't going to die."

"You can't promise me that." I sniffed and rubbed away my itchy tears. "I always thought I'd have time to prepare. Now I'm afraid to face God. I'm not ready to be judged." I squeezed the crucifix. "I pray, but I'm still afraid. I know I'm no saint."

"But you try, and that's got to count for something. Everything you've suffered—you can't tell me that doesn't count for something."

"It's all too little, too late," I replied flatly.

I sensed him frowning. "Listen to me, Charlene." His hand still sat on my shoulder, and I felt an increase in pressure. "I'm far from an authority on this, but even I know that it's never too late. You're not dying today, but if you did, you wouldn't have to be afraid. God's merciful."

"You're just saying that." I sucked in a shuddering breath. "You don't really believe it. How could you? After everything you told me earlier—"

"I'm telling you now," he broke in. "I may be a lost cause, but you're not. So don't give up."

I swallowed salty tears. "Then you can't give up either. Please. You're not a lost cause. You said yourself that it's never too late."

He made no reply, but his hand remained on my shoulder, strong and comforting. As my focus shifted from myself, my panic and fear subsided to a manageable level.

Silent moments passed.

But there was one thing I needed to ask. "Clay?" I attempted timidly. "If I die, will you do something for me?"

"You aren't going to die."

"But if I do," I whispered. "Will you . . . do you think you could, if it's not too much to ask . . . would you say a prayer for me?"

Not even pausing, he answered, "Yes, Charlene. I promise."

Chapter Seventeen

*T*he door's metallic clang startled me. My body went rigid, but Clay squeezed my arm reassuringly. We both looked up.

Abner's large form lumbered down toward us, gun already aimed, flashlight clamped between his teeth. Dropping to the ground with a tremendous thud, he grinned. His hollow eyes remained on us as he tied the rope ladder up out of reach.

"How's the blushing new bride this morning? I trust you had a wedding night to remember?" He turned his flashlight on Clay's face like an interrogation spotlight. "Well, boy? Have you made me proud for a change?"

Clay blinked in the overwhelming brightness.

"Lost your tongue?" Abner swept the light over me. "She doesn't look too emotionally damaged. In fact, she doesn't look damaged at all. Boy, I think you've failed once again."

"Think what you want. I did what I had to." A vein pulsed in Clay's temple. A warning.

Abner narrowed his eyes. "You know the terms of this agreement. I made it very clear. If you can't do your duty by your wife, then you don't deserve to have her." He took a hungry step toward me.

Clay stepped in front of me. The brothers stood mere inches apart, Abner towering over Clay. "Face it, boy, you failed. You're going to have to step aside. I brought some rope with me, and I think I'll just have your little wife here tie you up. And then . . . you can watch a real man in action."

I held the crucifix ready behind me while I trembled from head to foot with anger, indignation, and humiliation. My tongue couldn't even form a word, let alone speak a sentence.

But Clay's did. In fact, he spoke very calmly and coolly. "Abner, what would Lydia think of you right now?"

Rage flashed across Abner's features. "Do not speak to me of her."

"You vowed to be faithful to her," Clay continued, "and I know you meant it. That bond of commitment doesn't dissolve just because she walked out on you."

Unidentifiable emotion rippled over Abner's face.

"If you ever truly loved Lydia, don't mar her memory like this."

I was amazed at Clay's composure and tactical approach. He knew his brother well enough to know just where to strike. Abner's nostrils flared wide and the tendons in his neck stood out like steel cables. He seemed to be battling within himself. I waited with pounding heart to see what would happen next, but what happened next was completely unexpected.

"Fire!" someone yelled from up above. Max.

With a curse, Abner pulled the ladder free and scrambled up it. Even in his urgency, he remembered to lock the door behind him.

I sniffed the air, but smelled nothing. Of course, why would I, deep down in this hole? "Do you think there's really a fire up there?" I asked, while trying to decide whether that would be a good or bad thing.

Clay shook his head. "No idea. But if so, that's some timing. Guess I'm not the only one trying to redirect Abner's attention."

I turned to him and looked steadily where I believed his eyes to be. I imagined their rich brown-gold coloring as I said, "You were doing a great job. Thank you."

It felt about fifteen minutes later that the door above opened. My breathing paused as I waited to see who would come down the ladder. No flashlight accompanied the person, and I saw with relief that it was Max.

Behind him, Abner's voice ricocheted from the dryer.

"Clay, get up here! You can thank that punk for the damage you're going to have to spend the rest of the day cleaning up."

Clay touched my hand as he left. "Keep digging," he whispered.

When the door closed behind Clay, sealing off all light, the first thing Max said was, "Are you okay, Char?"

"Yes, I—"

"They didn't touch you?" Anxiety stiffened his voice. "Neither one of them?"

"No. I'm fine. Clay never had any intention of hurting me. He really came through this time."

Max grunted. "Maybe, but now he's back up there doing Abner's dirty work."

Before I could say anything, he went on. "I caused quite the diversion, though, hey?"

"Awesome. Tell me how you did it."

"Sure, but first, let's get some light so we can dig while we talk. Where's the flashlight?"

"It burned out," I admitted regretfully. "We've got some candles, but I couldn't find the matches."

I heard a rustle, a snap, then a sizzle as a single flame illuminated Max's face and hands. "That's 'cause I swiped 'em on my way out yesterday. How do you think I started the fire?"

But I let out a cry of dismay as I took in his bloody nose and the wicked bruise under his right eye.

"It's nothing." He sniffed and wiped away some blood, smearing it and making it look worse. He turned, found the black candles, and lit them. "Look what else I got." He turned back to me and pulled a metal spoon from his coat pocket. "Now we can work twice as fast. And we're going to need to," he added grimly. "I have a strong feeling Abner's patience is wearing dangerously thin."

He approached the escape hole and did a double-take. "What happened here? Why'd you fill it back in? Abner didn't find it, did he?"

"No. This was to help make sure he didn't." I hurried over

and began scooping the loose dirt from the hole. It cascaded out easily, like a dirt waterfall. "Clay's idea."

"Clay knows about this?" Max swore.

"It's all right, really. He won't give us away. Look what he did—he dug all this for us. We're a lot closer to escape thanks to him."

"I still don't trust the guy," Max muttered. "But this is our only chance, so let's dig."

We each gripped a spoon, and I was glad for the slight padding of my gloves. It helped to insulate the pain in my palm from the pressure of the spoon handle. Meanwhile, my cut finger throbbed dully. And the shallow slice on my throat barely bothered me at all.

While we worked, Max began telling his story, beginning with Abner handcuffing him to the foot of the bed. "I wasn't on the bed, though; I was on the floor. When Abner returned, he seemed to take a lot of pleasure in telling me what he did down here, the whole ceremony thing—the guy's a maniac. He kept taunting me with what he was going to do to you in the morning. I knew I had to keep him away from you. I was racking my brains for a plan. I had the matches, so I knew I could start a fire when he left, but being cuffed to the bed, I knew that idea wouldn't do me any good unless I wanted to burn with the room. I thought about picking my cuffs—skilled magicians can do that, obviously—but I needed something to pick with. Finally, I was so exhausted that I laid my head down, and I spotted a fishing pole under the bed."

"A fishing pole? Let me guess—you used the fishing hook to pick your lock?"

"Not quite." Dirt flew from the hole as Max worked eagerly.

I smiled at how thoroughly he seemed to enjoy telling the story.

"Abner barely slept all night, just stayed in bed reading a black book. When he finally started snoring, I made my move. I pulled against the handcuffs and stretched my fingers and just managed to reach the pole. Sure, I considered the hook, but it was no good. Too short, sharp, and bent. Then I noticed that the closet door was open about an inch. Since it's not a large room, the closet wasn't too far from me. I used my legs to inch the door open wider. Then I held the pole between my feet and lifted my legs, trying to use the tip of the rod to snare one of the wire coat hangers. It wasn't easy, but I finally got one. From there, it was a simple matter to unbend the wire to pick my cuffs.

"Abner woke up while I was doing that, and I shoved the pole and wire under the bed and pretended to sleep. When he left to visit you, I quickly finished the job. Free of the cuffs, I lit the bed on fire, shouted down to him, and raced out of there, grabbing a spoon from the drawer as I went. See, I figured he'd catch me—I can't move too fast with this dang foot—and I didn't want to leave you alone, anyway."

"You're the best twin ever," I gushed gratefully.

Max gave a crooked grin, but kept digging. "Abner doused the fire pretty quick, then caught me, and we grappled, as you can see, then he shoved me back down here. But I'm happy; I accomplished my goal—I got him away from you, and now I'm back to protect you. I'm just hoping he'll be occupied with the repairs for a little while. 'Cause I saw the bedroom when he dragged me back to the dryer—the bed was a complete loss, the carpet and walls a mess. Yeah, I think he'll be busy. So we've got to make the most of this time and work like crazy."

I agreed, and despite the pain radiating through my branded hand, I continued digging. We even picked up our pace, working side by side in candlelight. Even when the candles eventually burned out, we didn't slow down.

———

The next evening, we broke through the dirt wall. It took us a moment to realize it in the dark, but my spoon scraped at air and I let out a triumphant squeal. "We're through!"

"Let me feel it." Max pushed his hand into the opening eagerly. "All right! We're close now. All we have to do is enlarge this enough so we can squeeze through."

We carved away at the dirt perimeter, our spoons clinking into each other now and then. My heart thrummed with excitement. By the time we got the opening wide enough, Abner would likely be sleeping. And once outside, we'd have the advantage of hours of darkness to aid our escape. I could practically feel the hot shower and taste the gallon of water and pounds of food I would soon enjoy. As my stomach growled, I noticed our opening became more visible, as if a light glowed somewhere beyond. "That's weird—"

Max pushed his dirty glove over my mouth, then pulled me eye-level with the hole. There was just enough room for us to peer through together. A sound like heavy footsteps came pounding down the cellar stairs, and through our peephole, I spotted Abner. I thanked God we hadn't made the hole any wider yet. With luck, Abner would never notice it or us. Because though he carried a black candle, it didn't give off much light, just a dim halo. He also carried a bouquet of red roses. I would have exchanged a baffled look with Max, if we could see each other, but I knew we exchanged one mentally.

Beyond Abner, all I could see of the cellar was an old shovel propped in a corner and a wooden shelf holding some small cans and a rope. Abner knelt down on one knee in the middle of the room, and I shivered because he was now closer to our level, but I prayed that the shadows in the cellar and the thick darkness of our prison would camouflage us.

Carefully, Abner set the candle and the roses on the dirt floor. "Your favorite flowers," he whispered, just loud enough to reach my ears. He set a hand softly on the dirt and bowed his head sadly. My eyes riveted on him, unblinking. Who in the world was he talking to?

I felt a million spiders creeping up my spine. *Or is he talking to someone* not *of this world?*

"Three years, Lydia. Three years to the day since we parted. I still miss you so much. Our little one would have been two. Was it a boy or a girl? I still wonder, every day, but I'll never know, will I? And we'll never have that happy family that we dreamed about . . ."

185

My gloved fingertips braced the dirt wall as my mind swirled, uncomprehending, and yet comprehending too much.

"We lost everything. All because of old Perigard and his accursed God. Well, we're getting our revenge, slowly but surely. We're eliminating the old man's family, one by one. The first one was easy, almost too easy." His slight chuckle ripped through my heart. "A faulty parachute? Happens all the time, an unfortunate accident."

I almost gasped out loud, and Max nudged me sharply. I gripped his arm in return, needing his support. How did he remain so composed? Surely, he'd heard what I had, and knew what it meant. Our father, our dear, wonderful, loving father, had been murdered. By Abner. Tears leaked from my eyes and gathered in the corners of my mouth. I tasted salt, yet was too stunned to swallow.

"So far, that's only one Perigard down," Abner muttered, and he clenched his hand into a fist. "It's not enough! And it was too fast, too painless. I've had a long time to plan and prepare since then. Now I've got the grandkids, and I promise you, they will suffer as much as possible before they die. And when they're gone, it will finally be the old man's turn."

My heart was beating so loudly in my ears now, I almost couldn't hear what he was saying. I didn't want to hear. And yet, I had to.

"We'll save the very best treatment for him. We'll strip him down, make him cower and cringe, drag him through the snow and ice, douse him with boiling water, slice up his flesh." Abner licked his lips, then exhaled.

"But one thing at a time, my dear, one thing at a time. First I need to finish off the kids. Send them to meet their God they love so much."

He stroked the dirt lingeringly before rising to his feet. "Justice will be done. Watch and wait, my love, watch and wait. I'll join you in the darkness when my mission here is complete, I promise." He lifted the black candle. "I'll be your prince, and we will be together forever, in the kingdom of power."

He melted away from view, but I heard his steps retreating up the cellar stairs. Max and I remained staring into the black hole, and that was what I felt inside—an empty, gaping black hole. In the next instant, my soul overflowed with fear and grief. I pushed away from the wall, feeling as though the dirt was filling my lungs. I covered my face, shuddering with sobs. Abner hadn't just ruined our past week, he'd destroyed our past two years. If not for that evil man, our lives would have been completely different.

Dad would still be alive.

A strong grip on my shoulders preceded Max's voice. "Char, I know." The depth of emotion and meaning in those three words were a balm to my soul. He did know. He was my twin. He knew exactly how I felt. I heard him inhale. "But now, you've got to pull yourself together. It's what Dad would want. We still have to widen this hole before we can escape. And we've got to escape. We've got to get Abner arrested, not for ourselves, but to get justice for Dad."

"That won't bring him back." I gulped. "That won't bring him back."

The pain was so fresh, it felt as though our dad had just died. Discovering this new information changed everything. I'd grieved for him years ago, but now it didn't count. I'd grieved for a dad who had died in a tragic accident, not one who'd been vengefully murdered.

I became aware of a scraping sound and realized that Max had gone back to digging. Strong and composed, he was directing his emotions productively. I sucked in a deep, trembling breath, swallowed my tears, and joined him.

"I think it's big enough now," Max decided. "Go ahead and give it a try."

I wriggled through the narrow dirt tunnel, feeling much like a worm. Max attempted to follow, but couldn't quite make it.

"Still too tight," he declared. So he handed me a spoon and

I worked on enlarging the cellar side, while he worked on his side. At last, he made his way through, joining me in the cellar.

"We did it." He clasped my hand briefly, but the excitement of reaching this long-awaited goal was clouded by urgency. We still had two more doors to pass through before we could consider ourselves free.

I glanced around the cellar, and our surroundings seemed just a shade less black than the pitch darkness we were used to in the prison hole. We headed carefully to the stairs and crept up them, keeping our hands along the dirt wall for guidance.

Max, in front of me, stopped at the trap door and listened for a full minute at least. "Nothing," he whispered finally. "Let's go." I heard him push against the wood. "Darn it, it won't open." There was a long pause as he examined the problem. "The doors move just enough so I can fit a finger between the crack, but there's a wooden bar on the other side, locking us in."

"The wood can't be very thick. You could break it, right?"

"Yeah, but I don't think we want to risk the noise."

"Here, let me feel; my hand is smaller." I pulled off my glove and exchanged places with him. Indeed, I could fit my fingers through the narrow space that was created by pushing up against the shutter-like doors, but then I felt the slat of wood running firm across the center. I tried twisting my fingers to get a grip on the slat to slide it out, but the only way I could grip the wood was by pressing against the door, and that same pressure wedged the wood too tightly. It wouldn't budge.

"We can't break it, and we can't slide it out," I muttered. "There's got to be another way."

We became silent, thinking. A faint noise, coming from far away on the other side of the door, intruded on the silence, and I put my ear to the crack. The distant, deep rhythmic rumble confused me at first, then made my lips quirk. "I think I hear Abner snoring up a storm."

"Could be Clay."

"No, it's way too ugly sounding. I'm sure it's Abner."

"Fine, but that doesn't solve our problem. I guess maybe we could just hope Abner's a deep sleeper and risk breaking the door open."

"No. We've come too far to do something stupid. What about going back down to check this place out? We didn't search it. Aren't cellars usually places to store things, like tools? Let's go see if we can find something helpful."

So we headed back down and searched blindly with our hands. I felt the shovel, rope, and shelf of cans that I'd seen earlier, when Abner had been down here. Then I searched the opposite wall, the one where we had broken through, and discovered a shelf stood above our opening. I ran my hands over the surface and tried not to think of mousetraps or razors catching my vulnerable fingers. The last thing I needed was another wound.

Suddenly, I felt the prick of a sharp-toothed blade. My hand drew away, then returned cautiously. "A saw," I hissed. "Max, I found a saw! It's the perfect thing. Narrow enough to fit through the crack, and sharp enough to do the job. All we have to do is saw through the wooden bar!"

He approached me, and I carefully guided the handle of the saw into his hands. "Great find," he agreed. "But this is still going to make some noise."

I smiled. "Yes, but I think it will blend right in with the snoring."

"Good point."

We climbed back up the stairs—hopefully for the last time—and Max went to work while I prayed silently. It was an awkward way for Max to work, I was sure, sawing something above him, with sawdust probably falling in his face, but he made no complaint.

Many moments later, the sawing stopped. "Char, we're good to go."

I transitioned mid-prayer to *Thank you, thank you, thank you*, then followed Max up and out of the cellar, into the darkness of the cabin kitchen.

But this was not really darkness. Not to us. The glowing night made its way through the outside tangle of trees and filtered sporadically through the small cabin windows. To us, deprived of sight for so long, this was magnificent visibility.

I cocked an ear and was relieved to hear snoring still going strong. As it was impossible to tiptoe in our boots, we walked flat-footed, making little noise. We crossed the small living room, a room which taunted lurid memories of torture, and reached the front door. Max turned the knob, inched the door open, and indicated with a sweeping gesture for me to pass through first.

He was right behind me as I stepped out onto the snowy porch. He closed the door quietly while I pulled in a deep breath of clean icy air. An owl hooted somewhere above, as if rooting for our escape.

Giddy energy trilling through me, I padded down the few steps, then broke into a run.

As I fled the cabin for the rustic road, blue, black, and gray shades of night blurred before my eyes, eyes which smarted and teared in the cold, a coldness which chapped my lips and dried my tongue. Running my tongue over my gums, I could even taste the cold, a slight metallic flavor.

The glorious taste of freedom.

Chapter Eighteen

Snow crunched underfoot as I bounded down the slope of the narrow road, exhilarated by the rush of frigid fresh air. Not pausing, I headed left, following the road's sweeping curve. It bent left again, swooping past towering, snow-capped pines, before straightening and ending abruptly at a wide open vista of white. There before me lay a magnificent, open expanse of snow-blanketed ice.

"The lake." My eyes roved in pure wonder. After my captivity, the largeness of the world astonished me.

Hearing no response, I turned. "Max?" Panic billowed in my chest. "Max, where are you?" Suddenly afraid, I hurried to retrace my steps. I'd been so caught up in my breathless dash, I'd just assumed Max was right there with me. Overcoming my hesitation to make noise, I yelled with full power. *"Max!"*

"I'm here. I'm coming," he panted.

I hustled up the road and found him moving along at a pace closer to a jog than a run. He shook his head. "This is no good. I'm weak. I'm slow. My foot's killing me, and my legs won't do what my brain tells them." His eyes were pained. "Char, I'm sorry, but you'll have to go without me. I refuse to hold you back." He looked past me and spotted the lake. Relief touched his voice. "But it's okay. We'll be okay. You can cross the lake in a flash. Look." He pointed.

At first, I saw nothing. With no moon or stars visible, the sky seemed to be spread with tar. Snow, which lay pure as beaten egg whites, seemed to be the only thing lighting our surroundings. Then as I stared, I caught sight of a pinprick of light across the lake. It was a more welcome sight than any light the sky could have held. *It's a house light.* In the house, I was sure to find understanding people and, most importantly, a telephone.

"You see that light?" Max asked. "Go there. Get help."

"But what about you? You can't just stand here waiting. What if Abner—"

He left the road and began pushing through tangled brush, into the forest. "I'll crouch down and hide out in here. I'll hibernate." He laughed shortly. "Now get going."

"But—"

"*Go,* Char. It's our only chance. Whatever happens, don't come back unless you bring the cops."

Even as I stepped away, I reached out toward him. "I'll find help, I promise. Pray for us," I added.

With a nod, he ducked into the underbrush.

I turned and raced for the promising light. Just a speck, but it grew as I tore across the crusty surface of the lake, never once looking back. Icy wind battered my face. Visions of Grandfather snuggled in his comforter-laden bed pushed their way into my mind. *At least he doesn't control the cops up here.*

I forced my legs to keep moving. The muscles cramped painfully, not used to such exercise. I shoved my thoughts away from the pain. *I need to be free not just of Abner, but of Grandfather. I will be,* I promised myself.

Though I kept a strong pace, I didn't seem to be making any progress. The light, as irresistible as the light at the end of a tunnel, remained unreachable, making me wonder if I was caught in a dream.

Had the light moved? Was it some kind of star after all? It appeared to have risen. But no, I had finally reached land, and the light stood on a post at the top of an almost vertical embankment. So it wasn't a window light; still, I held onto hope. Grasping prickly branches and wiry shrubs, I struggled to the top, where the grand form of a large stone house made me sigh with relief.

Snow squeaked underfoot as I passed a tire swing which

hung, like a frosted black donut, from a tree in the front yard. The house's windows were dead of light. Of course, at this time of night, that was normal. I'd have to wake the occupants, but I trusted they'd be more than understanding once I explained my situation.

When ringing the glowing doorbell failed to bring any response, I figured the owners must be sound sleepers. I began knocking. This soon turned to pounding. With a savage blow of my fist to the wood, the thought finally struck me that no one was home. Most likely, this was a vacation house. The lamppost probably turned on automatically at dusk.

Refusing to accept this devastating truth, I beat harder. There very well could be other residences along this lake, but I didn't have all night to search. I rattled the doorknob. I battered the windows. Maybe there was no one home, but I was still determined to get inside to find a phone.

I snatched up a brick lining the sidewalk, not pausing to think that I was, in my desperation, resorting to vandalism, and aimed for the window. Before the brick had a chance to fly, a voice startled me.

"Charlene!"

My hand wavering, I turned to see a shadowy silhouette, one I had seen enough times in darkness to recognize. It was Clay, hurtling toward me with manic speed, snow flying from his feet. My grip tightened on the brick as I scanned the shadows for Abner. "Are you alone?"

"Yes." He dropped his hands to his thighs, catching his breath beside me.

"Good, you can help me get the police." I pulled my arm back to throw the brick, but he seized my wrist.

"No, you don't understand. There's no time. You've got to come back or Abner—"

I tore myself from his grasp as a violent mixture of devastation and anger filled me. "Come back? Are you insane? Why are you still helping him? Did he threaten you this time, or did you just volunteer? Unbelievable! I thought you'd changed, but I was obviously wrong." My fierce tirade cut into his protests, and I heard nothing he said. My grip on the brick tightened as I backed away. *I should just throw it at him.*

But what if I hurt him?

"I'm not going back!" I hurled the brick at his feet, then took off running. "Help!" I screamed at the top of my lungs. "Someone please help me!" The words rattled through the air, like stones in a tin can, and I knew there was no one to hear them.

Glancing over my shoulder at the wrong moment, I ran smack into the tree that held the tire swing. Dizzily, I grabbed for the frozen rope, and it was the only thing that kept me from falling. Snow flaked from the rope in delicate slivers. Clay, a wavering strip of black before my shaken eyes, approached.

My head had to clear before I could run again. I needed to buy some time. "You're a double-double-crosser," I spat. "I bet you heard us escaping and told Abner."

"Think what you want. Just quit wasting time. Your brother's life is at stake. Abner gave me exactly ten minutes to bring you back before he kills him. We've probably got less than five left. So *come on.*" His eyes blazed with urgency as he extended his hand.

"Stay away!" My brain still woozy, I clutched the tire. "Why should I believe you? What if this is a trick?"

"It's not. But since my word means nothing to you, answer this: Are you willing to gamble with your brother's life?"

"If you're telling the truth, and Abner has Max, then he's already good as dead. My coming back won't stop that," I said flatly. "My only chance is to get help. I'm so close. I have to try. There won't be another chance. Help me," I surprised myself by pleading. I recalled Clay's kindness from when we were last together in the hole. *I know there's good in you.*

"You don't get it, do you?" His voice was gruff. "You don't have a choice. You're coming with me, one way or another." He stepped forward, suddenly looking very strong.

Without warning, I hurled the tire at him. I heard the *Mmmph* as it socked him in the chest, saw chunks of snow fly, and heard a thud as he hit the ground.

I ran from the twinge of horror at what I'd done. *I had to do it. He was lying. Max is safe; he's hiding. Abner couldn't have found him.* I pounded over the snow, thinking, *But Clay found me . . .*

Desperately wishing another house would appear, I ran aimlessly, burdened by fear, and my pace was too frantic for my eyes. Something—a log or a rock or a root—tripped me, and I went sprawling, smacking my face into the snow.

As I lifted my head, I saw Clay coming, and a wave of terrifying déjà vu struck me. This had all happened before—only now it was twisted, wickedly contorted. He was no innocent ice fisherman, and he was not my rescuer; he was my enemy.

I'd barely struggled to my knees by the time he reached me. In one quick, fluid motion, he scooped me up and tossed me over his shoulder like a sack, knocking the breath from me as he did so. He carried me swiftly through overhanging branches that snatched at my hat and hair. In a flash, we were out of the forest and facing the lake. He skidded down the bank and onto the ice, bumping and jostling me.

"Put me down!" I screamed, beating his back with my hands and his front with my knees. His only answer was to grip me tighter. I tried writhing and twisting, but his arms were iron bands around me. The blood rushed to my head, and as I strained my neck to look up, I saw the shore, my one chance of salvation, fading rapidly away.

"I'll find help, I promise." Those had been my last words to Max. I'd failed him yet again. But no, those hadn't been my last words. Not quite. *"Pray for us,"* I'd added.

Bitterness filled me now as I joggled upside down, completely demoralized. *God, we've been praying so hard. You obviously don't want us to be free. I know I'm supposed to accept Your will, but I can't accept this. I can't.*

"We might still make it in time," Clay puffed.

I tried again to struggle free, hoping his strength was wearing down, but it did no good. Finally, I went limp. "I hate you, I hate you," I said pointlessly, defeated.

"I'm sorry." There was a long pause—time for him to gather breath. "But I don't want Max killed." Another pause. "Abner threatened my ma, too. Said the cancer won't be what gets her," another puff of breath, "if I don't bring you back."

"Your mother will be so proud of you, I'm sure."

He cursed. "You're impossible to please."

"No, I'm not. I like simple things. Freedom. The ability to walk on my own two feet. And a man who has the guts to act like a man."

"I'm trying," he huffed, "to do what I can for you and Max, considering the circumstances."

My laugh came out raw and ragged. "You had me fooled for a little while, but no more. There's no question in my mind what you're bringing me back to: Death. Abner killed my father, did you know that?" I thought I felt a jolt run through his shoulder. Perhaps if I shocked him enough, I could still escape. "He killed Lydia, too. She's buried in the cellar; he goes down at night to talk to her. Did you help him with those deaths, too?"

For a second, I thought Clay was going to drop me. He shuddered, adjusted his grip, and plunged on. "I know what you're doing, but your wild accusations aren't going to free you. I know Abner's evil, but the one thing I'm sure he's not guilty of is Lydia's death." He heaved a deep breath. "He loved her too much."

"Maybe that's why he killed her."

Instead of answering me, he bellowed, "Stop! Abner, stop! I've got her."

A moment later, I was tumbled unceremoniously to the ground. Aching all over, I looked up to see Abner with his ever-present gun in one hand and a switchblade knife in the other. I shivered convulsively and reached instinctively for a blanket to wrap around myself. Of course there was none, only shrubs poking through snow.

"You're lucky, very lucky." Abner flicked the blade. "I was just about to start slicing up your brother."

Max sat on the ground, head down in his hands, and he didn't even look at me. I'd never seen him so defeated, and my empty insides rolled. "What did you do to him?" My voice quavered. I should have come running the second Clay told me to.

"Just kept myself entertained," Abner said dismissively. "Now get up and get moving." He kicked Max, then me. Motioning with his gun, he directed us onto the road.

"How did you find us?" I was beginning to think that evil spirits appeared to him, guiding him. It wouldn't surprise me. I just wanted to know what we were up against. *But I already know. We're up against evil. Utter evil. And it's going to win.*

Abner laughed. "I'm a hunter. Tracking footprints in the snow is second nature. Clay's not bad at it either, are you boy?"

Tears hovered in my eyes. *We would have been free but for the chance factor of fresh snow?* It was too excruciatingly ironic to stand. *And it wasn't chance. God sent that snow. Why, God? Why?*

Abner marched us up the driveway, Clay included. Instead of ordering us into the cabin, he directed us to the left, up a slope to a grove of trees located yards from the building. "This will do nicely." He pulled a long coil of rope from his coat and dropped it at Clay's feet. "Tie them up against the trees."

Clay hesitated. "You're not going to leave them out here all night? You know how the temperature drops, and if they can't move—"

"Precisely. They wanted to escape into the outside world, so now I'll let them enjoy it."

My eyes met Clay's and narrowed into I-told-you-so slits as Abner's deep, resounding laughter shot through the night and ricocheted off the ebony tree trunks.

"This has been so much more enjoyable than hunting mere animals. With you two Perigards, I get to savor the kill. See the fear in your eyes."

I tried to will the fear from my eyes, but I knew I failed.

"What are you waiting for, boy?" Abner demanded. "I said

197

tie them up."

The muscles around Clay's eyes tensed. He bent as if to pick up the rope, but instead he went for the gun in a lightning quick move. Yet somehow, Abner anticipated the move and smashed his elbow into Clay's stomach.

"You never learn." Abner hardly sounded angry, just exasperated, as Clay doubled over. Abner clouted him on the back, and Clay dropped to the ground. "You cannot defeat me. It is physically impossible. Now tie them up, and I'll deal with you later." As he spoke, his gun flashed from Clay, to me, to Max, always expecting something, always ready, and I barely blamed Clay as he picked up the rope and followed Abner's directions. What was the point in resisting? It only brought pain. *Death will be a relief,* sighed my mind.

For a finishing touch, Abner produced two handkerchiefs and made Clay tie them around our mouths.

"I'm sorry," Clay whispered.

"Tighter," Abner ordered. "Make it hurt."

The fabric cut into the corners of my mouth and into my cheeks. Not much material was in my mouth, though, so maybe I'd still be able to talk. Not that it would do any good. But even as I thought this, Abner used his grimy fingers to push a wad of handkerchief into my mouth until I literally started gagging. He did the same to Max, who was tied to the tree on my right.

"Good night, sleep tight, don't let the frostbugs bite." Abner chuckled all the way back to the cabin, his gun pressed to Clay's back. They disappeared through the front door, and I listened, thinking maybe Abner would smack Clay around a bit. But if he did, I heard nothing.

I tried not to think about the way the ropes cut across me with vice-like pressure. Relaxing brought more pain as the ropes chafed against my weight. But I had no energy left to keep from relaxing. No energy to try working at the ropes, no energy to fight the pain. And above all, no energy to pray.

Yet my eyes lifted wearily, skyward. The murky black firmament belied the thought that up there, somewhere, existed brightness and goodness and happiness. A place called heaven. And God, a supposedly merciful God.

My head dropped.

Have mercy.

———

Unconscious or asleep (I wasn't aware of a difference, only that I was free from pain on some level), I became aware of a noise pulling me rudely from my partial refuge where senses were dulled and energy not needed. A growling noise. *An animal, perhaps? Yes, a bear. At last, the means of our death . . .*

I sighed, but the breath would not leave my mouth. *How very annoying. But where was I? Oh yes, being eaten by a bear . . . I suppose it will hurt a lot, but maybe it will be over quickly.*

My head lolled against the harsh tree bark, and I snapped out of my fuzzy thoughts to agonizing reality. My eyelids parted, and I still saw darkness. Still night. Though it had felt like eternity, not much time had passed. Groggily, I saw that the source of the growling noise was only a car.

Only a car? My eyes flew wide. I yearned to yell out and race toward the vehicle. Because this was not just any car. It was a cop car, rumbling to a stop as it parked behind Abner's truck. The engine cut, giving way to the sound of whispering wind. A tall officer in a warm dark coat stepped out and surveyed his surroundings casually. Much too casually for my liking.

Help! We're over here! I tried to scream, but I could barely move my tongue against the saliva-saturated handkerchief. I watched with sinking heart as the officer headed not in my direction, but toward the cabin. He didn't move particularly stealthily, either. In fact, his movement suggested routine boredom.

But his being here had to mean something. Maybe Grandfather was finally coming through for us. I strained my neck to look to the road, hoping for a swarm of cop cars—FBI would be nice, as well—to come fishtailing to a halt, armed men leaping out to surround the place.

Max's eyes met mine. His grave expression warned, *Don't get your hopes up.*

But they were already up. My heart thundered against the ropes. My focus turned back to the officer, who now stood at the cabin door, knocking politely.

No! At least pull out your gun!

The door opened, spilling a meager puddle of light over the officer. I couldn't see who stood in the doorway, but of course it would be Abner.

The officer showed his badge and appeared to be conversing calmly, courteously, with no sense of urgency. My teeth chomped on the material in my mouth. *How can he look at that barbaric thug and not know the truth?*

Maybe it was Clay at the door, but that made no sense. Abner would never allow it, and there was no way Clay had overpowered him. Still, he was in there somewhere. Now would be the perfect time to try something, make a racket, call out—he could save us all. But nothing happened. The officer talked some more, nodded, then turned and hiked back to his squad car. Half expecting Abner to plug the man in the back, I braced myself for a gunshot, but that didn't happen, either.

I watched the officer climb into his car, start it up, and snap on the headlights. As he pulled around, I willed the lights to hit us, to find us through the crowd of trees, but the illuminating beams merely bounced off other trees before focusing on the driveway.

Crimson taillights soon became a blotch of red in the corner of my eye. When even that vanished, my shoulders slumped—or tried to. The ropes still had no give. But my pain was no longer so acute. The combination of cold and lack of circulation was numbing my body, bringing me one step closer to my destiny of becoming a frozen corpse. I let out a sigh through my nose.

Wearily, my eyes wavered over the cabin. How nonthreatening it looked. A cozy cabin snuggled in snow, its tiny windows emitting a lemon-butter glow while warm wisps of smoke curled from the black stove pipe. The scene was straight off a Christmas card.

No wonder the officer had been fooled.

That's the way of evil. It's crafty. It takes on all forms, particularly the most appealing.

My eyelids fell heavily, and I let my tear-iced lashes rest on my cheeks. *But once the evil has you in its clutches, it drops the façade. It unleashes claws and fangs. It strikes. And nothing and no one is strong enough to stop it.*

It destroys.

Chapter Nineteen

$\mathcal{I}$n my near-frozen state, I was barely aware of being re-leased from my bonds. My fogged mind conjured up a rescuer bathed in holy light, but this immaculate image was shattered, plunged into muck by the brutal touch and rough handling of very real, cruel mortal hands. When the gag was yanked free across my cheek, the icy material sliced like a knife.

My body was bent and twisted, my neck pressed into a clamp, my wounded throat smarting rawly. I gulped wintry air, and awareness swept over me. Abner held me in a head-lock, squeezing with one thick arm; his other arm imprisoned Max. Half my face was squished into Abner's scratchy coat, but I could see enough to know that we were being dragged toward the cabin. He pulled us up the few steps, which tripped my blundering feet. Cursing, he yanked me all the more viciously.

Then we were inside the cabin, but before I could begin to appreciate the warmth, Abner kicked open the cellar door and shoved us down the steps. Max and I fell, bumping and bruising our limbs on each other and on the wooden steps, until we thudded onto the dirt floor in an injured heap. More darkness. A sound to my left, a human groan, but it didn't come from Max.

Light glimmered from behind, sending beams of pain flashing through my head. Blinking, I turned to see Abner pounding down the stairs with the LED lantern in one hand. Setting it on a middle step, he descended to stand at the foot of the stairs, blocking our escape route, brandishing his gun.

Hearing another groan, I turned back to see the cellar

swathed in gray shadowed tones. Clay, trussed awkwardly with his wrists tied to his ankles, sat uncomfortably against the wall—the wall with the hole that led to our previous prison, through which Max and I had broken through with such delight mere hours ago. A couple of fresh red and purple lesions marked Clay's face, evidence of further trauma courtesy of Abner, and I winced. *You do keep trying,* I thought before lightheadedness took over. My knees pulsed with pain.

Max, beside me, began to haul himself to his feet.

"No, don't stand," Abner said. "Not yet. Not till I tell you."

Max dropped back down beside me, mute, his fight and fire gone, beaten away by too many cruelties. Seeing him this way ignited a spark somewhere deep within me, but I wondered how long it could survive. How long *we* could survive. This dank cellar emitted a musty sense of finality, like a crypt or a coffin.

Desperately, I scanned our silvery-brown surroundings. The shelves were bare now, the cans removed, as if Abner thought we might use them to bombard him. Perhaps we would have, given the chance, though they would have been futile against a gun.

Lydia's red roses were gone, too, as if I'd only imagined the morbidly striking scene earlier. All that remained in this bare dirt cellar was a shovel, propped in the far corner. *A nice weapon for someone with the strength to hoist it.* Attacking Abner without the gun going off would be a problem. But then, what about our situation was *not* a problem? I eyed the shovel, its wooden handle and battered rusty blade. *It might be worth a shot.* My lips twitched stupidly at the unintentional pun.

"Your time is up." Abner pronounced the words like a death sentence, as indeed they were. The lantern glowed behind him, hooding his face in shadow. He looked as menacing as when cloaked in his black robe. He was the Grim Reaper, a Demon of Death, come to collect our souls.

"You're scared," I countered boldly, "scared because the cops were here, and you know they'll be back. Any moment.

If you kill us, it will only be worse for you."

He chuckled heartily. "You know very well that it was only one meager cop who came snooping. Yes, he asked nosy questions. I could have finished him off, but it wasn't worth it. He had nothing to go on. A vague report of a car seen miles from here, days ago. Might have been yours, might not. They'll never know, because that car is long gone; and soon, I'll be long gone, as well. Once I'm finished disposing of you."

"No, Abner," Clay spoke up, "you don't mean that. You aren't going to kill them. You're not that evil—"

"How stupid are you?" Abner cut in. "How did you think this was going to end? Even these two knew; that's why they kept trying so foolishly to escape."

"You could leave them somewhere, in a field or a parking lot," Clay argued. "You could be gone from the country before they're found. Please, Abner—brother—" His voice almost broke. "They've suffered enough."

"Not possible," Abner replied darkly. "No one has suffered the way I have, and they have to pay. The old man has to pay. So yes, Clay, I am going to kill them. And yes, I *am* that evil."

Clay shook his head. "You were a hero once. More than once. You saved me from the fire. You—"

"The fire," breathed Abner, his tongue caressing the word. "How very well I remember the fire. You've been in the dark about that all these years, carrying the guilt like only you can . . ." He thrust back his shoulders and puffed out his broad chest. "I'll tell you what, boy. For you, because you're my brother, I'll give these good-for-nothing rich brats a choice. One choice," he eyed me, his pupils like flint, "and one choice only."

He directed his words at both me and Max. Words hard with hate. "Deny your God, get on your knees, and cower before me," he rasped. "Ask the Prince of Darkness to save you. Do that, and I'll let you live. You can join me in revenge against that so-called grandfather of yours. You know you hate him. You know he deserves death." Abner bared his teeth.

"So what will it be? Life and Satan, or death and your feeble Jesus?"

With no hesitation, I replied, "I choose Jesus Christ."

"Jesus Christ," Max answered at the same moment.

A righteous fury fueled my blood, warming my body as I added, "Christ conquered death. He's the only one Who can give life. What you have—what you propose—that's death. But you can't kill our souls."

"How eloquent," Abner said. "You've been studying your catechism."

My gaze crept to the shovel. If I could only reach it without being shot.

"I see you eyeing that shovel, girl," Abner said. "Go ahead, pick it up."

When I didn't move, he barked, "I mean it."

Slowly, I rose to my feet, my arms and legs tingling with a pins and needles sensation. Pain pressed into my temples.

"That's right. Grab ahold of it. See, I have a plan. You thought if you chose death, that I'd use this gun, and it would come swift and painless, but what I have planned is so much more slow and torturous. Give me the shovel."

Trying not to tremble, I did so. Then he surprised me by backing up the stairs with the shovel and lantern in hand. "You've got five minutes. Then I return with this shovel, and if you haven't changed your answer, you get to see just how this shovel fits into my plan for your last moments. I promise it won't be pleasant."

We were left in utter darkness. And the zealous bravery I'd felt flare up mere moments ago, was snuffed out.

"He's just torturing us more, dragging this out." I gulped. "Five minutes left to live."

"Untie me," came Clay's voice through the dark. "It will be three against one. And if you go down, we'll all go down—but at least we'll do it fighting."

I expected a caustic remark from Max in response. Instead, I heard him move to Clay's side. I joined him, and without a word we both began working blindly at the ropes. I had no anger left against Clay, only dim sadness that he was in this nightmare with us, and even an appreciation that now that we were obviously defeated, he was willing to stand by us and take one last beating.

It meant something, and I sensed Max thought so, too. So we tried our best, fingers working the ropes frantically in the dark, fingernails practically ripping with the effort.

"It's no good," I said at last. "Abner knew we wouldn't be able to untie you in this short amount of time. The five minutes must be almost up, and we haven't made any progress." A sob surged its way from my throat. "Dear God, I can't take any more torture!" My hands dropped from the ropes and I covered my face, shuddering and weeping.

An arm came around me, firm and comforting, and held me while I cried. I thought it was Max's, but then I heard him mutter, "These ropes are tough, but at least I got one of your arms free."

And that, I realized, was the arm that held me. Clay's arm. It felt good, very good.

"I wish I could do more," Clay said. "I admire you both for your faith. I wish I shared it, I really do." He touched my cheek briefly. "And I wish I could truly protect you. I wish I could take all your pain and suffering. God, I'm sorry I ever brought you here."

And for once, I had no biting comeback. I didn't want to hurt him anymore. Why had I ever thought I did? I rested my head on his shoulder, like I'd done once before in the fog of sleep after our dark "wedding" night.

"I'm sorry we can't do more for you," I whispered, "and I'm sorry we were so hard on you. Thanks for everything that you did do for us."

"She's right," Max put in. "No hard feelings, man. I wish I could get you loose." He stopped working the ropes and rested a hand on my shoulder, and I took a deep breath, savoring both Clay's and Max's comfort. In some odd way, although this was one of the worst moments of my life, it was also one of the best.

When we heard Abner open the cellar door, none of us panicked or screamed. We waited calmly, hearts beating heavily, to be sure, and yet, if we must die this way, a whisper in my soul told me we would all meet again, free of the suffering and pain. And it would all be worth it.

"Well?" Abner boomed. "Have you come to your senses? Or are you sticking with your Jesus?" Lantern light bounced off the crusty old shovel in his hand.

"Christ sticks by us." I straightened. "We'll stick by Him."

"Same goes for me," Max said.

"So be it." Abner spoke in Clay's direction. "They've made their choice. Now break it up, you fools!" He stomped to the bottom stair, brandishing the shovel.

Suddenly, he threw the shovel at me. "Take it, girl. Now step over there—" He motioned for me to move to the left side of the room—"and start digging."

I felt the weight of the shovel in my grip, assessed my chances of smacking the gun from Abner's hand. But he was too far away.

"You heard me." He trained his gun at Max's head. "Dig, or your brother gets his brains blown out."

I swallowed and thrust the shovel into the ground. The packed dirt was hard, and I had to stamp on the narrow top of the shovel to pierce the earth. My muscles felt like old rubber bands, brittle and ready to snap. After several minutes, sweat trickled down my forehead, and I voiced the question that infested my mind. "Am I digging my own grave?"

"Smart girl."

Clay, who was twisting futilely with his ropes, began struggling frantically.

"Calm down over there," Abner told him. "You won't be getting free till I let you. Even if you weren't tied up, you really think you could stop this? Don't forget, this is your doing, too. You signed on with Satan from the start, when you agreed to be on my side. So sit back, relax, and enjoy the show."

"You're a fiend, a devil," Clay fumed. "I never wanted

this. You know that!"

Abner shrugged. "It's what you get for compromising. If you'd remained pure and untainted like your dear friends here, you would have the privilege of soon becoming a martyr." He twiddled the fingers of his left hand in a fluttery motion. "You'd be strumming a harp up in heaven before this night is done."

At last, once the hole was large enough to fit me sufficiently, Abner ordered me to stop digging. "Drop the shovel."

I did.

"Now lie down in the hole."

By this time I was so weak and trembly, I couldn't help melting down into the trench, as if it were a warm soft bed, instead of a cold hard grave from which I'd never rise. *But I will rise,* soothed my mind. *"I believe in . . . the resurrection of the body, and life everlasting."* I crossed my hands over my heart and closed my eyes.

"Okay, kid, your turn. Dig yourself a nice grave, or I shoot your sister between the eyes."

I kept my eyes closed, not wanting to peer up and have my last view of this world be Abner's wicked face. Calmly, my mind danced over my life, my relatively short eighteen years, and I prayed for forgiveness for all the times—so glaringly clear now—that I had done my will over God's.

I listened to the rhythmic *sluice, sluice* of the shovel, the *patter, patter* of loose dirt until, all too soon, Abner said, "That'll do, boy. Now lie down and make yourself comfy. You're going to be in there for a long time."

Max cursed. "You're nothing but a coward. Let my sister go. She doesn't have to die, too. You don't need her. She never should have been a part of any of this."

"But she is; she's a Perigard," Abner said mockingly. Changing to a brutal tone, he commanded, "Now do as I say and lie down."

"You'll burn in hell," Max continued. "You'll burn in—"

Whack. My eyes flew open just in time to see Max fall into his gaping grave. The position of Abner's gun hand told me he'd cracked Max on the head. *I'll never hear Max's voice again,* I realized, *not in this world.*

Abner's sparking eyes turned to me, and I shrank back down in my grave. He stood above me, and I saw his free hand produce the switchblade knife. I heard him stalk over to Clay. "Here's where you prove yourself, boy. I'm cutting you free so you can finish this job."

As I was about to leap up and dash for the steps, Abner returned to his strategic location at the base of the stairs. From my low position, I could just see his upper half, but he loomed larger than ever.

"That's right, Clay. Start with the girl. As her husband, it's your duty to bury her."

"No, it's my duty to save her."

"Pick up the shovel and bury her," Abner said smoothly. "Otherwise, you're next." He ran a finger over the barrel of his pistol. "I'll kill you. Don't think I won't. Don't think blood ties will protect you. I'll kill you just as surely as I killed dear ol' Dad all those years ago."

Clay gasped. "What?"

"You heard me. You may be stupid, but you're not deaf. I killed him, not you. And I had the pleasure of doing it on purpose. Well, not from the start, but it came to me quickly as I lit the holy cards. You see, as I stood there watching you praying while Dad lay stinking drunk, passed out on the bed, I wanted nothing more than to destroy those useless religious pieces. But first I waited for you to leave.

"You did blow out the vigil candle, by the way. I saw you do it. Then I went in and relit it. I'd had enough of it all: Enough of Dad, enough of the useless religion, and I grabbed those holy cards on the altar and burned them. It felt good." He heaved a deep breath. "Real good. When the cards dropped to the carpet and the fire got out of control, I didn't care.

"I watched it for a little while, watched it creep up the bed, catch on Dad's clothes. Then I went outside and waited. I assumed you were sulking in your tree fort, like usual. But

209

when you didn't come out to watch the smoke and flames, I discovered you weren't in there. That's when I ran back inside for you. I had no reason back then to want to kill you. You were just a pesky kid brother." Abner grinned. "It all worked out real well for something that wasn't even planned. No one suspected a hero of starting the fire. And we were all free of Dad's oppressive hand."

"And now you're worse than he ever was," Clay said coldly. "And all these years, you let me think I'd started the fire, you let me carry the guilt—"

"You wanted to carry it," Abner scoffed. "No one has to tote guilt around if they don't want to. You just toss it away. Guilt is for weak people. People who bow to God, and that's why I don't."

"But you still went to the seminary? It makes no sense."

"On the contrary. Old habits die hard. I was indoctrinated, still just a kid. Oh, I knew Dad deserved killing, but I actually felt some guilt. It's not surprising I fell back onto the crutch of religion. I wasn't as strong then as I am now. Besides, it beat working a job, and it didn't hurt that my piousness pleased Ma, either. She was always the most important person in my life."

"Until Lydia," Clay said. "But you never really loved her either, did you? You couldn't have. A monster like you could only love yourself."

Abner's nostrils flared. "Watch your tongue. You know nothing about me and Lydia. Nothing."

"Why don't you tell me then." Clay came into view, skirting the edge of my grave with care. "Starting with why you killed her."

A tempest brewed in Abner's eyes. Lightning flashed. Thunder boomed from his throat. "I did not kill her. It was all Perigard's fault! If he hadn't fired me, I never would have gone to the bar, never would have had those drinks, never would have fought with Lydia when I got home." His fists trembled. "She stormed out. It was a black night, icy roads. I was worried about her, like any good husband, especially with her in her condition—I was going to be a father—you never knew that, either—we'd only recently found out. I went looking for her in my truck—"

"So you were driving drunk," Clay said stiffly.

"No. I was aware, in complete control, until God interfered, sabotaging the road with ice, sending the truck sliding—slamming right into Lydia." Abner shook his head, his bloodshot eyes unreadable. "It was too dark. I never saw her walking on the shoulder of the road. Didn't see her till the headlights hit, and then—it was too late."

"You killed her," Clay concluded, his chin jutting defiantly. I noticed that he had the shovel in his hands. When had he picked it up? "What I want to know is how you got away with it."

"It was late, an isolated road . . ." Abner mumbled, before snapping, "I didn't kill her! It was Perigard. Perigard, and God."

"Your mind is warped," Clay said, "and so is your conscience. You really have thrown away your guilt, convinced yourself you weren't at fault by blaming others, blaming God. But look at the price you pay. You reek of evil and death." Clay's expression radiated disgust. "Face the truth: You killed your wife."

"I didn't," Abner repeated, his face clearly blanching, despite the shadows.

"Oh yeah?" Clay indicated the ground. "Then why are these two graves spaced apart like this? There's room between them for another grave. A grave, and a body. If I dig here, I'll find her bones, won't I?" With that, he thrust the shovel into the ground.

With a beastly cry, Abner leaped at him. "Don't you dare desecrate her grave!" He yanked the shovel from Clay's grasp and shook it in his face with rage. "Yes, I took her back here to bury her. She's my wife; I had the right. No one else cared. She had no other family."

Realizing Abner's concentration was all on Clay, I sat up carefully.

211

"This is where we had our honeymoon, and she loved it here. But she won't rest in peace until we get revenge!" Suddenly Abner swung his gun at me, and I leaped from the grave as he squeezed the trigger. A bullet zinged past my ear. Clay landed a well-aimed punch at Abner's temple, and the monster reeled, but didn't fall. He lurched forward and cuffed Clay's jaw.

While the brothers grappled for the gun, I plunged to Max's side, tugged at his arm, and patted his face frantically. "Wake up, Max, wake up!" He stirred and groaned, put a hand to his head, and sat up.

"What's going on?" He blinked dazedly at the brothers, scuffling and wrestling wildly, kicking dirt onto us.

"This is our chance," I hissed. "Come on!"

There were too many of us for Abner to keep track of and gain control of. His mistake had been in having us all unrestrained in the same room. As I tugged Max from his trench, I saw Clay seize the gun. But the next second, Abner knocked it from his grasp, and it fell, skittering away, lost in shadows. Abner crashed a fist into Clay's face, and he fell backward. I turned and ran toward the stairs, pushing groggy Max as I went.

"Not so fast." Abner grabbed for me. I swerved and darted, zipping randomly, avoiding his fatal grip, yet glad I was distracting him from Max. Maybe Max would make it out of the cellar.

As I rounded the perimeter of the room, I saw the hole Max and I had dug through the cellar wall. At the same time, my foot struck something—the gun—kicking it into my empty grave. No chance at reaching the weapon before Abner caught me, I dove through the hole in the wall. Abner roared and lunged for me, seizing my boot, but I kicked and pulled free. While he bellowed behind me, I assured myself that the hole was too small for him. Indeed, when he tried to follow, he became wedged in the tight earthen passage. Seething, he clawed at the dirt with his talon fingers. I backed away and prayed Max had made it up the stairs.

I had no exit from this prison, but at least I could stay free of Abner's clutches. I gulped. Unless he dug his way in. But that would take time. Time for Max to get help.

I put my hand to my face. The stench in our old prison was overwhelming, and I realized how close I was to the waste bucket. Familiar with its location in the dark corner, I hoisted the bucket easily. Then I turned and hurled the contents in Abner's face.

Spitting and spewing muck and profanity, his rage spiked, and he twisted himself free of the hole. Needing to see what was happening, I crouched down from a distance and saw him heading for my grave. For the gun. My heart hammered. He'd return to the hole and shoot at me like a caged animal. Yes, I could dodge, press myself against the walls, but for how long? And what if a bullet ricocheted? *Dirt walls,* I comforted myself. *That can't happen. Can it?*

Maybe he wouldn't come after me, maybe he'd go after Max. But that would be even worse.

Where was Clay? If Abner had knocked him out, why didn't I see him lying on the ground somewhere?

Suddenly, I did see him. But he wasn't lying on the ground. Shovel in hand, he crept up behind Abner, who was kneeling at the edge of the grave, reaching down to pick up the gun. Clay hoisted the shovel and slammed Abner on the back of the head. The strong *thwack* resounded through the cellar and oscillated into my hole. I watched Abner topple, like a felled tree, into the grave.

Dropping the shovel, Clay turned to me. "Come on, I don't know how long he'll be down."

I clambered into the passage, nasty now with leftover waste, but I barely cringed. Clay reached for my hands and tugged me through so I popped out into the cellar like a cork from a bottle. "We should get the gun," I said breathlessly.

Clay shook his head. "Can't. He fell on top of it."

As I hesitated, he pulled me to the stairs. "Let's get out of here!" We raced up the steps, knocking the lantern over as we went. I heard it clatter down the steps behind us.

As I emerged from the trap door, a figure lunged toward me. A knife-blade flashed, and I shrieked.

A hand clapped my shoulder. "Chill, Char. It's only me."

"Max?" My knees trembled. "You should be out of here by now. Gone for help."

"You think I'd leave you?" He lifted the knife. "I was just getting this." He made as if to move past me, and came face-to-face with Clay.

"You don't need that anymore," Clay said, eyeing the blade. "I bashed him with the shovel. He's out cold."

"Then I'll finish him off."

Clay met his gaze. "You can go back down there if you want, but we're getting out of here."

I nodded. I wanted to get far away from Abner and this cabin, but I wanted Max with me. My eyes snagged on the sharp blade, my mind envisioning blood. No matter how much Abner deserved it, I couldn't fathom returning to the cellar and carrying out such a horrible task. "Max, come with us."

He hesitated, and I took his arm. "Please. Don't make yourself do that—"

Our debate was cut short, because at that moment we heard an unearthly groan rise up from the depths of the cellar. Our eyes flew wide as we realized Abner was already awake. We raced for the front door.

My rapid footsteps matched the pace of my heart as I bolted from the cabin and hurtled down the driveway with Max and Clay right behind me.

As we fled, my ears pricked. All too soon, I detected a sound behind us like a cabin door crashing open. *Dear God, no.*

Shots pierced the night.

"Go ahead, run, you fools," Abner thundered. "I'll hunt you down and skin you alive!"

A few more shots whizzed past, then eerie silence settled around us, although our feet pattered madly and air whooshed past my ears.

Was Abner following us? Would we run till we fell, exhausted, into his clutches? And where were we even trying to run to?

As if in answer, Clay yelled, "Head for the lake!"

Yes, the lake. I felt a twinge of hope. Clay fished on the lake. He knew it well. He would know where the other houses or cabins were, which ones would contain people. People who could help us. People with bolts on their doors and phones to call the police.

We ran along the edge of the narrow road, camouflaged by tree shadows. Any trees that weren't pines were skeleton hands, reaching up with bony black fingers to snatch the moon from the sky. My heart raced like one of Grandfather's model trains, pumping with incredible power despite my small size.

Where did my energy come from? It certainly didn't come from food or water. Sprinting down the snowy road, I became a fleet-footed deer. A hunted deer. That's when I knew where the energy came from: Fear. I had looked into the eyes of evil and only narrowly escaped. Thanks to Clay. I glanced at him, jogging beside me, then turned my attention to Max.

Can he make it? My heart squeezed. He was panting, barely keeping up, and he began to fall behind, clearly in pain. I slowed slightly. My boots soon became bricks strapped to my feet, and the swift deer image vanished from my mind. Several times I tripped and skidded and almost pitched head over heels.

Just as we reached the ice, I heard a sputter and a roar behind us. Distant at first, but the sound grew as if an avalanche was approaching. Legs still pumping, I chanced a glance back, and my alarm increased exponentially.

A truck growled with rage as it tore around a bend.

Abner's truck.

He's going to run us down.

Chapter Twenty

Snorting with wicked glee, the truck pursued us onto the ice. Popping and pinging sounds pierced the air as the ice protested the weight. Headlights hit, exposing us like specimens under a microscope. I saw my shadow, a contorted black image of myself, running before me, yet bound to me. *Even my shadow can't escape.* My mind laughed sickly.

Any moment now, heavy tires would grind my flesh and bones into the ice. My heart beat itself into my throat, and I couldn't swallow.

My eyes gazed desperately ahead and swept the tree-shrouded shoreline. *So far to go yet. No shelter to dive for. Just this wide expanse of ice.*

Behind us, the mad zooming roar became deafening. The metal monster would be on top of us in seconds. As if realizing this simultaneously, we fanned out. This way, at least only one of us could be hit at a time. Maybe one of us would even escape. Hearing the raging increase in motor volume behind me, I realized that I would not be the one to escape.

I would be the first victim.

Somehow, I forced myself to run faster. At the same time, I knew how futile it was to think I could out-race a chariot from hell.

It will be over soon. He can crush me and kill me, but at least he can't drag me down with him to hell.

As if I wasn't already startled out of my wits, an ear-shattering *crack* startled me further, making me turn, despite myself. I was just in time to see the front of the fierce truck plunge through the ice and splash violently into the lake. The back tires spun uselessly on the remaining ice, spitting snow.

The glare of the headlights now gone, I saw nothing but blue, black, and purple blended with shadows.

Then the rest of the truck shifted, slid, and dove into the dark watery abyss.

Taking Abner with it.

Instead of relief, fear and urgency still tugged at me, and I ran.

Cracking noises followed me, and even as I continued to move my legs, I realized I was not running. I was falling. I flailed my arms for balance, but only lost it more. The ground shifted beneath me. Even as I thought, *But it's not ground, it's ice!,* I tottered, slipped, hit the ice, and kept on falling.

Water! I felt myself being sucked into the frigid depths of the lake. I grappled for the edges of the broken ice, but only succeeded in splashing myself. Freezing droplets stung my face like splinters of glass.

My heavy clothes weighed me down, but I treaded water ferociously while gulping nasty mouthfuls. My teeth chattered so hard, I thought they would break. My voice froze and I couldn't scream. The truck had been too close to me when it broke the ice, and the cracking must have spidered outward. Abner was still trying to get me.

Even now, I heard his wretched voice calling out.

I'm delirious.

But no, my head bobbed above water, and Abner's voice carried through the air, a yell—not vengeful, but fearful. "Clay! Clay, help me!"

Between my up-and-down dance in my patch of ice water, I caught sight of Abner's head, yards away, bobbing like a rotten apple.

Somehow, he had made it out of the truck. I was vaguely impressed. *He really must have a deal with the Devil. But will Satan save him?* My head dunked into water, choking me. *I should be worrying about myself.* Deathly cold, I coughed and sputtered. *Christ, save me.*

Through my watery struggle, I saw Abner wrestling for a hold on the ice, but he couldn't pull himself up. "Clay!"

Glub, glub, lake water filled my mouth and ears. I thrashed my arms and legs and bounced back up. Again, I heard Abner.

"Clay, brother! Don't let me die!"

Glub, glub.

"Brother, I'm begging you!"

Glub, glub.

"Have mercy!"

My legs kicked, and the effort was so feeble, I assumed this would be my last moment above water. I caught sight of someone on the ice, carrying something like a long stick, running for the wreckage, just before my head sank underwater. *Clay, you've gotta be kidding . . . still trying to save your brother . . .*

I was barely aware of my consciousness shimmering, drifting away, and I had the shadowy impression my body, too, would simply drift away into an unknown, watery grave. Someday my bones would wash ashore and some vacationing child would find them. I was too numb to panic at the idea. Instead, I thought wearily that it was too bad that the last thing I had to hear in this world was Abner's voice.

But the last person I had seen was Clay. Somehow, I didn't regret that, and I began to pray that he wouldn't fall into the water when he tried saving his brother. But the ability to think slipped away from me. My legs and arms slipped away from me, too. And my heart . . . my heart didn't seem to be beating anymore. Maybe I was already dead . . .

—————

Something poked me in the cheek. A slightly uncomfortable sensation, but it made me realize that I had a cheek. And a head. Arms. And legs. But I couldn't breathe. My lungs burned, bursting for air. I struggled upward, flailing toward a quivering light.

I broke through water, gasping and sputtering, buoyed up only a moment before sinking.

"Char! Grab the stick! Grab it!"

The urgent voice, so close, jolted me, forcing my legs into

movement. A glimmer of awareness returned. Clay stood on solid ice, several feet from me, holding out a branch. I grappled for it with my numb, wet, gloved hands. Useless hands. *I can't. I can't hold on.*

"Max, she can't grab it. I've got to get it farther out. Hold my legs." Suddenly the branch dove under the water, bumping my body. "Put your arms over it!"

My arms?

"Char, you can do it!" Max's voice.

I tried. I willed my muscles to be muscles, instead of these heavy slabs of useless meat. My arms slid over the branch, and I curled myself against it. The stick supported me, and suddenly, I was no longer sinking.

In fact, I was moving, gliding through the water. Chunks of ice parted before me, and I was riding a water chariot under the moonlight. Riding toward my rescuers, glowing in the night. One reached out and hauled me from the water. I almost managed to say, "Thank you," before I sighed and slipped away.

Like shards of ice, noises slid past me until one voice struck with such force it shattered me out of my delirium. "Char! Fight it! You've got to wake up!"

I sputtered ice water and opened my stiff eyelids to see Clay and Max kneeling beside me. My head swirled. Which one had spoken? Which one was speaking now?

"You've got to keep moving. We've got to get out of here."

Out. Yes. We're always trying to escape something. The cellar. Abner. Death. I shivered. No, I'd been shivering all along. When was the last time I hadn't shivered? My body knew nothing but this constant trembling.

I felt myself being hoisted by Max on one side, Clay on the other. They wanted me to walk, but I couldn't feel my legs. The water that coated me was turning to ice, glazing me with a glassy shell.

My eyes felt frosty, like little snowballs. But they could see, for a moment. They saw what was left of the wreckage, the liquid lake within the solid lake, the fragmented ice floating like flat, desolate islands. The cracking turmoil had settled into eerie silence, as if this lake had never known such things as vehicles. As if the terror had never happened. The truck was nowhere to be seen. Neither was Abner.

My mind spinning, I tried to speak, but nothing intelligible came out. I had so many questions, but . . .

Cold, so cold.

If I could just move . . . I was wobbling, stumbling. My heart was fluttering, my breathing rapid, but not sufficient.

Voices . . .

And then, silence.

The smashing sound shocked me, and I flinched, my frozen eyelids ripping open. My confused brain vaguely registered a dark door, a broken pane of glass, the door opening . . . more darkness.

I was moving into it, into the darkness. Shapes. I heard sounds from a distance, as if my ears were stuffed with snow. How was my body moving when I couldn't feel my legs?

At last, a slim relief as I felt myself sink onto something soft. Sleep would be nice.

I jolted, cried out as bright light hit me. I blinked. Blinked again. Shifting images, a figure in white and blue. *Mother of God . . . help me.*

Voices, gentle but urgent, trying to reach me. I shook, shaking the clogging cold from my ears. *Clickety clack, clickety clack.* The clicking in my brain, my head . . . my teeth chattering. Something heavy and dry settled over me, a huge mantle of blue, covering my shoulders, my body.

Then I heard the muffled voice, the urgency in it. "Char, use the towel. You need to get out of those wet clothes. Now."

I clutched at the towel with clumsy fingers. Threads of sense wove their way into my mind, into my limbs. I moved awkwardly under the giant towel, plucking and peeling off the stiff wet layers, swaddling myself in the fluffy dryness. I heaved air into my lungs and coughed.

Finally settling, I blinked until I realized I was sitting on a quilted bed in a small room. My tongue bumped around in my mouth like a crazy creature in a cage. At last I managed to get out a word. "Max . . ."

He looked up from where he knelt, wrapping a fuzzy green towel around my bare feet. He gave a lopsided smile. "You're gonna be all right, Char."

I gripped my blue towel closer, smelled an unfamiliar fabric softener. "Where am I?"

He shook his head. "Not exactly sure. Some cottage on the lake. No one's here. We had to break in to get you dry and warm before . . ." He stood abruptly and dropped another towel on my head. "How do you feel?"

"Some numbness. But I'm fine." Slowly, I rubbed the towel against my thawing hair. "What happened?"

His eyes were serious. "You went through the ice. We pulled you out just in time."

We. I looked around and truly took in my surroundings: A single spindly lamp on the bedside table cast light onto the cream walls, the narrow closet, the closed door, the squat pine dresser with a Virgin Mary statue standing on a crocheted doily. And, of course, I saw Max. I twisted a corner of towel in my fingers. Max, but no Clay.

No Abner.

But . . . I remembered him calling, calling out for Clay. And Clay had heard him, had mercy on him, and was going to save him. I saw him running . . .

Realization washed over me in a warm wave. *He came running to save me.* Suddenly, panic gripped me, my blood pumping. *Where is he now? Where's Clay?*

Just then, there was a knock on the bedroom door. Max opened it, and Clay stepped into the room holding a steaming red mug. I stared at him, relief raw in my chest. He gave me a small smile while his injured face strained to hide fatigue, pain, and sorrow. Chilled as my eyes were, warm tears leaked from them. As warmth wound around my heart and soul, I felt as though ice inside of me was melting, producing the tears. And from there, prickly sensation began to return to my limbs.

"Here, drink this, Char," Clay urged gently, unaware of the thoughts pounding through my head as he nudged the mug into my hands.

I never said you could call me Char. But I don't mind.

His hand lingered, warm on my cold one, helping me lift the mug.

I took a small sip. Hot chocolate slid down my throat and pooled warmly in my stomach. Max and Clay both watched me with intense concern. My chapped lips cracked into a smile, and I saw relief settle in their eyes.

Overcome, I bowed my head, thinking, *I'm alive.* And in the perfect position to thank God, if only my hands would figure out how to fold themselves. Steam billowed warm and moist into my face. I sent a feeble prayer heavenward, but knew there was someone else I needed to thank, someone whom God had arranged to be the hand that pulled me from the water and saved me from drowning.

"Thank you," I said, turning to Clay, "thank you for saving me."

The words seemed to distress him, and his hand fell away from mine. "Don't thank me for doing what I should have done from the start. And it only worked this time because I had Max's help."

"We made a good team," Max conceded.

When I thanked him as well, Max gave a nod and something like a grunt as he moved to the dresser and began opening drawers. He soon turned to me with a shapeless green sweater, gray sweatpants, and wool socks. "Here, put these on." He dropped them beside me on the bed. "Let us know when you're done." Then Max and Clay filed out of the room and closed the door.

I set the mug down and sucked in a quivery breath before shedding the towel and pulling on the clothes. Relieved that the large sweatpants had drawstrings, I tugged them and tied them securely. Too long, the pants pooled at my ankles. I heard Max and Clay talking in the other room, their voices muffled, but as soon as I opened the squeaky door, they both stopped speaking. They hurried to my side and guided me onto a sofa draped with a brown afghan.

The broken windowpane in the front door leaked swooshes of cold air into the cottage. Through it, I thought I caught the shadowed shapes of pines, and I imagined the lake lurking out there. I pictured how Max and Clay had guided me away from the disaster area, across crusty blue-white snow to this cottage. If I looked outside, I would see our footprints in the moonlight. But I didn't look. Didn't need to. I was content right where I was.

Footprints only show where we've been—I heaved a deep breath and turned my eyes to Max and Clay, a flutter in my breast—*not where we're going.*

"We're finally free," I said with wonder.

They remained standing beside me, watching me, both so unusually silent and still. Why wouldn't they meet my eyes? I followed their shifting gazes to a black telephone. "Does it work?" I asked.

"Time to find out."

Confused by Clay's clipped tone and the frown that creased his brow, I glanced questioningly at Max, who put a detaining arm on Clay's shoulder.

"We're even, man," Max said gruffly. "You came through in the end. That's all we care about. So get out of here. Disappear."

I jumped up from the couch. "Max, what are you saying? Why would—" Then it hit me. *We're about to call the cops.* There would be a tirade of questions, reports, an investigation, and details would come out. There'd be no hiding who Clay was and what part he'd had in the kidnapping. Max and I might pardon him, but others wouldn't. The law would see the facts.

The law would prosecute.

"Max is right," I said softly. "You need to go. You can't risk—"

Clay shook his head. "I'm not running." He set his jaw firmly. "I'm going to face this."

"But they'll take you to jail—they'll lock you up—"

"I'll survive."

"But you could be free."

"No, Char." He looked me in the eye. "Not really free. Not by running, not by hiding."

"It wouldn't be wrong," I almost sobbed, surprised at the intensity of my desperation. "You could move far away and no one would ever know—"

"But it wouldn't be right," he said, adding, "and I would know."

"But—"

"He's made up his mind, Char." Max took my arm and tugged gently. "Respect the man's decision."

Biting my tongue, I halted my words.

Clay seized the phone while anxiety ate at my empty insides. Maybe the phone wouldn't work. Maybe we would have just a little more time—

He started dialing.

I swallowed and made my way past a cluttered knickknack table. A brass-framed mirror caught my eye and I shrank from my appearance. Shapeless baggy clothes. Bedraggled stringy hair, red eyes underscored with hollows, and pasty, blighted skin. *The cops won't even recognize us.*

"My name's Clayton Morrow. I need to report . . ."

I ducked into the bedroom, not wanting to hear the rest. The towels lay crumpled in a pile on the floor, beside my wet clothes. Crouching on my heels, I gathered the towels in my arms and squeezed them against my chest, buried my face. I needed to think about something else, anything else. But my thoughts had been filled with darkness for so long now, I didn't know how to find the light.

Lifting my head, my gaze swooped around the simple room, and I wondered who lived here, what kind of people, and what they would think when they found out about our intrusion.

My eyes fell on the Virgin Mary statue. She held Baby Jesus in her arms, so young and chubby, unscathed by the horrors that were to come. But He knew they would come, and so did His Mother. And yet . . . they both smiled.

Shivering again, I looked away, down at my soggy discarded clothes. I began folding and stacking them. My fingers touched something hard and cold; it was the rosary dangling from my jeans pocket. Strange to think that it had made it through the whole ordeal with me. I pulled it free and dropped the beads into my palm, closing my fingers around them.

I retrieved my mug from the nightstand and carried it into the narrow kitchen. I added a splash of hot chocolate from the saucepan to warm my drink. The fresh heat burned my branded palm, and I quickly adjusted my hold on the mug so that only my fingers clutched the handle. My body told me to drink, but I couldn't just yet. I stared out into the tiny living room—at Max sitting on the sofa and Clay hanging up the phone—and I felt like I was waiting for a verdict.

"They're on their way," Clay said.

Max nodded.

I said nothing.

Clay's hand still lingered over the phone. At last he picked it up again. "I'd better call my ma. I'd rather break the news to her than have her find out some other way."

I moved to sit next to Max on the sofa. Clay's conversation this time was too quiet to hear, not that I wanted to. His back was to us, so we couldn't even read his expression. But I couldn't help wondering how his mother was reacting. She was already very sick, and now she was learning that one son was dead as a result of criminal activity, and her only other son was turning himself into the cops for his part in that activity. It seemed too cruel of a burden to dump onto a dying woman.

When Clay returned, I whispered, "How did it go?"

He sank down beside me, shaking his head. "She's praying,"

he said wryly.

We were all silent. A clock ticked.

"There's still time," I attempted. "You could still go."

Clay shook his head. "I can't. Someday I hope you'll understand."

I stared into the murky hot chocolate. *Why is he making this worse than it has to be? We should all be so happy right now. We could all be going home.* But even if Clay took our advice and left, how could he go home? The cops would find him, take him away. His only chance was to disappear, and that would mean never seeing his mother again. She probably didn't have much time left. I thought about me and Max, the rich home we would be returning to, and sighed.

Still, we are free. This is what we wanted, what we prayed for. I noticed the spindly hands of a mantle clock pointing to 1 a.m. *A new day,* I realized. *A Sunday.*

I squeezed the rosary in my fist, and the crucifix poked my palm. I flinched and let the beads trickle out between my fingers. There was nothing left to do now but wait.

Wait, and pray.

Clay's mom has the right idea.

I bowed my head, crossed myself, and murmured a plea for us all. Looking up, I caught Clay's eyes. They seemed to question me: *Praying again?*

I spoke over the ache in my throat. "Someday I hope you'll understand."

Chapter Twenty-One

"Just look at this!" thundered Grandfather several mornings later as Max and I sat at our dining room table working trigonometry problems. I jumped slightly, making the large New Year's champagne glass centerpiece wobble as Grandfather appeared like an angry apparition between our chairs. I hadn't heard him enter the house.

At the commotion, I saw Joy and Gwen peek in from the hall. Both their mouths formed little "Os." I imagined the cook and maids crowding near the kitchen door to eavesdrop.

But my attention was redirected as three newspapers slapped on top of my notebook, textbook, and calculator. "What do you have to say about this?" Grandfather demanded.

Fanning out the skewed papers, I read the varied head-lines:

Grandkids Kidnapped, Perigard Didn't Care.

Cold-hearted Grandfather Allowed Perigard Teens to be Tortured!

Perigard Too Greedy to Pay Ransom for Own Grand-children.

I pushed the papers away, not interested in reading the slanted accounts, and glanced up at Grandfather, whose taught, veiny neck poked turtle-like from his body. "Well?" he barked.

"Well what? We didn't write the articles." I picked up my pencil and returned to my notebook.

"Don't get smart with me. You've obviously been talking to reporters."

"No, we haven't. You know we've barely left the house since we got back." From the tiny cottage tucked among the pines, the police had taken us to the nearest hospital, where we were treated. Clay, we heard, had been treated also, then taken into custody. Max and I spent weary hours answering police questions, then returned home to crash. Other than meeting with Father Selton for much needed confession and Holy Communion, we ate and slept and tried to avoid answering more questions. We hadn't felt up to returning to school yet, so we were completing assignments at home and online for now. The principal had been understanding.

Grandfather was not.

I gave the newspapers another shove. "However they got their information, it wasn't from us."

"It's all vicious lies," Grandfather said. "I did what I could. It's not my fault the police are imbeciles. And now my company stock is taking a nose dive. I may never recover the losses!" Again, as he had when he'd first seen us at the hospital, Grandfather sputtered with anger. "You two have caused a blasted load of trouble."

My tone prickled. "It wasn't exactly a holiday for us, either."

Grandfather smacked a fist on the table. The champagne centerpiece teetered menacingly, sending curly metallic blue strands shivering. "I know that! And that's why retribution must be paid. The dead one's the lucky one; the other one will face my wrath." He rubbed his hands together. "That scum's going to face so many charges, he'll wish he never heard the name Perigard."

I dropped my pencil. "We told you we don't want him prosecuted."

"Nonsense. You were delirious and sleep-deprived when you said that. Surely now that you've had time to recover, you've come to your senses." His eyes challenged us to deny it.

Max, surprisingly silent and controlled thus far, spoke. "We meant what we said. We're not changing our minds. Clay saved Char's life, and we can't ignore that."

"But you'll ignore everything he did to me—to us?" Grandfather blustered. "Don't be a fool. He knew he was a goner, and letting her die wouldn't help his case. He just wanted to win your sympathies to save his own skin. But you've already given your statements to the police about what happened. You can't change that, and the facts go against the scumbag. I'll see that he gets life in prison. The worst prison there is."

"You can try," Max said evenly, "but you won't have our support."

Grandfather grabbed the newspapers, crumpled them, and waved the wads in our faces. "You'll do as I say, and that's final."

I opened my mouth, and he almost stuffed the paper into it.

"You'll do as I say," he repeated, "or you can say goodbye to your rich, cushy life. If you defend that worthless criminal over your own flesh and blood, I'll disinherit the both of you—and you'll be out on the street."

His head whipped around to face Joy and Gwen, who had crept into the room but stood mutely near the china cabinet. "I know two very perfect candidates who would be more than grateful to receive your inheritance. Don't think you'll be missed. These two never give me trouble. They understand the value of money more than you two ever have. What do you think of that? Who's it going to be, the criminal, or me? Choose wisely." The cold intensity of Grandfather's bulging, bloodshot eyes reminded me of Abner.

Steadying my nerves, I stood. "I choose to do what's right."

Max rose as well and put an arm on my shoulder. "I'm with her."

"You ungrateful, spoiled brats. All these years I've supported you, and this is the thanks I get?" Grandfather's mustache quivered. "Get out. Get out now." He pointed to the door. "The newspapers want to write garbage about me? Fine, let them rave about this. 'Grandfather Disinherits Worthless Grandkids.' See if I care!"

As I reached for the math textbook, Grandfather's hand

slapped down on it. "Nothing! If you leave, you'll take nothing! No clothing, no books, and certainly not the new Lexus. I own it all."

I nodded. "But you don't own us." I crossed to the front hall and reached for my coat.

Grandfather scuttled after me and snatched the coat away. "I said nothing! That means no coats. If you don't change your mind and support me in prosecuting this case, you can leave now and freeze to death, for all I care. It's no worse than what would have happened if you'd stayed with your precious kidnapper."

As I opened the door and exited into a blast of arctic air, he shouted spitefully, "This also means you'll get no help for your hideous wounds, no plastic surgery. That means no prosthetic toe, Max. And Charlene—no skin graft."

"We never asked for that," Max said, joining me on the porch.

"Then you'd better get used to your ugly hand, Charlene," Grandfather sneered.

I glanced at the cross on my palm. "It's not ugly."

Max and I walked down the drive and out the gate, letting it slam shut behind us with a final, freeing clang.

———

We should have taken a stand together and left Grandfather a long time ago, I thought as Max and I walked down the sidewalk. For all the old man's raging and threatening, it hadn't been difficult at all. Especially not with Max standing strong beside me. His arm looped around me, supporting and warm, and I relied on him to lead the way.

And I actually felt sorry for Joy and Gwen. *Grandfather's focus will be all on them now.*

As we continued walking, I could tell Max had a destination in mind. A shelter? A friend's house? A bus station? It didn't matter. *We'll be okay. We're in this together.*

We ended up at Wayne's house, where the family had just returned home from vacation. Upon hearing our story and learning that Grandfather had kicked us out, they insisted we stay with them. Max shared Wayne's room, and I was given a small room in the rear of the house, near the laundry—it was really more of a closet than anything, but I didn't complain. It had just enough room for a small air mattress. Shelves of books lined the walls, and I enjoyed perusing the titles. When I discovered a worn copy of *Gone with the Wind*, I settled down with it right away.

Wayne's sisters, ages fourteen and fifteen, occupied a bedroom on the other side of my room and liked to play country music at all hours. The sad songs wailed through the wall, and sometimes the tunes reminded me of Clay. When that happened, I put a pillow over my head. I didn't like thinking about him sitting in a jail cell somewhere, alone. Or worse, not alone.

The case was scheduled to go to trial in May, but was delayed until late August to give the defense more time to prepare. Meanwhile, Max and I continued with life. We returned to school. Max was more popular than ever, and I received some attention as well, but I knew it was because of the kidnapping, and I had no desire to talk about the experience.

Detective Donnelly kept us posted with any details worth knowing. The cottage we had sheltered in belonged to a nice retired couple who lived in the city but liked to come up every couple of weeks for peace and quiet. Abner's body was retrieved from the lake by divers. Investigation unearthed a dead body with remnants of a wedding dress in the cabin's cellar. The body was identified as Lydia Morrow, Abner's wife. She had been three months pregnant when killed by trauma wounds—wounds, they deduced, that had resulted from being hit by a vehicle.

Tight-lipped as Max and I were about our ordeal, publicity still found us. Job offers rolled in, invitations to appear on talk shows, "fan" letters, even a few proposals of marriage. It was crazy, and I couldn't wait for it to all subside. But I supposed there'd be no chance of that happening till after Clay's trial.

Of course, Max and I didn't want to be a burden to Wayne's family, so we did take jobs. We selected low-profile ones. I worked in the local college library, and Max worked at a sporting goods store. It would take time for us to save enough money to be able to move out into our own place.

In the meantime, I helped Wayne's mom with grocery shopping, cleaning, and—worst of all—laundry. It was a very strange, unnerving feeling, reaching into the dryer for a load of clean clothes. But I made myself do it, over and over.

Graduation came, and I wasn't surprised that Grandfather didn't show up. He had been strictly true to his word, and we hadn't seen him since "That Day," as I called it. But when Max and I descended the stage with our diplomas, I was surprised to see a familiar face in the crowd: Joy, my stepmother. I had not seen her since "That Day," either. At school, Gwen avoided me.

I didn't really blame them. I knew that Grandfather had commanded them not to associate with us, and now as the sole heirs to his fortune, he had them in his complete control. Life back with Gwen, Joy, and Grandfather now seemed like another lifetime.

Diploma in hand, Max moved off to talk with some friends. A moment later, Joy approached me timidly, glancing over her shoulder. "I can't stay long," she said in a hushed tone, "but I have something I need to give you." She placed a dark wooden box in my hands. "I was saving this for your twenty-first birthday, but I thought you'd better have it now."

Curious, I lifted the golden latch and opened the box. My breath caught in my throat. A stunning assortment of jewelry rested on a bed of wine-colored velvet: A ruby pendant, a diamond cross necklace, a string of pink pearls, and a various rainbowed assortment of jeweled rings and winking silver and gold bracelets.

"Your grandfather would be furious if he knew I gave these to you." Joy tittered. "But they were your mother's, and they belong to you. They're very valuable. I thought that maybe you could sell some of them . . . get your own place.

It's no fun living in someone else's house." She gave me a light kiss on the cheek before flitting away.

I touched the pink pearls, admiring the smooth, creamy color. These were them, the pearls I remembered my father giving my mother so long ago, the pearls I had loved above all my mother's jewelry.

A memory I had long forgotten, returned to me, an image of my mother getting ready for a party. I watched her, leaning my knobby six-year-old elbows on her white frilly dressing table as she glided crimson lipstick onto her smile.

"Now all I need to do is choose a necklace, and I'll be ready to go," she said, opening a wooden jewelry box.

"Let me, let me!" I pleaded, bouncing on my heels. "Let me choose it, please?"

She laughed, her musical, piano-scale laugh. "Go ahead."

I plucked up the pink pearl necklace with no hesitation. "This one," I breathed.

She smiled. "A lovely choice. But pink pearls with a yellow dress?" She laughed again. "You have your father's fashion sense."

"It's so pretty!" I cried. "Please wear it, Mommy, please?"

"Of course," and she looped the strand around her neck as my dad strode in.

"A vision of beauty," he said, "the both of you," and he swooped us into a bear hug.

Now, closing the jewelry box, I hugged it to my chest. I couldn't have received a more wonderful graduation gift.

―――

When I brought Max to the doorway of my room and showed him the jewelry and told him my plan, he was delighted.

"That's awesome, Char. So's the timing. Now I can go and I won't have to worry about you being stuck here. You can get your own apartment and make it exactly the way you want it."

I backed up, almost stumbling over my air mattress. *My own apartment? I thought it was going to be* our *apartment.*

233

But something else he'd said was even more disturbing. "So you can *go*? What do you mean? Go where?"

He moistened his lips. "I didn't say anything earlier because I didn't think I could manage it, but now—this is perfect. Me and Wayne have been talking. We're finally done with high school—we want to hit the road and try making a go of our magic act. We really think we can do this. And now with all the publicity—well, it's bound to help. We might as well take advantage of this while we can."

"But what about college?"

"There'll be time for that later," he said dismissively. "You know this is what I've always wanted to do."

"And the trial, in August?" I added softly. He and I had met with the lawyers on both sides; they knew how we felt, yet they both wanted us on the stand.

"I'll be back for that."

What else could I say? "It sounds so impractical. What if you don't make enough money? And where will you sleep?"

"We'll rough it. That's half the fun. I've got some money saved, but you never know; we might make it really big. We won't know unless we try. I could buy us a house of our own." He grinned. "I could even get a new toe."

I nibbled at my lip.

"I need this, Char. Life's been too serious for too long. I need a break. A change."

I met his eyes. He read me, like he always could.

"You could come with me. Be our assistant or something. You need a change, too. Between here and your job at the library, you spend all your time cooped up with books. What do you say?"

I searched his eyes, then dropped my gaze. As he could read me, I could also read him, and I knew he didn't really want me to come. "No, but thanks for asking. This is your and Wayne's thing. I really don't want to tag along, sleeping in a crammed car, eating gas station food three times a day with a couple of belching guys. And besides, I happen to like my job. I like a calm, orderly life." I lifted my head and met his gaze, realizing the truth of my words. "We can't always be together. So you go be a traveling magician, and wow everyone." I forced a smile. *It'll be good for you to keep busy.* "Send me some postcards, and I'll hang them in my new apartment."

———

A month later, I tacked my first postcard from Max on the wall of Wayne's old bedroom. Ever since he and Max had left, his parents had insisted that I move into this larger room. I wasn't having much luck yet finding an apartment. It had torn my heart to part with any of the jewelry, a legacy from my mother, so I sold as little as I possibly could and searched for cheap places. The pink pearls, I would never sell.

Finally, I moved into a rundown mud-colored complex on the far side of town. Wayne's parents were not a fan of it and pleaded with me to stay with them. But I told them this was something I had to do.

The first thing I did when I moved in was stick Max's Grand Canyon postcard on my whirring fridge. Then I spent a weekend scouting Goodwill, Wal-Mart, and rummage sales for furniture bargains. I ended up with two mismatched oak chairs, a worn kitchen table with water rings, and a simple nightstand with a nicked drawer that tended to stick.

As I climbed into bed at night, I wondered how long it would take before this apartment felt like home. The nights were the worst.

Dear God, I prayed as I pulled a single bed sheet over my body, *keep the nightmares away.* It was really too warm for the sheet, especially without a window or fan in my room, but without it, I felt too exposed, too vulnerable. *As if the sheet would stop anyone or anything,* I chided myself.

The dreams came. And Abner starred in every one of them.

Around me, ice shattered, giving way to a watery black pit, from which Abner rose. He cackled fiendishly, his arms reaching from the water to grab me from my shaky little ice island. And the blackness was his skin, wrinkled, fire-burned, devil skin. "Cold, are you?" he snarled. "You won't be for long, not where I'm taking you."

A crash startled me awake. *That wasn't ice. It was glass breaking.* And it had come from somewhere in my apartment. I trembled in sweat.

There's no one here. No one but me.

The suspense finally drove me from bed. I snapped on a light and surveyed my surroundings. In such a small apartment, it didn't take me long to find the cause of the crash.

I let out my breath and stepped gingerly. The bathroom mirror had fallen and shattered on the yellowed tile floor. *That's all. Seven years bad luck.* I choked on a laugh. *Good thing I'm not superstitious.*

I swept up the mess and returned to bed, finally falling asleep with the light on. *Light keeps away darkness,* I told myself logically. *Darkness is evil. And evil is Abner.*

<hr>

Maybe I should have gone to counseling, I thought as I carried the Tupperware of chocolate chip cookies into the church basement after Sunday Mass, my head foggy with sleep deprivation. I'd been attending St. Paul's Catholic Church ever since I'd left Grandfather's, and I had thought that if I went to church, I shouldn't need counseling. Wasn't God supposed to be able to take care of all things? Turn to Him with our fears, and He would comfort and protect? He'd promised not to give us more than we could handle. So why were the nightmares getting worse? *I can't handle them, God.*

I set my bake sale contribution on the blue countertop, behind which a middle-aged lady with abundant brown hair smiled and thanked me.

A glass bottle of holy water, which I'd filled this morning from the church's reservoir, sat heavily in my purse. Now I needed a holy water font. I turned away from the fattening array of goodies and wove through the mingling parishioners to reach the shelves of "for sale" Catholic goods.

The selection was surprisingly large, and I ended up

choosing two fonts. But I didn't stop there. Seeing all the religious items, so holy and protective looking, a kind of fever hit me. *If I cram my apartment full of religious things,* I reasoned, *I'll feel as safe as I do in church.*

I picked pieces up like I was grocery shopping. In fact, I secured a plastic shopping bag from the bake sale and loaded it with my purchases: A Virgin Mary statue, a votive candle, another rosary and scapular, a Miraculous Medal, a crucifix, a Bible, a Sacred Heart picture, a Saint Michael holy card depicting the warrior angel conquering a scaly green devil dragon, and a book enticingly titled, *Why Must I Suffer?*

"Wow, you're really stocking up," came a male voice over my shoulder. "You starting your own church or something?"

I flushed and turned, the heavy bag straining from my hand. Maybe I had gotten a little carried away. But I'd be glad for it tonight.

A young man dressed in a well-fitting suit smiled at me. For a moment, I thought his hair had a premature gray streak, but it was only the light reflecting silver off his very shiny dark hair. "Since you're buying everything in sight, are you going to buy something from the bake sale, too?"

"Ben, you dummy!" called a small girl perched on a nearby table, her white stocking legs swinging, her blue skirt ruffling around her like giant flower petals. "She doesn't have to buy anything from the bake sale—she donated to it."

With a twinkle in his eye, Ben said, by way of introduction, "That's Lucy, my kid sister, the most precocious nine-year-old you'll ever have the unfortunate pleasure of meeting."

She grinned at me, showing a missing tooth, and held up a cellophane-covered paper plate. "Wanna buy some cookies? I made them. They're sugar fish."

Approaching the table, I saw that the cookies on the plate were indeed fish shapes sprinkled with golden sugar.

"I love fishing," she explained.

Ben winked at me. "Sorry to break it to you, Sis, but your cookies aren't the only fish in the bake sale sea. I've sampled

237

every cookie here, and I have to say that the chocolate chip cookies in that Tupperware on the counter are the very best."

I followed his pointing finger and couldn't help smiling. *He obviously knows I made them.*

"Ben," Lucy said, "you're such a pig. How do you not weigh a thousand pounds?" She shook her head at me. "I would have been able to sell *twice* this many cookies if my brother hadn't eaten half the batch last night."

"Still going on about that?" He flicked one of Lucy's pigtails. "I promised to take you fishing tomorrow, didn't I?"

Lucy's smile widened, but she turned to me. "What's your name?"

"Charlene." I never gave my last name unless absolutely necessary.

"Do you like fishing?"

I gave a small shrug. "I don't really know."

Lucy bounced the plate of cookies, probably breaking a few of them. "You should come with us. You'd love it!"

"Oh," I began awkwardly, "I don't—"

"Ben wants you to come," she said knowingly, "but he's afraid you'll say no."

I blushed and forced a light laugh.

"What did I tell you?" Ben nudged Lucy so hard, she almost fell off the table. "Precocious." He shrugged. "But she's right. I would like you to come. I know you don't know me, so it's no big deal if you say no. But if you come, I promise I won't make you put any worms on hooks."

"That's the best part," Lucy interjected.

Fishing. Worms on hooks.

"My dad brought us here a few times for fishing and hunting." Clay's words came unbidden to my mind. *"I remember this one time, when I was six, he locked me in the cellar overnight . . . because I didn't want to stick a worm on a hook."*

I felt my blushing color drain away. "Maybe some other time."

"Sure." Ben bounced right back. "Maybe you could hang

around after church sometime, give us a chance to get to know each other first."

I wasn't sure if I responded or not. I threaded my way through the crowd, clutching my purse and heavy plastic bag as I exited into the late June sunshine. A fresh warm breeze caressed me, clouds billowed in a blue sky, birds twirled and twittered. I gulped a breath and worked to steady my nerves.

Clay hated the cellar. And now he's in a cell. A jail cell.

What would it take for me to forget?

But I'm not meant to forget. The trial's coming up.

Walking home, I listened to the birds sing, but they were all songs about happiness, songs about freedom. I both anticipated and dreaded the trial. I wanted to see Clay and I didn't want to see him. I wanted to defend him from the stand, but I didn't want to relive the kidnapping. I wanted to know the verdict and I didn't want to know it.

It was like part of me was waiting in that cell with him.

Two more months to go.

Chapter Twenty-Two

*D*o you have a moment, dear? I'd like to talk to you."

I'd just stepped out of church, ready to make my customary getaway, when the matronly voice stopped me. I swallowed and turned to see the same plump, abundant-haired middle-aged lady who had taken my bake sale contribution a few weeks ago. Her dress was one huge splash of colorful flowers.

What could she possibly want? Had someone complained about my cookies?

"I'm Helen," she introduced herself with a smile, "and I'm on the Altar and Rosary Society here."

Maybe she wants me to join. Or maybe she's soliciting donations.

"Your name's Charlene Perigard, isn't it?"

Suddenly damp with perspiration, I backed into a shaded corner formed by shrubs and the stone church wall. "That's right," I admitted as I struggled with an irrational, gripping fear. I'd enjoyed my anonymous attendance here at Saint Paul's, and had hoped it could continue. But if this woman knew who I was, how many others knew? Now they would all stare at me funny and whisper about me.

"Please," Helen said, "don't look so distressed. That's exactly what we don't want."

We?

"I only wanted to tell you, on behalf of us all here at the parish, that our hearts go out to you and your brother, and if there's anything—anything at all that you need, any type of help, please let us know."

They know. They all know. Oddly, I felt humiliated, as if I'd been caught sinning. "How long have people known?"

"Oh, for quite some time, I would imagine."

Then why haven't I noticed anyone staring or whispering?

"But we don't want to bother you," she continued. "We only want to offer our support. You belong here with us, and we like to take care of our own. That's why we'd truly appreciate it if you would accept this little card and gift from us all."

She held out a blue envelope, and I took it hesitantly. I was glad she had brought it out in private and that I hadn't been called up to stand in front of the entire congregation or something.

Inside the envelope I found a religious "Thinking of you" card, signed with so many signatures, my mouth dropped open.

And then I saw the check.

My gaze flew to Helen. "I can't. I can't accept this."

"Of course you can." She beamed.

"But I barely even know anyone here. It wouldn't be right—"

"Of course it would. It's what God wants. Look, even Father Villateshire signed it and contributed. You don't want to throw this all back in our faces, now do you?" She chuckled.

Blinking, I shook my head and swallowed my pride. "But how could I ever thank everyone? I—"

"By accepting it, my dear. That's all we ask. Use it for anything you need. There are no strings attached . . . though we'd love to see you smile sometime." She winked. "God bless you." And she turned and strolled away before I could reply.

As I walked home thoughtfully, I passed a "for rent" sign outside of a pretty apartment that I'd long admired (and had tried not to covet) on my previous walks home. Now I stopped and studied the check in my hands. *It's possible now.*

The rays of sun shining down on me felt extra warm. I turned my face to them, soaked them up, an antidote to the chill that had lingered in my bones and soul for too long. Gratitude filled me. *Thank you, Jesus.*

And maybe now that I could move into a cheery place, the nightmares would stop.

—————

I awoke in my bed.

That was my first mistake.

Opening my eyes was the second.

If I had kept them closed, I wouldn't have seen the dark hulking figure across the room. The shadowy hood kept me from seeing his face, but I knew who it was: Abner.

He moved. Glided, really. Coming closer to the foot of my bed. I crossed myself, fumbling, using words and the sign of the cross as a holy shield. "*In the Name of the Father, and of the Son . . .*"

But Abner laughed and kept coming. When he reached the foot of my bed, a white apparition appeared beside him. It wasn't any form of heavenly help. On the contrary, it was another fearsome figure: A half-rotting woman in a tattered wedding gown. Horrors, I could even smell her. The brittle bones of her fingers crackled as she stretched them toward me.

My voice trembled. "*. . . be our protection against the wickedness and snares of the Devil . . .*"

Abner held a glowing, red-hot branding iron, moving it toward my face.

Praying didn't stop him.

So I stopped praying.

I jumped up and fled. I raced to my parents' room, expecting them to save me, but their bed was vacant. In fact, it hadn't even been slept in.

That's right, they aren't alive anymore.

How had I forgotten?

Next, I raced to Max's room, but he was snoring deeply and would not wake up no matter how hard I shook him. And still I heard the evil spirits coming for me, calling my name in ghastly tones.

Cornered, I hoisted my scapular and Miraculous Medal and held it toward them. "Begone Satan!" I screamed.

Then I awoke for real, but I was moaning in my bed, and the fear was not lessened by thinking it was only a dream. Because I was alone. In the dark. And I was convinced the nightmare was about to happen all over again.

I switched on a light and clutched my sweating head. Despite my lovely new apartment, the nightmares were becoming more real than reality. Would this be Abner's ultimate revenge, to haunt me the rest of my life, or till I went insane? Why would God allow such a thing?

I never should have moved out on my own. If only Max had stayed with me.

Max.

I picked up my phone and dialed his number with shaky fingers before looking at the clock. As his phone rang, I realized it was one in the morning. But the last I knew, he was in California, so the time zone difference would mean it was only eleven for him. He'd be awake.

"Hello?"

"Max, it's me."

"Char, hey."

I heard background noises, a thumping of music, people yelling. Probably a party.

"What's up?" he asked. "You okay?"

I clenched and unclenched my sweaty bed sheet. "I'm fine. Just wondering how you're doing."

"I'm great! The shows are going great. And listen to this— I was going to call you tomorrow to tell you—we just got the most awesome opportunity. We've been booked to open for David Copperfield in Las Vegas. Can you believe it? This is our big break! Man, I still think I'm dreaming. But it turns out a show featuring a magician who escaped from a maniacal killer is projected to be a big hit, go figure. We'll see. Say a prayer."

He talked on for a minute or two. I barely heard him. All the while I was thinking, *I'm not fine. I'm losing my mind. And you're my twin; you're supposed to read my mind.* I swallowed a laugh. My paranoia, combined with insomnia, was not a good combination.

"So . . ." he tapered off, "if there's nothing else, I'm gonna get going."

I nodded, caught myself, and whispered, "All right." I hesitated. "You'll be home in two weeks, right? For the trial?"

"Two weeks?" There was a pause.

"Max?" I prodded uneasily. "When does that Las Vegas show open?"

"The sixteenth."

My heart squeezed. "But that's the start of jury selection."

"Man, Char, I'm sorry. If there was any way around this, I'd be there—but I can't blow this chance. And Wayne's counting on me—"

"*I* was counting on you. And I can't believe you're taking our horrible experience and—and—cashing in on it!"

"And why not? Why shouldn't we get something good out of it? Should we just hide for the rest of our lives? I've got a chance to do something positive, and I'm taking it. God gave me talent, and I'm using it. And if I make a lot of money in the process, I'll put it to good use—and you'll be first on my list."

<hr>

So it was that two weeks later, Max was not by my side as I approached the courthouse. That was okay with the prosecution, they didn't need him on the stand yet, but it wasn't okay with me. I'd counted on having Max's moral support. Yet as much as I dreaded this, nothing could keep me away.

I passed through the metal detector and found the courtroom. Early as it was, the room was already filling. The way the media was covering this case, you'd think it was the entertainment of the year. I expected most of the people had come merely for sensational thrills.

Whispered voices and not-so-hushed voices buzzed as I entered. Some people noticed me, and some hissed, "That's her, Charlene, one of the Perigard twins who was kidnapped!" I averted my eyes and walked stiffly up front to my reserved seat.

Grandfather sat across the way, flanked by spiffy lawyers, and though I carefully kept my eyes away from him, I could feel his heavy glare. Not knowing quite where to look, I alternated keeping my eyes on my clenched hands and on the clock. Time crawled.

I hadn't watched enough courtroom dramas to know how court proceedings went, but I had a gut feeling that Clay would be brought in sometime soon. My heart started beating faster and faster in dreaded anticipation.

My eyes lifted to the door at just the right moment to see him being led in by a policeman. His face had healed well, but his nose seemed slightly crooked, as if it had been broken and healed wrong. His hair was much shorter. His skin, paler. He wore a simple, ill-fitting black suit, and had lost weight.

But these were all the superficial things. The things I really wanted to know—how he was doing, how he was feeling, how he was being treated—I had no way of knowing. Until he looked at me. His expression was smooth and composed, but his eyes revealed something. They weren't angry, afraid, or haunted, but they did look older, weary and weathered. And yet at the same time, there was something in them—something of strength, like you'd expect to find in the eyes of a soldier. He didn't acknowledge me—gave no nod or smile—but then I didn't expect that, and I did nothing to acknowledge him, either.

And yet.

And yet, there had been a connection. A pulsing in my veins, an understanding of, "here we are, at last. Not where we want to be, but where we have to be." *We. We're in this together.* I rubbed the white, raised scar on my left ring finger, recalling how our blood had been mingled, and I shivered.

Everyone rose when the Honorable Judge Whitman entered, and my heart sank. He was a hawk-eyed man with a narrow face. He also looked like he had a constant bad taste in his mouth.

We were informed that Clayton Morrow, twenty-one,

faced multiple charges of kidnapping, abduction, torture, assault, battery, and conspiracy to murder. I swallowed.

The business of the day was jury selection, and as the candidates were presented and questioned, I assessed them myself. A steely-eyed construction worker. *Please, no.* Young, gentle-looking ballet teacher. *Yes.* Twenty-two-year-old computer science student. *Possibly.* And on and on till my head spun.

By the end of the day, I left the room wearily. *And the real action hasn't even begun.*

A mob of reporters surged toward me as I exited the glass doors.

"Is it true that you were forced to eat dead mice while in captivity?"

Microphones were shoved at my face.

"Did your grandfather really disinherit you and kick you out of your home?"

"What do you think the verdict will be? What do you want it to be?"

"Miss Perigard, are you in love with Clayton Morrow?"

I almost tripped on the cement steps.

God, get me out of here.

I was actually relieved to enter my apartment. I took a long, roundabout way there, just in case any kooks or hounding reporters tried to follow me. I double-bolted my door and went straight for the refrigerator. My stomach told me I was starving, but it was so twisted in knots, it only let me eat a few bites of my microwave dinner before I felt like gagging.

While I washed my fork and glass, a knock sounded on my door. Hoping Max was finally arriving, I dried my hands hastily. Forgetting to check the peephole, I cracked open the door, leaving the chain on.

"Yes?" I peered at a harmless looking old lady wearing a soft blue scarf over her head. Her hands held a white plate on which perched a Bundt cake under a clear plastic dome.

A new neighbor introducing herself, I surmised tiredly.

"Hello, my name's Margaret," she said brightly. "I hope

I'm not disturbing you."

I noticed that the cake looked green.

"Oh, don't worry, the cake's not moldy," she assured me, apparently reading my suspicious gaze. "It's a pistachio cream cake, my specialty. Very delicious, but I can't help the color. Would you like to try a piece?"

My eyebrows raised. *You've got to be kidding. Food from a stranger? I'm really not looking to be poisoned.*

"I hope you're not allergic to nuts," she added, almost shyly.

As I studied her guileless face, the wrinkled skin smoothed, the scarf was replaced with lustrous chestnut hair, and the features became somewhat familiar, as if I'd known her in her younger days . . . or seen a picture.

I glanced again at the cake, and it came to me. Clay had told me pistachio cake was his mother's specialty. And now I remembered the picture that he'd shown me from his wallet.

"You're Clay's mom."

"Goodness, you figured that out fast! I was still wondering how to break it to you." She took a deep breath, as if speaking tired her. "I have so wanted to talk with you, but didn't know if you'd be willing . . ." Her words trailed off with a hopeful, unspoken question.

I didn't even take the time to wonder if talking with her was legal or not, considering the trial. The cake looked like a burden, a dead-weight in her thin arms, and I recalled her frail condition. I unlocked the door and let her enter, thinking, *How is she so composed?*

After securing the door, I relieved her of the cake and showed her to a seat, where she sank down gratefully, like a wilting flower. Scanning the room, I was glad I had my many religious goods prominently displayed—my holy water fonts, Bible, pictures, crucifix, and statues. *She'll appreciate them.*

I set the cake on the table, where we promptly forgot it.

"Did Clay send you?" I asked, still standing.

"Goodness, no! He wouldn't be pleased if he knew I was here."

"Why not?" I tried not to sound offended as I dropped into a wooden chair.

"You know," she waved a feeble hand, "busy-body mother interfering, and all that. Besides, he thinks he's caused you enough trouble."

So why are you here? To plead for mercy for Clay? Since I was already on his side, I didn't need anyone trying to sway me. And another thing: "How did you know where I live?"

"Forgive me." She bobbed her head slightly. "I didn't know until today. I followed you home from the courthouse."

So . . . I hadn't done a very good job of jumbling my tracks after all, not if a sick old lady could trail me home. Although, I realized now as I sat across from her, she wasn't really that old—not more than fifty-five—but something about her gave her the appearance of having lived many years. Many hard years.

"You walked?" I asked, incredulous.

"Gracious, no! These legs aren't what they used to be. I took a cab. I'm sorry, may I have a glass of water?"

"Of course." I rose and got one hastily, ashamed I hadn't offered.

She took a long, slow drink, as if very parched. "I'm not here to plead Clay's case, if that's what you're thinking," she said perceptively. "No." She folded her pale hands. "I came because I want to tell you how very sorry I am for all that you've suffered." A deep trembling pain came into her voice, but she gained control and continued steadily. "I wanted to apologize personally for my sons' behavior, both of them," she clarified, "and ask your forgiveness."

I struggled to keep from swallowing my tongue. Forgiveness for Clay, I could extend. But for Abner? No. Fortunately, she didn't press me. In fact, I began to sense that she was actually referring to forgiveness for herself. "You're not to blame," I attempted.

Her eyes looked past me and she spoke wistfully, in a very soft voice. "Sometimes, I wonder. Sometimes, I doubt. I think, if I had raised them better . . ."

Her face was wan, her eyes distant. "I lost them long ago. I grieved for them then. But I haven't given up hope. If you don't have hope, you have nothing." Her words became resigned. "In the meantime, I pray for them."

I thought of Saint Monica, how she had prayed all those years for her wayward son, who became Saint Augustine. I felt like I should say something, but Margaret leaned toward me.

"And then I saw you, and I thought, you've suffered so much, especially for someone so young. You looked so alone and afraid, and I wanted to comfort you. Offer you hope."

Shifting uncomfortably, I asked, "How's Clay holding up?"

She nodded once. "He's doing well, all things considered." I thought I caught a glimpse of a haunting shadow in her eyes. "In fact, he's changed from the Clay I knew last year, before all of this . . . but it's a good change. The Lord works in mysterious ways."

I compressed my lips. *He works in painful ways.*

The look in her warm brown eyes made me feel as if she'd heard my disrespectful thought. Her gaze traveled the living room. "You display many Catholic things."

"Yes." I felt a strange urge to defend myself. "Shouldn't I?"

"That depends. There are those who do it for show, the 'holier-than-thou' types—definitely not you, my dear," she added—"and there are those who do it out of pious love. But most of us fall in-between. We do it out of habit, or because we think we should." She took a breath and a drink. "Others gather sacramentals like a lifeline, because they are lost or struggling, and it's something material that they can hold on to. They think it will help bring them closer to God, or protect them from evil."

"That's me," I blurted, "and it's not working. I have nightmares, horrible, evil nightmares." *I'm plagued by the ghost of your son.* "And I thought . . . maybe these things would keep them away."

"Ah, yes. But outward things cannot replace inner strength. You said it yourself: They are things. Good things, yes, with graces attached to their use, but things, all the same. They have to be used right, as a means to help us increase our faith, not substitute for it. They're not magical."

"I know that."

"And yet," she continued, unruffled by my sharp retort, "you expect these things to make your problems disappear, like magic." She shook her head, her blue veil wafting. "My dear, my dear, I was just like you. I thought if I was good enough, careful enough, followed all the rules, God would surely reward me by answering my prayers. And every time something bad happened to me, I thought it was punishment for some sin. I felt I couldn't win."

Yes. My mouth began to drop open, and I shut it.

"Finally, I resigned myself to the fact that we're not meant to 'win.' We're not playing a game with God. He knows what He's doing with us, and we have to trust Him. What can I say?" She spread her palms. "There are no easy answers. We won't understand God's ways till we get to heaven. That's why we need faith."

"Faith," I muttered. "Just when I think I have it, something happens to prove me wrong."

"Yes, that's just the way of the world. You have to pray every day to keep strong. And God knows we'll both need to keep strong in these coming days . . ."

Surveying her, I thought, *She looks anything but strong.* Worn out, weak, decrepit. And yet her soul, her faith, they were strong. *That's all that really matters.*

"But I didn't come here to give you a sermon," she said, rising carefully, "and I'm sorry if I have."

"That's all right." As I stood to help her, I suddenly realized I didn't want her to go. "Please, won't you stay a little longer and help me eat some of this cake?"

Her eyes smiled. "I'd love to."

After she left, I prayed, climbed into bed, and continued thinking about all she had said, until I drifted off into a nightmare-free sleep.

But the following days in court were nightmarish enough to make up for it.

Chapter Twenty-Three

*T*he prosecuting attorney, a cement-haired man named Gauntley, spoke to a full courtroom. "I call Charlene Perigard to the witness stand."

My dreaded cue.

Feeling all eyes on me, including Max's, I rose and walked over the diamond-patterned carpet to the dark wooden witness box, my heart buzzing like a cicada trapped in my chest. The bailiff, a bald-headed man, brought the Bible to me. "Please raise your right hand."

I did so, and there was a ripple of reaction from the on-lookers as they saw the cross scarring my palm.

"Do you swear to tell the truth, the whole truth, and nothing but the truth, so help you God?"

The "I do" froze in my throat. I was back in the bitter cold depths beneath the cabin, in the midst of a Satanic wedding ceremony.

"Say, 'I do,'" Abner growled.

The bailiff cleared his throat. "Ms. Perigard?"

I blinked myself back to the moment, touched my throat, where I felt the faintest thread of a scar, and swallowed. *He's gone. Abner's gone, and he can't hurt me anymore.* I pulled my hand away from my throat. *But he's still hurting Clay, and I have to stop him.*

"I do."

I clasped my hands together, looked steadily at Gauntley, and waited for his first question.

"Please state your full name for the record," he directed.

"Charlene Elizabeth Perigard."

"Ms. Perigard, please begin by describing your first encounter with the defendant, including the date and location."

I took a moment to collect my thoughts and words. Looking out at the sea of faces, I saw Clay's mom, a pale waif of a woman, a pastel pink scarf swathed softly about her head.

"It was a Sunday," I began, "December twenty-eighth of last year. I was lost in some woods up north, outside of Cedar Hills, after being run off the road by Abner Morrow. He chased me and was yelling at me, threatening me, and I managed to lose him, but then he found me at the cabin and he—"

"Thank you, Ms. Perigard," Gauntley cut in, "but you need to stay on track."

"I am," I shot back. "You said to describe what happened, and this is important."

"I'm only interested in hearing about the defendant," Gauntley said firmly, "not his brother."

"But it's his brother who's the guilty one—not Clay. Abner was pure evil, a maniac. You have to hear the whole story." My voice rose to a strange pitch. "You have no idea!"

"Please, Ms. Perigard, contain yourself."

"No!" I realized I was shaking, but my mouth just kept moving. "I can't be quiet anymore. The court needs to hear the truth. The whole concept of this trial is ridiculous! It—"

"Ms. Perigard," Judge Whitman cut in, a warning.

I glared at Gauntley.

"Your Honor," Gauntley said, "I'd like to request permission to treat Ms. Perigard as a hostile witness."

Mortified, I stopped glaring and shrank in my seat. My cheeks burned. What in the world had I been thinking to create such a scene in court? Sounding like a hysterical, irrational person would not help Clay's case.

"Counsel for both sides," Judge Whitman said, "please approach the bench."

My ears roared with rushing blood, so I only heard snatches of the quiet discussion being carried on before the judge.

". . . evident that this witness . . . defensive," Gauntley said. ". . . clearly prejudiced . . ."

Clay's public defender lawyer, a thin red-head named Pharris, said something in return, but I couldn't hear him at all.

The judge, however, I heard loud and clear as he officially declared me a hostile witness.

With something like a smug smile on his face, Gauntley returned to my side and picked up where he had left off. "Please describe your first encounter with the defendant."

This time when I spoke, I was careful to keep my tone subdued. "It was evening. I was freezing and lost in the woods. I spotted someone walking through the trees, and it was Clay, on his way back from ice fishing." My eyes forgot the room crammed with people, and landed on Clay's face. His expression was intent, but impersonal. His mouth remained in a firm line. I wished I could see him smile.

"Ms. Perigard?"

I snapped back to attention. "Yes?"

"Did he approach you?"

"No, I called out to him."

"How did you end up in the cabin?"

"He brought me to it."

"I see." Gauntley's tone told me he saw something I didn't. "Did you pause to think that this strange man might not have had noble intentions?"

My face flushed.

"Objection," put in Pharris. "Calls for an opinion, not fact."

"Sustained," the judge said.

Unperturbed, Gauntley resumed. "So you went with the defendant, alone and willingly?"

"Yes." My hands clamped together painfully. "I had no choice. I was freezing, lost. It was snowing so heavily, and getting dark. I needed shelter. I thought I could call for help from the cabin."

"Did you?"

"No."

"Why not?"

"There wasn't a phone."

"Tell me what happened next."

"Clay's brother, Abner, came home. I recognized the truck and tried to escape, but Abner caught me."

"You were forced into a cold, underground prison, and locked up, correct?"

"Yes, but—"

"You were subsequently forced to watch your brother get his toe cut off, correct?"

"Yes, but Clay didn't do it. He—"

"He didn't stop it, though, did he?"

"Objection!" Pharris said. "Counsel isn't giving the witness a chance to finish answering."

"Sustained." The judge gave me a nod. "Continue, Ms. Perigard."

I swallowed. "Clay was tied up when that—the toe—" I cringed "—happened."

Gauntley nodded. "You and your brother were locked back up after this incident, but the defendant was not, correct?"

"Yes, but . . ." I shot a desperate look at Pharris, wishing he could help me in some way other than objecting. As Gauntley continued, reigning me in and redirecting me to suit the prosecution's case, I knew I was doing a horrible job. I was barely able to say anything in Clay's defense.

―――

The one bright spot in the long hours of court, was that Max had made it home, and I had someone on my side to talk to at the end of each weary day.

Max's time on the stand was no more promising than mine had been.

Back at my apartment that evening, heat raged through me, and I vented to Max. "Gauntley's picking us apart, making us seem so traumatized that we're incompetent."

"I know, I can't wait for this to be over, but we've gotta hang in there. We owe it to Clay. He doesn't deserve this."

Then Max tried to cheer me up with talk of the future. He had achieved the magic success on stage that he'd hoped for, he and Wayne were now in demand, and it didn't look like money was going to be an issue for him any longer.

I stared at Max, the brightness of the future he described hovering just out of my reach. When he asked, "What kind of house should we get?", I shook my head and massaged my temples.

"I can't think about anything else right now. Not with this trial going on."

He put an arm around me. "I know. I wish you and Clay were both free. I think . . . you'd be good for each other."

The next day when I picked up my paycheck at the college library, I was summoned to the dean's office.

This is highly irregular, I thought suspiciously as I entered his large, orderly office. A gnawing deep in my stomach told me that now with all the trial coverage, maybe the college didn't want me working for them anymore. *I'm bad publicity.*

I waited nervously, but the dean looked up and smiled at me from under his bronze mustache. "Sit down, Charlene," he said kindly before introducing himself as Dean Rowland. Instead of firing me, he said, "I've been told you are a very good worker, and I have a proposal for you. I'd like to offer you a full four-year scholarship to our fine college. We would be honored if you'd accept."

I blushed. "But—but why?" I stuttered, taken completely off-guard. "I didn't even apply for a—"

He shook his head. "That's not always necessary. We keep our eyes and ears open for worthy candidates. Simply put, the Scholarship Association and I believe you deserve it, that you would work hard, and that you would make good use of it. Now, there is a condition attached: You'll need to keep your grades up. Do you think you can do that, Charlene?"

"Yes." Bewilderment gave way to wonder. "Yes, I would work very hard. I would be extremely grateful. But—I just don't know if I should accept." Suddenly, I felt like I was once more in front of Helen from church, being offered charity that I didn't deserve.

"And why not?"

Because I don't want it because you feel sorry for me. I don't want to be a charity case. "I don't think I deserve it."

His eyes registered understanding. "Take it. You deserve it. And we'd be proud to have you as a student."

A new thought struck me. "But my brother," I began. "He'll probably be able to put me through school. So there's really no reason—"

"Yes, there is," he cut in. "We're aware of your brother's situation, but we want to do this. For you." He held out a fat white envelope, and it found my hand.

"You may not know it, young lady, but you've got a lot of people rooting for you."

Something like tears gathered in the back of my throat. "Thank you," I managed before turning away, the precious envelope clasped in my hands.

Not all the world is bad, after all.

—⁓—

Back in court, Gauntley continued his merciless tactics. I shared my concerns with Pharris. "This is all wrong. There's not enough focus given to Abner and his part in all this—he was the mastermind, the one who made us all suffer."

"It's not his trial," Pharris said.

"But Gauntley seems to think that by showing that Max and I were tortured and almost killed, it's all Clay's fault. It's illogical."

"The trial's not over yet." Pharris then promised me that our time would come. Once the prosecution was through with presenting their side, Pharris would put us on the stand to testify as witnesses in Clay's defense.

Still, I worried.

The prosecution gave an impressive presentation of evidence. The ransom note was shown as Exhibit #1. The wicked metal pruners were Exhibit #2.

In addition, enough disturbing pictures were shown to fill a grisly photo album. The vivid pictures included Max's severed toe; his foot minus the toe; my scarred palm, finger, and neck; our dark prison; and two gaping graves in the cellar. The prosecution even showed highly unflattering pictures of me and Max right after our escape—pitiful pictures I didn't even remember being taken.

But the prosecution's prized piece of evidence was more disturbingly effective than any still picture could ever be; it was the video that had been sent to Grandfather.

It was about to be shared with the world.

I'd known this was coming. Pharris had been given a copy of the video as part of the legal discovery process long before trial, but I still wasn't ready.

For this special feature, a giant screen was brought into the courtroom. I felt like I had front-and-center seats in a movie theater premiering the worst horror movie ever, with me as the unfortunate star.

Static specks snowed onscreen for a few moments before a dark hooded, masked figure appeared.

Abner is back.

I trembled in my seat.

Abner's red eyeballs looked out from the screen and seared into me. He spoke in a slow, raspy voice. "Greetings, Mr. Perigard. It has now been five days since you received the first ransom note, three since you received Max's special package . . . and you've still failed to meet my reasonable demands. I warned you about involving the police, but you ignored me. Big mistake, old man. This is your last chance, your last warning." He paused.

"Perhaps your cold heart is not swayed by your grandson. Therefore, this time, I'm going to use your granddaughter." Abner made a sweeping gesture toward me.

There I was, back in the nightmare, bound to the chair. In real-time, as well as on film, my breathing became labored and sweat trickled from my forehead.

Abner continued. "Perhaps your granddaughter's screams will persuade you to finally cooperate. If not, this is the last you will ever see of her. And now . . . on with the show." He opened the stove door and stuck the black branding iron inside.

As it heated up, he circled around me, chanting eerily in Latin while, onscreen, I twisted in my bonds. Now in court, I twisted in my seat. Why didn't I just close my eyes against this wretched rerun, cover my ears? But it was as if I was bound once more.

Abner removed the glowing red-hot iron from the fire.

He brought it toward me. Onscreen, I started screaming.

In court, I stuffed my fist in my mouth as I watched the brander pushed onto my palm. Once, then once more. Suddenly, the scene shook, flipped, and disappeared from sight with a rattling bang.

Clay dropping the camera, I recalled.

When things steadied, the screen showed only a dark shadowy blur as the camera lens focused on nothing. My screams could be heard, though only faintly, before Gauntley switched the film off. Then there was only stunned courtroom silence.

The third witness whom the prosecution called to the bench was none other than Grandfather, who didn't have anything of much worth to say, but he sure thought he did. After answering predictable questions (about me, Max, the ransom, and the video), he began spouting off about how it was all a conspiracy, and Max and I were probably in on the scheme from the start, and that's why we wouldn't go against Clay now.

"Silence!" Judge Whitman ordered. "I will not allow such wild and irrelevant opinions and accusations. You will stick to answering the questions, or I will have you removed from my courtroom. Is that clear?"

Grandfather looked like he wanted to shoot the judge, but he replied in the affirmative. I heaved a sigh of relief when he stepped down from the bench.

Other witnesses the prosecution called included Detective Donnelly and the officer who had visited the cabin the night of our escape. Pharris had the chance to cross-examine each man when the prosecution was through, but it seemed like a waste of time to me. So many of the questions and answers seemed so irrelevant to the main issue of Clay's innocence.

Why do they call them "witnesses?" I wondered indignantly. *What do they know? They weren't there to see any of it.*

———

"The prosecution calls Robert Crew to the witness stand."

It took me a few moments to register who this latest witness was. Then I saw Rob, wearing a suit and polished black shoes, walk confidently up to the witness box and be sworn in. Max and I exchanged glances, wondering what in the world Rob would say. Would it help us, or would it hurt us? Knowing Rob's allegiance to Grandfather, I feared the latter.

Gauntley began. "You are employed by Mr. Perigard, correct?"

"Actually, no," Rob announced coolly and clearly. "I was, but as of now, I'm giving my resignation. Mr. Perigard wanted me to swear that he took this kidnapping seriously from the start, but nothing could be further from the truth. He even had me switch out the ransom money for counterfeit."

"Why, you—you—" Grandfather sputtered, rising from his seat. "You can't quit—you're fired! And furthermore—"

"Silence!" Judge Whitman commanded. "I will not tolerate outbursts in my courtroom, Mr. Perigard. This is your second and final warning. Another outburst like that, and I will have you removed."

I was surprised I didn't see steam shooting from Grandfather's ears, nose, and mouth. Gauntley whispered something to him, and he sat down sullenly.

Judge Whitman turned his focus back to Rob and told him

to continue.

Rob nodded. "So right after Mr. Perigard sent Charlene off with the ransom money, he tells me he changed his mind about paying, that Max didn't deserve a single dollar—even if it was, quote, 'a crafty scheme that Max cooked up.' So Mr. Perigard sent me to make the switch with fake bills. He was sure that Max, unlike Charlene, wouldn't be able to tell the difference."

When Rob left the stand, he grinned my way and mouthed, "Good luck."

Chapter Twenty-Four

Gauntley had a strange smile on his face. "I call Dr. Bach to the witness stand."

An elderly gentleman dressed in a navy blue suit took the stand and was sworn in.

"What is your occupation?"

Dr. Bach sat up very straight. "I am a psychiatrist."

Uh-oh.

"Tell us, Doctor, what is 'Stockholm Syndrome'?"

The doctor steepled his fingers. "Stockholm Syndrome is a term used to describe a paradoxical psychological phenomenon wherein a kidnapped person develops a positive emotional attachment or relationship with his or her kidnapper. Hostages may be affected to such an extent, that they will even defend their captor."

"Very interesting," Gauntley said, as if he were surprised to hear this information. "Is this a rare occurrence?"

"Actually, it happens more often than you might think. In fact, the FBI's Hostage Barricade Database System shows that roughly twenty-seven percent of victims display signs of Stockholm Syndrome."

The doctor went on to cite a case of a thirteen-year-old girl who was kidnapped, then located ten years later, living as a wife to the kidnapper. They even had two children together.

Listening, I felt sick.

But I certainly didn't want Dr. Bach coming to my aid.

"This is so twisted," I whispered to Max. I felt a million eyes on me. "And I hate all these people for feeling sorry for us."

"Don't worry," Max laid a hand on my shoulder, "they won't all fall for this crap."

At last the tables turned, and it was the defense's turn to present evidence and testimony.

The handcuffs that Abner had bound Clay with were entered into evidence, as was the sliced rope that had been found in the cellar. Flecks of blood had been identified on the rope fibers, and DNA testing proved that it belonged to Clay. When Pharris showed pictures of Clay from January fourth, the day he was arrested, his wounds spoke more than words.

Magnified, the pictures gave evidence of Clay's chafed wrists, proving my testimony of how he had struggled against his bonds in the cellar so he could help me and Max. The picture of Clay's face, however, didn't need to be magnified. The many wounds were obvious. I watched the jury's hardened faces soften gradually, and I felt hope that they were truly beginning to see the truth.

Max gave testimony about how Clay had saved me from the lake. *Powerful stuff,* I thought. *But of course, I'm biased.*

Pharris also drilled Max about what took place after the lake rescue. "Did the defendant enter the cottage of his own free will?"

"Sure did. He was helping me carry my sister."

"Who made the phone call to the police?"

"Clay did."

Pharris played the recording of that phone call for the entire courtroom to hear before continuing with the questions.

"After the call was made, was the defendant kept in the cottage against his will to wait for the arrival of the police?"

"No."

"Thank you," Pharris said. "That's all, Your Honor."

This time when I took the stand, I was determined to have my say.

"Ms. Perigard," Pharris began, "When you first encountered the defendant, did he threaten you or assault you, or in any way force you to enter the cabin with him?"

"No."

"And when his brother, Abner, entered, what happened?"

I described the scene, explaining how when Abner grabbed me, Clay jumped in to stop him. "Then Abner hit him with his rifle and forced him down into the prison with me."

Pharris continued to question me on key points, giving me freedom to describe what had really happened, though we were interrupted with quite a few objections from Gauntley. Still, the truth came out, how Clay was restrained and beaten, locked up, held at gun-point.

"Clay may have made some mistakes," I said calmly, "but I'd like to see any one of you stand up to Abner, and even live to tell about it. Clay stood up not just once, but many times."

"Objection!" Gauntley barked.

"Overruled," Judge Whitman responded, before Gauntley could even say what exactly he was objecting to.

The judge nodded for me to continue. I took a deep breath. "So don't condemn Clay for not succeeding the first time, or the second." As I spoke, I looked each juror in the eye, willing them to understand. "Don't condemn him for not being physically stronger than Abner." I rubbed the thin raised scar on my ring finger. "He failed to save us at the start, but he kept trying, and eventually, he succeeded."

I cleared my throat. "Even then, he could have run. He knew what he'd be facing if he was caught. But he purposely chose to stay and wait with us for the police. Then he waited in jail for seven long months for his case to come to trial. Don't you think he's paid enough?" My voice broke. "Don't you think it's time he finally went free?"

"Hogwash!" Grandfather shot up from his seat. "Balderdash! She's brainwashed!"

"Silence!" The judge's gavel pounded. He pointed a severe finger at Grandfather. "Three strikes, you're out, Mr. Perigard." Judge Whitman nodded to two police officers, who promptly took hold of Grandfather's arms and began forcefully escorting him from the room. Grandfather's angry struggle and protests were drowned out by an eruption of applause from the courtroom crowds. I could hardly believe it.

"Order in the court!" The judge's gavel pounded, but even as the clapping subsided, most everyone was smiling. Max gave a jaunty wave in Grandfather's direction.

"Joy, Gwen," Grandfather barked, "come on! You're leaving too!" Joy and Gwen gave me an apologetic glance before rising to do his bidding.

"You'll all be sorry!" was the last the court heard from Grandfather before he was dragged out the doors.

"Awesome," Max said when I returned to my seat beside him, and when he gave me a high-five, I had to muffle a laugh.

Now I was becoming optimistic, but Pharris didn't share my enthusiasm. "Don't count your verdict before it's decided," he cautioned dully as we met privately between court sessions. "It could go either way. The prosecution's evidence is very compelling, very emotionally provoking. Our sympathy angle's good, but we don't have any evidence strong enough to counter the video. That's a clear depiction of an accomplice."

Pharris's words ran through my head as I fell into bed that night.

The video. An accomplice.

But Clay wasn't. If only they could have been there. Seen, or at least heard, what came after the camera fell.

I snapped up in bed. My mind whirred as I replayed the video. There had been no fuzzy white static snow indicating that the film had truly ended. The screen had been dark; you couldn't see anything. You could barely hear my scream— but it had been there. And that's when Gauntley had turned the film off.

But what if there was more?

I knew there was, because I had been there.

No one else knew, because they couldn't see it or hear it. But if the volume was turned up, way up—maybe using some kind of special equipment—just maybe, the court would be able to hear the rest of the scene. Why hadn't I thought of this sooner?

I kicked off my sheet, grabbed my phone, and called Pharris.

All eyes in the courtroom watched the dark gray screen, but it was their ears that mattered. Eventually, we heard what I knew was there. The words were dim, but decipherable.

"Are you completely insane?" came Clay's horrified voice. "You *are* a monster!"

There was a clang.

Abner dropped the branding iron, I recalled.

I braced myself for Abner's voice, and when it came, it didn't shake me.

"And you're a weak kid who can't stand the sight of pain. That's where the power is. You still don't get it, do you? I'll do whatever it takes to make the old man pay."

"It's not worth it," Clay cried. "It's just money. Just dang money!"

"That's right," Abner sneered, "you still think this is all about money. What a fool. Of course it's not. It's about revenge."

Thud, thud, smack. The sounds of fists hitting flesh were obvious to me and, I hoped, to every person in the courtroom.

Wham, the final powerful punch. In my mind, I saw Clay crumple to the floor.

Now, a buzz of voices filled the courtroom. I couldn't keep myself from glancing at Clay—something I usually tried avoiding so there would be no more talk of the "Stockholm Syndrome."

As if sensing my eyes on him, Clay turned to face me. The words he couldn't speak were unmistakably evident on his face: *Thank you.*

Max nudged me, making me break eye contact with Clay.

"Good job, Char. You should go into detective work. You

could team up with your favorite guy, Detective Donnelly," he joked.

I nodded absently.

At last, Clay was given the opportunity to testify in his own defense. I held my breath, wondering if he would take it.

He did.

"We've heard a lot of testimony over these past days, Mr. Morrow," Pharris said. "Do you have anything you'd like to add?"

We all knew that whatever words came out of Clay's mouth, they would likely be the most pivotal in the case. Most people probably expected a long, detailed, defensive account of every action of his that had been questioned. Instead, we heard:

"It's all been said, and I thank Max and Charlene for saying it." He glanced our way. "I want to ask their forgiveness. The truth is, though I didn't mastermind the kidnapping, that's not good enough. I *was* an accomplice." He ignored Pharris's glare. "Maybe not so much by action, but by inaction. I was a coward, compromising, making excuses, twisting the truth. I didn't stand up for what was right. Max and Charlene could easily have been killed." He bowed his head. I almost didn't catch his hushed final words:

"God forgive me."

"To convict Clayton Morrow of these criminal charges, the prosecution must have proved beyond a reasonable doubt . . ." As Judge Whitman gave the jury their final instructions, my mind wandered. Today, the long wait would be over. For Clay, it would be a bitter end or a new beginning. For me . . . I didn't know. I couldn't think past the verdict.

Finally, it was time for the two sides to make their closing arguments. Max kept his arm around me protectively the whole time.

The prosecution went first, Gauntley emphasizing Clay's guilt and asking that justice be done. He finished by saying, "Remember, just because the victims decide that they like the defendant, that doesn't make him any less a criminal or a threat to society. He's still culpable for his crimes, and must be locked away. Think of the other Perigards." Gauntley's gaze swept the jury. "If it were your grandkids or kids who had been kidnapped and mistreated, wouldn't you want the kidnapper behind bars—even if your kids didn't?"

Murmurs spread through the room.

Next, Pharris stepped forward to address the jury. "Good morning, ladies and gentlemen," he began blandly. "The prosecution would have you believe that Clayton Morrow is a ruthless kidnapper, a dangerous criminal. But what does the evidence tell us? Starting from the beginning, the ransom note, Exhibit # 1, is clearly written in single person form, the 'I' referring to Abner Morrow. What this entire case comes down to is that the prosecution would have you condemn the defendant for his brother's crimes."

I sat straight in my chair, my muscles tense, as Pharris continued.

"Look at the facts: Clayton Morrow helped Charlene Perigard out of a cold snowy woods into the shelter of a cabin. Here, he opposed his brother and subsequently suffered beatings. He was tied up and held captive. When able, he assisted the Perigards in digging for freedom. Hardly the acts of a criminal." Pharris took a few steps and smoothed a hand down the front of his suit. "If he was guilty, why didn't he flee the cottage before the police arrived? For that matter, why did he go there at all?"

After a significant pause, Pharris added, "He went there so that Charlene Perigard wouldn't die of hypothermia. He helped her brother bring her out of the cold, and then Clayton Morrow called the police himself."

At that moment, I changed my opinion of Pharris. He had fire in him after all, and it ignited his words.

"Above all," he continued, "the defendant saved Charlene

Perigard's life—you have this testimony from her own lips. Clayton Morrow saved her. Will you not save him?"

Please, I prayed. *Please.*

"By now," Pharris said, "I know it is clear to you that the only thing Clayton Morrow is guilty of is being in the wrong place at the wrong time. Yet has anyone stopped to think what the Perigards' fate would have been if the defendant had *not* been at the cabin? Perhaps Clayton was, in fact, in the right place at the right time."

My blood pumped hotly through my veins. Pharris's words streamed into my ears, words which I hoped convinced the jurors, compelling their minds and moving their hearts.

"I have presented the facts," he finished. "It is now up to you to use these facts and come to the only logical, just conclusion: A 'not guilty' verdict. Thank you."

My heart fluttered with hope until the judge informed us that the prosecution had the final word. As I listened to Gauntley's powerful voice, I thought, *No, no, he's ruining everything!* My heart wrenched with distress.

It wasn't fair. Of course the side with the last word would have the most influence. The prosecution's bias would be seared freshly in the minds of the jurors as they departed to decide the verdict.

"Ladies and gentlemen of the jury, do not be deceived," Gauntley pleaded. "The defense and the two unfortunate Perigards would have us believe that Mr. Morrow is a victim, instead of a very real and dangerous criminal.

"Do not forget, dear jury, the film recorded by the defendant. His fingerprints were found all over the camera. The female victim, in her sworn statement, affirmed that the defendant did indeed film the torturous event." He paused. "The video should leave no question in your mind about the defendant's guilt. Despite what came after, only a monster would film such a thing."

Abner was the monster! He forced Clay to do it, I wanted to cry, but it was no use. The judge would reprimand me. Besides, I remembered my own blinding anger and hatred toward Clay at the time.

"The defense wants you to think Mr. Morrow was 'made' to do it," Gauntley continued, "but as you know, it takes free will to hold a video camera, press record, and film for any length of time. And the brother, whom they say 'made' the defendant do this dastardly deed, was obviously occupied while the filming was taking place. This would have been the perfect opportunity for the defendant to make a move—if, indeed, he was victimized—which he obviously was not.

"Yes, the young man may look innocent and harmless—even charming—but you all know what the evidence has shown: He's evil, not fit for society. The only place he is fit for is a prison cell."

Gauntley's words rang with the finality of a prison door clanging shut.

―――

The jury deliberation took over three hours. I spotted Clay's mom sitting in her usual spot, her face pale, her eyes closed, rosary beads slipping through her fingers, her lips moving slightly.

A very good idea.

I pulled out my own string of beads. Mine, because Gwen had never wanted it back. Fingering the smooth tear-droplet shapes, I remembered how Max had tied Clay up with this rosary, and how I had released him. I recalled the conversation we had shared, and how later, Clay had called religion "just another form of captivity."

Time dragged, but when the doors opened, there suddenly didn't seem to be enough time. The paper with the verdict was handed to the judge. A collective intake of breath swept through the room.

Now was the moment of truth.

My eyes went to Clay, who stood facing the judge—facing the most serious moment of his life—but his posture showed no cowering, no fear. In fact, Clay, who had been beaten and broken so many times in his life, stood waiting with a sturdiness that baffled me.

Judge Whitman cleared his throat.

What happened next made my rosary slip from my fingers.

Deliberately, with a steady arm, Clay lifted his hand and made the sign of the cross.

An act of faith.

And suddenly, the verdict didn't matter. Because, after all, it was only a piece of paper, only the judgment of men.

Whatever it may be, Clay has the strength to deal with it. He's not alone anymore.

And neither am I.

Slowly, I lifted my branded hand. My fingers brushed the cross imprinted in my skin, then touched my forehead. With thanks in my heart and a prayer on my lips, I too made the sign of the cross.

A wondrous act of faith.

A Note from the Author

Dear Reader,

When *Frozen Footprints* was first published in 2012, I had no definite plans to write a sequel, though I certainly left the possibility open for one. However, the characters lived on in my imagination and this, combined with reader response, compelled me to write a sequel. I'm now very excited to announce its impending release in early 2016.

After the Thaw continues the story of Charlene and Clay while introducing some new characters and, of course, new danger. The majority of the story takes place about four years after *Frozen Footprints* ends.

Once *After the Thaw* is published, you will be able to read the first few chapters online for free. And yes, I promise you'll find out Clay's verdict.

If you enjoyed *Frozen Footprints*, please take a moment to leave a review online—even if it's only one sentence. When you help spread the word, it makes a world of difference to the success of my books and writing career.

I hope to write many more novels, and knowing that there are readers for my stories is a wonderful encouragement. Thank you from the bottom of my heart.

God bless,

Therese Heckenkamp

Acknowledgements

To all those who made this book possible, I send a deep and sincere thank you. I'm especially indebted to:

My dear husband for reading my manuscript and being honest about the flaws, offering suggestions for improvement, and for not minding when I left the light on to write while he slept.

My sisters Monica and Cassandra for reading this so many times over the years it took to reach publication, for listening to my frustrations, brainstorming, and never hesitating to point out problems.

My brother-in-law Chris Eckert for reading the manuscript in one day (wow!) and giving me valuable feedback from a guy's perspective.

And of course to my three wonderful children for enduring a writer for a mother.

Huge thanks also go to: Regina Doman, who helped shape the story in so many ways—you know how very much I owe you! Andrew Schmiedicke, if not for you there would have been no prologue. Vincent Frankini and Stephen Frankini of Tumblar House, for believing in this book and making my dream come true when they first published it in 2012.

And to my dearly departed ones, with heartfelt gratitude for your prayers: My cousin Mikey (thanks for being a fan of my first book and for interceding for this one); my loving grandmothers; and my two tiny babies who never got to take a breath in this world but moved right on to a better one. I love you and miss you.

Above all, I thank the Good Lord, Who works in such mysterious ways.

About the Author

*T*herese Heckenkamp was born in Australia but grew up in the United States as a homeschooled student. She lives in Wisconsin with her husband and three energetic children. A member of the Catholic Writers Guild, she enjoys writing during naptime and at night (when the house is finally quiet).

After the Thaw, her third novel and the sequel to *Frozen Footprints*, is scheduled for release in early 2016.

Visit Therese online to share feedback and to keep up-to-date on free ebooks, new releases, and more:

Therese's website: www.thereseheckenkamp.com

Facebook: www.facebook.com/therese.heckenkamp

Twitter: www.twitter.com/THeckenkamp

Book website: www.frozen-footprints.com

Made in the USA
Las Vegas, NV
27 May 2021

23681612R00157